D1494381

100 Reasons to Celebrate

We invite you to join us in celebrating
Mills & Boon's centenary. Gerald Mills and
Charles Boon founded Mills & Boon Limited
in 1908 and opened offices in London's Covent
Garden. Since then, Mills & Boon has become
a hallmark for romantic fiction, recognised
around the world.

We're proud of our 100 years of publishing
excellence, which wouldn't have been achieved
without the loyalty and enthusiasm of our
authors and readers.

Thank you!

Each month throughout the year there will
be something new and exciting to mark the
centenary, so watch for your favourite authors,
captivating new stories, special limited
edition collections…and more!

THE COMMANDER

Kate Bridges

MILLS & BOON®
Pure reading pleasure

First published in Great Britain 2008
Harlequin Mills & Boon Limited,
Eton House, 18-24 Paradise Road, Richmond, Surrey TW9 1SR

© Katherine Haupt 2006

ISBN: 978 0 263 86245 4

Set in Times Roman 10½ on 12¾ pt.
04-0208-74819

Printed and bound in Spain
by Litografia Rosés S.A., Barcelona

Kate Bridges is fascinated by romantic tales of the spirited men and women who tamed the West. Growing up in rural Canada, Kate developed a love of people-watching and reading all types of fiction, although romance was her favourite. She embarked on a career as a neonatal intensive care nurse, then moved on to architecture. Later, working in television production, she began crafting novels of her own. Currently living in the bustling city of Toronto, she and her husband love to go to movies and travel.

Recent titles by the same author:

THE DOCTOR'S HOMECOMING
THE SURGEON
THE ENGAGEMENT
THE PROPOSITION
THE CHRISTMAS GIFTS
    (part of *A Season of the Heart*)
THE BACHELOR

This book is dedicated to my family,
for always being there.

Chapter One

◦◦◦◦◦

June 1895, Calgary, Alberta

Even after all these years, at the mere mention of his name, Julia O'Shea still felt the urge to slap his face.

On the day the memories of Ryan Reid came flooding back to her, Julia was working in her print shop, racing to meet her noon deadline. With an hour left, she was organizing stacks of freshly printed newspapers while her reporter worked the cylindrical press. Two of her distributors walked in. Julia smiled in greeting, but from their dampened expressions, she knew their news wasn't good.

"Business is slow at the mercantile," old Mr. Rossman whispered in shame. He pushed a pile of clean rags across the counter. "The drought's affected a lot of ranchers and no one's buyin' much of anything. Can I pay you with rags again?"

Julia ran a finger beneath her sticky velvet choker. She'd

lost five pounds in the past month from working so strenuously, and her loose gray skirt dragged along the floor.

She glanced at the gent's worn shirt, elbows patched ten times over. Why, he was no better off than she was, and he had *three* children to feed compared to her one. "No need to fret, sir. Thank you for taking the amount of papers you do."

When he left, the stooped man who owned the diner next door offered her a crate of tin scraps. With a pinch to her stomach, Julia accepted the tin as payment. At this rate, she'd be closing her presses within a month. But she remained cheerful, walked him to the propped-open door and waved goodbye.

A hot prairie breeze swirled around her skirts. The smell of dust seared her nostrils and permeated her thin blouse. Outside, a team of groaning oxen pulled a wagon full of homesteaders. Dozens of settlers in wagon trains had been arriving all day, and the shifting landscape made her restless. Change disturbed her, and always had since the age of five.

Life never seemed to get any easier. What she wished to give her son, Pete, was a bit more than she'd had as a child. A hot meal once a day. A bed with a real mattress, not a straw one. Parents who didn't go to prison. All the love he needed.

Behind her, her assistant and sole reporter, David Fitzgibbon, turned a large drum. A clickety-clack filled the air. Last week, she'd shamefully had to let go of her other two reporters due to dwindling business, which left her and David to do the bulk of the work.

But she could turn this around. She *knew* she could. She'd spun bad luck into good before.

"What we need around here," she said, approaching

David, "is a big story to increase sales. Something to make folks feel good. Something that's got nothing to do with the drought or the wildfires."

Blond hair poked out from beneath his plaid cap. "As soon as people read your personal advertisement in today's paper, tongues will flap and—"

"My ad was not intended to increase sales."

"But placing an ad for a husband—"

"A *gentleman* husband. You and Grandpa always forget that word."

Julia picked up the newly inked front page of the *Calgary Town Crier*. The news would be out by midday. Seeing her ad at the bottom, in black and white, made her hopes flutter. Meaning no disrespect to her late husband, Brandon, she'd been five years now without a partner at her side, and it was time.

For the past five months, Julia hadn't had any luck with suitors on her own. Some men disapproved of her running a business and had demanded she quit to concentrate on the home. Some hadn't been able to accept another man's child. One unemployed drifter had the gall to assume she'd consent to any man who walked up to her door. Many men placed ads for mail-order brides, so Julia saw no harm in placing her own ad for a husband. Being frank ahead of time about the type of man she wanted would save on hurt feelings later—his and hers.

"We should concentrate on our society page. There's nothing more interesting to people than other people." She turned the focus back to her newspaper and to drumming up sales.

"Then we should write about a prominent family."

David heaved the last papers to the counter so they could fold them. The weakness in his left arm, caused by a gangrenous wound he'd suffered a few years back, caused the pile to shift. "Ryan Reid's back in town. We could write about him."

Heat flashed through her face. "What did you say?"

"Do you know him? Ryan Reid."

Julia stumbled, dropping the paper. "Donovan Ryan Reid?"

"That's right. According to the hotel clerk across the street, most folks call him Ryan."

The day had finally come. She fumbled with her lace collar, trying to block the vivid memory of Ryan standing in her grandpa's bar. As she recalled their last conversation, anger stiffened her spine. A bead of sweat trickled down her neck beneath her heavy auburn braid. She peered across the street, past the rolling covered wagons, toward the Prairie Hotel. "He's there?"

"Walked by two hours ago. When I saw this big wolf of a man leap off a wagon and enter the hotel, I followed. He walks like he thinks he's important, so I figured he might be. Even beneath the scraggly hair and beat-up clothes."

Gone ten years and now forty feet away.

"The hotel clerk said he's the long-lost son of Joseph Reid," said David. "I couldn't stay longer to ask more questions due to our deadline. But a maid told me he's the black sheep of the family. Any idea why they call him that?"

Julia braced herself. "He once killed a man."

David dropped onto a stool. "A murderer. How?"

"It was a—a stabbing."

"What a great story this would make. No wonder his

family disowned him…both his brothers are Mounties. And good God, his father was a copper back in Ireland. How long was Ryan in prison?"

"He didn't go to prison. It was self-defense."

David whistled. "Imagine the headline: The Black Sheep Returns. Folks would buy us out."

"What?" Julia frowned at David. "No…that's not what…"

David grabbed his camera. "Your grandpa and Pete will be here soon enough to take over. Bring your notebook. Let's go."

She ran a shaky palm along her cheek. Over the years, she'd promised herself she'd never again get close enough to see the light reflecting in Ryan's eyes. But if she didn't act on this bit of news, there were three other papers in town that would. She had Grandpa and Pete to support. She had an obligation to pay David his wages. She had her pride in proving that a former barmaid did have the business savvy to pull through any hardship.

Blood pounded through her veins. And a secret part of her wanted to show Ryan that she had survived just fine without him.

"Your timing is awfully bad."

"When do you figure they'll be back?" Shirtless from his recent bath, with a towel slung around his bare shoulders, Ryan Reid strode past his narrow hotel bed to the open window. A hot breeze stirred the fine damp hairs on his chest. Rubbing his beard, he turned to the skinny clerk who'd introduced himself as Ned.

Ned huffed beneath the weight of Ryan's suitcase. He

flung it onto the mattress beside Ryan's two most precious things—a beat-up leather bag and the violin, in its hard leather case, that was causing him so much grief.

"The manager says your pa and brothers are deliverin' two hundred head of cattle west of Red Deer. They're supposed to be back within a week, same time as your sister and mother. The ladies went south to visit relatives."

Ryan stiffened at the talk of his family, more nervous than he thought he would be about seeing them again. This was the time of year for cattle drives and Ryan had suspected the men might be gone, but he had hoped for better luck.

While the clerk straightened bedsheets and filled the water basin, Ryan spun around to peer out of the second-story window. Moving stiffly from his old wounds and his long ride, he leaned over the squat sill and pressed his left shoulder against the frame.

Dusty air stung his nostrils. Ryan stared out beyond the shifting wagon trains. Calgary had tripled in size since he'd last been here, but to him, the town still felt like a tight fit.

In the far west, a faint ribbon of smoke curled above the foothills, against the backdrop of the Rocky Mountains. A wildfire. This year seemed more parched than most, folks had told him, and the drought was aiding and abetting the flames.

"Pray for rain," the settlers he'd ridden with kept saying.

A knock at the door pulled Ryan in that direction. When he opened it, a young Scottish maid, her pretty face turning poppy-red as she looked at his chest, handed him four folded newspapers. "As ye requested, sir."

Newspapers were inexpensive to start up, and therefore most towns had several, but Ryan knew many didn't survive long in business. "Which is the most recent?"

"The *Calgary Town Crier* is fresh off the press."

He shuffled it to the top of the pile and read the headline: Wildfires Burning Closer. "Thanks."

After another flustered glance at his scarred chest, the maid raced away. He reckoned she didn't like what she saw. Or maybe she liked it extra. He never knew with women.

He tossed the papers on the bed. The bath had done him good, but his hair was tangled from weeks of riding, and his beard was too long to look respectable.

Another knock on the door drew him to it. "Yes?"

The barber stood in the hall.

"Come on in. Set up anywhere you want."

The old man nodded and headed toward the dresser and chair. His greased-back hair shimmered in the orange sunlight. He wore a brown satin vest buttoned over a white shirt. "Sir."

Ryan squinted at him. "Good to see you again, Todd."

"Holy hell, is that you? Ryan Reid?"

The barber glanced at the scar running across Ryan's nipple, then coughed. The clerk glanced away.

Ryan gave the old man an uneasy nod, recalling how much Todd Mead used to enjoy prying into other men's affairs.

The clerk and barber set up an area by the window where the lighting was best. Ryan slid onto the chair and told Todd to cut it all off. As the barber snipped, wads of hair fell onto the towel wrapped around Ryan's shoulders.

"Say, there's a good fighting match going on later tonight behind the saloon. A man could make some extra money."

Ryan's jaw tightened. "I no longer fight."

"But you were so damn good with a knife." With glee,

the barber explained to the clerk, "We used to call him 'The Edge' because he'd scrape the blade right along someone's chest—"

"I said I don't fight." Ryan's brisk tone halted the conversation.

Someone pounded on the door. The wiry clerk dashed to get it.

A thin blond man wearing a plaid cap poked his head around the pine slab. He reminded Ryan of a scarecrow. When he eased into the room, he was carrying a boxlike portable camera.

A woman inched in behind him. Her floppy straw hat concealed most of her face, but Ryan could see her journal and pencil.

Reporters? Ryan balked. What did reporters want from him?

A plait of auburn hair flowed over the woman's shoulder. Three blue feathers adorned her hat. Her thin white blouse clung to the corset reining in her curves, and a sagging gray skirt draped softly against her thighs. Her clothes were well-worn, but she was dressed like a proper lady.

Ryan's muscles tightened in response. Proper ladies had been scarce on his journeys.

Her hat dipped while she looked him over, then she recoiled and gasped. She was reacting to his scars.

His neck burned with hot anger, with the sting of being rejected. The reaction of a proper lady bothered him more than the maid's or the clerk's or the barber's.

But it served her right. It was her fault for barging in. The shock of seeing him undressed was no more than she deserved. This was *his* hotel room. He was getting his hair cut, for hell's sake.

"Hello, sir," said the scarecrow.

"Who are you?" boomed Ryan, jumping to his feet. He stalked across the floor, clumps of shorn hair flying from his shoulders. His muscles shook as if he were a grizzly defending his territory. "What the hell do you want?"

"Ryan," Julia breathed silently, stepping back in alarm as he lunged at them.

She stared at the wild beast. Hair trailed down his shoulders. His black beard glistened in the streaming sunlight.

With a tremor, she took in the guns and rounds of ammunition tucked into his belt, and wondered what war he was expecting. Still a fighter, she thought with an ache. He'd always be true to his guns or his fists or his knives, but never to a woman.

She heard David explaining their presence, and was grateful for the moment to recapture her breath.

"Sir, I'm David Fitzgibbon from the town's biggest paper, the *Calgary Town Crier,* and I'd like a moment to…to speak with you," he continued, while Julia watched Ryan.

Beneath his shaggy hair, droplets of water bounced across of his broad shoulders. Looking closely, she saw that Ryan's face was still recognizable: incredibly sharp, dark features and a sweeping gaze that took in everyone and everything in the room.

But his wounds…dear God.

They began with his earlobe—his partially missing left earlobe, which someone had apparently sliced off. She forced herself to look at his chest again. It was lightly matted with dark hairs, still damp from an obvious bath. She could well imagine layers of grime. There were more scars than she recalled, and she winced. Sunshine streaming from the window highlighted a long gash that cut from his right nipple across to the other side of his chest and down beneath his heavily muscled arm. Where in the world had he been?

She watched his muscles pulse, and tried to find a word to describe his looks. Nasty? Inhuman? His overbearing appearance created an aura of power, and an attitude that he didn't care much for the world.

He never had. He'd always been searching for meaning and direction in his life, even as a young man sitting on a stool in her grandpa's bar, trying to drink away his misery. He could drink longer and harder than any man Julia had ever known, and she'd served a lot of men in those lean years.

She forced herself to look lower down his body to his firm stomach, the coating of fine hairs, the muscled thighs encased in blue denim. His huge tan boots were as lined as his skin.

Had he found direction in his life? Had he found meaning?

She'd once heard Ryan's father, Joseph Reid, tell his son that he wouldn't amount to much in life. Even now, though she fought the reaction, her heart twisted as she recalled the look on Ryan's face when his father had berated him. But most folks in town, after witnessing the rage Ryan showed when he fought with his pocket knives, had said the same. They predicted he would die before he reached the age of thirty.

Her gaze traveled to the folded newspapers on the bed, piled beside a worn leather bag and a curious violin case.

Her paper was right on top. She groaned, thinking of her ad and wondering if Ryan had read it. She wasn't embarrassed about it in front of anyone else, but instinct told her to shield her vulnerability from Ryan. He wouldn't recognize her ad by her surname, but later, he might connect it to her. Placing a written request for a husband suddenly made her feel exposed.

If he saw it, Ryan would do what he always had: judge her.

David was still talking. "…if we might just…just snap a photograph or two, and ask a few questions, it could take the focus off the town's troubles for the moment. Sir."

Ryan turned toward Julia. A bolt of angry pride shot through her at the thought of how he might react if she lifted her brim to reveal her face. Would he be sorry for having treated her as if she'd meant nothing to him? Would he beg forgiveness?

She couldn't see *his* face, but his arms grew tense.

"And what about you?" he said to her in a vexing growl. "Do you speak?"

Her fingers gripped her notes while she fought the urge to slap him. "Only to people who are calm and reasonable enough to listen."

She heard the hotel clerk snicker. David gasped.

With a slow, deliberate sweep, she lifted her head, giving Ryan a full view of her face.

Their gazes locked. His dark eyes flickered, his stare penetrating her calm. The shock of knowing him raced along her skin. She braced herself for his reaction, expecting him to stagger back at the discovery. Heaven help her, for ten years she'd wondered about this moment. Goose-flesh rose on her arms and her heart drummed as she waited for him to crumble.

He did nothing. The spark of what might have been recognition vanished from his brown eyes.

"Reasonable enough to listen?" His mouth lifted in a slight grin. "Then maybe you should do the talking and let your friend sit down."

Julia struggled to grasp his meaning, then, slowly, her body slackened, her bottom lip dropped and a new humiliation swept over her. *He didn't remember her.*

Chapter Two

❧

Ryan Reid hadn't changed one blasted bit. He was still self-absorbed and completely unaware of how he affected those around him. With her pride toppled, Julia watched him dismiss the hotel clerk, while telling the barber to stay.

Her fresh disgrace only served to double the potency of ten years' worth of indignation. How many women had he been with these past ten years if he didn't recall her? True, her hair was different, her face had matured and she no longer wore the clothes of a serving maid, but still…

Fine. So he didn't remember her. It would be easier to get what she'd come *here* for then, wouldn't it? An interview with one of Calgary's *prominent* sons. Ha!

Julia tried to harness her temper as she took note of his room and its contents. A huge duffel bag sat propped in the corner; a boxy white shirt hung from the armoire door as if waiting to be pressed. The scent of the barber's lotions drifted her way. She should leave, instinct told her. She should walk out that door and down those stairs before

Ryan got the best of her. As a reporter, how could she ask him neutral questions in this explosive frame of mind?

Ryan walked to a small table that held refreshments and reached for a bottle of whiskey. Locks of cut hair clung to the towel wrapped around his thick neck. He was still half-naked, his haircut half-complete, but he didn't seem to care.

With haste, the barber cleaned his combs in the basin, discreetly withdrawing from the conversation but ready to continue the moment he was summoned. He sent Julia a strange grin. Oh, no, she thought, Todd must have read her ad. *Not now. Don't say anything now.*

Facing the window, Ryan held up the bottle of bourbon. His bare shoulder blades moved and the muscles on his lower back flinched. Remarkably, the skin on his back was unscarred, a total contrast to his front. "Anyone care to join me?"

David and Julia both muttered no. Her racing heart threatened to burst from her corset.

Ryan poured himself some liquor. "Tell me your names again."

"David Fitzgibbon, sir. And Miss Julia O'Shea."

"Actually," she said with a feverish snap, "it's Mrs., if you must know."

"Well, yes," said David, "but you're widowed."

Stop talking about me, thought Julia. Although David's talkative nature was normally a plus in reporting, it wasn't so right now. Fortunately, neither Todd nor David knew the true story of what had happened between her and Ryan. Very few folks in town did, except for Ryan's family, because the story had occurred twenty miles north in the town of Redwood, where she'd lived until five years ago.

She couldn't see Ryan's face now, so his mood was difficult to assess. His bulky silhouette filled the window frame. He lifted the shot glass partway to his lips, staring at the swirling gold liquid. "I knew an O'Shea once. He didn't live here. He lived in Redwood. Brandon was his name."

David spoke up. "That was her husb—"

Julia's glare stopped David cold.

With his hand on his glass, and still facing the window, Ryan hesitated. He swigged down his drink, then peered out at the street below, his voice low. "O'Shea's Printing Shop. Did that belong to Brandon?"

"*No,*" she snapped. "It belongs to me. I started it."

Ryan set his empty glass on the table and turned to face her. "In all my travels, I've never met a female reporter."

"It's about time, then, isn't it?"

A bolt of excitement, a thrill that she'd surprised him with her occupation, charged the air between them. She watched his muscles tense, his chest contract, his lips—those soft graceful lips that had once traveled all the hollows and dips of her body—part.

Julia couldn't seem to break free from the beast's gaze, but she heard David asking a question.

"In all your travels? Where exactly have you been, sir?"

When Ryan broke his lock on her to glare at David, Julia felt as though he'd left her body on fire.

David nervously inched backward. When he reached the bed, his knees gave way and he sank onto the mattress. "I'll just stay right here and let Miss O'Shea take over the questioning."

"That's a mighty fine idea," growled Ryan.

"Go ahead, Jul...Miss O'Shea." David looked from her to Ryan. "Let's start the questioning. We'll sit right over here on your bed, sir, if that's all right. Please continue with your haircut." David scooped the strewn newspapers into a pile near the footboard. "You won't be needing any of these other papers when you're reading ours."

Mercy. Her paper was precisely the one Julia wanted to cast away. Let Ryan amuse himself with someone else's ad. Now that he knew her surname, he'd know the advertisement was hers.

The bedsprings squeaked as David repositioned himself. The golden leather bag behind him tipped over. He patted the spot beside him, indicating she should sit, too, but her limbs felt too heavy to move.

The barber fidgeted, bringing his combs and scissors back to the towel beside the chair at the window, trying to look unobtrusive while he waited for his client to sit down. But he sent Julia another amorous glance.

She moaned. Todd was much too nosy for her liking, nearly three times her age, and had been trying to woo her for an entire year already.

Ryan didn't move his gaze off her.

Julia's first question came out as a hoarse whisper. "They tell me you've been out of town for a long spell. Where have you been?"

His deep voice stirred the air. "Overseas."

"What happened to you?"

"I joined the British army."

She wondered why. Living that far from home, he might as well have been on the moon.

He explained. "Anyone from a country aligned with the British Empire is allowed to join their military. Just like they can here with the Mounties. The Mountie ranks are filled with English and American men."

"True enough."

Ryan's presence, physically and mentally, seemed to take up the entire room. The space felt more like a box, and stifling hot. He lowered himself onto the barber's chair. Todd tilted Ryan's head forward to get at the back of it.

Julia was grateful for the release, a chance to tear her gaze away from the dark features. She sat on the bed, perched two feet away from Ryan's knees. He stared at her tattered hemline, the worn high heels of her buckle-down boots, and the torn kerchief poking out of her skirt pocket. A twinge of embarrassment shot through her, that she couldn't afford better.

The barber snipped around Ryan's ear. She tried not to stare at his slashed earlobe. A strand of black hair fell to the floor at her feet. She jumped away, as if contact might prove fatal.

"What are your plans, sir?" asked David, unable to restrain himself.

Ryan blinked at her boots. "I was hoping to keep them to myself until my family returns."

David leaned forward on the bed. "When will that be?"

"In a week."

"Problem solved. Our paper comes out weekly and this next edition won't come out till late Thursday, after they return."

Ryan shifted. The joints of the wooden chair groaned beneath his mass.

"I suppose my official plans will be out by tomorrow, anyway," he said, glancing at the snoopy barber.

Despite her apprehension, Julia had a job to do. "So you joined the British Army. Did that—that happen as soon as you left town? Did you go there directly?" Trying to suppress the trembling of her fingers, she raised pencil to paper.

Ryan took awhile to answer. Lord help her, she found herself both dreading and yearning to know every painful detail. As a reporter, she wanted to ask: *Why did you run that night? Why have you come back?*

As a living, breathing woman, she ached to demand: *How could your promise to me have meant nothing?*

The barber brushed the fallen hairs from his client's shoulders. "Your haircut's finished. I'll start the shave."

"I didn't go to England directly. It didn't happen right away, but soon enough."

Ryan's answer was so vague that she couldn't use it as a quote. She would have to ask more factual questions. "What…what did you do in the British Army?"

"Spent the first three years fighting for the colonies in Africa."

Africa. Half a globe away.

She must have taken too long to ask her next question, because David was staring at her. He scratched his temple. His cap shifted, then he blurted out another one. "What was your position?"

"Explosives expert."

David whistled. "Doing what?"

"Using dynamite and detonating roads. Bridges. The enemy's stockpile of ammunition. Whatever needed to be blasted to smithereens."

Julia detected displeasure in his voice, then something even deeper. Agony, perhaps. But *agony* seemed like such a strong word.

"And then?" she asked, taking notes. "What then, after those three years?"

Ryan's voice deepened. "I got tired of destroying things."

The violent Ryan Reid had tired of destruction? The daredevil who enjoyed doing everything to extremes? His ability to push everything and everyone to the limit was one of the reasons he'd been nicknamed "The Edge." Julia looked up from her notes. "Then you quit the army?"

"No," he said softly.

"I don't understand." She waited, but he didn't rush to explain. "What is it you do now for a living?"

Again Ryan paused, as if deliberating whether he should throw her and David out on their heels.

The ribbon beneath her chin that secured her straw hat seemed to tighten. She wiggled on the mattress, trying to find a better position, to sit straighter and appear more confident. When she crossed her legs, Ryan gazed at her thighs, and once again color rushed to her cheeks.

He leaned back, broad shoulders twisting to allow the barber to lather his beard.

She wondered how long he would make her and David wait for answers. Well, two could play that game. Ryan could wait until the roosters crowed if he thought she'd plead with him repeatedly for responses.

She waited for him to speak as if she had all the time in the world, but David lost his patience. He began a guessing game. "He's likely come back to try his hand at ranching. Like he used to with his father."

"Maybe," offered Julia with a touch of sarcasm, "he's become a professional fighter."

Ryan's jaw tightened and his stomach muscles flexed. When the barber finished scraping the razor down his cheek, Ryan straightened in his chair, and studied Julia. "I've enlisted with the Mounties."

David gaped. Julia quivered.

Did the Mounties accept such unruly men? A murderer—one not convicted of the crime, but who'd had a bad run-in with the law?

"Then you're a policeman like your brothers," said David.

"So I've heard."

"Will you work as an explosives expert with the Mounties?" Julia regained her focus and scratched some sentences on her paper. "And how long have you been enlisted?"

The barber scraped Ryan's other cheek, creating streaks of white and dark. A deep scar emerged, one that went from the left side of his jaw to his missing earlobe. No wonder he'd grown a beard. Looking at the scar made her eyes water. She glanced away, but not before he noticed her reaction.

His eyes flickered. "When I passed through Regina two weeks ago, I enlisted at headquarters. I requested to work in Calgary, so I report to the fort's commander tomorrow."

"A subconstable, then," she said in a rush.

He frowned at her assumption. "Why do you assume I'm starting at the very bottom?"

"Beg your pardon. What rank and position do you hold, so that I might get it right for the paper?" Exasperated, she poised her pencil.

Leaning back, stretching his long legs and crossing one

booted ankle over the another, Ryan tilted his head toward the ceiling rafters. She noticed him staring up at a spider web. The industrious spider dangled from a thread but was somehow trapped in suspension, much like Julia felt as she waited for this vexing character to answer her questions so that she might escape.

"All right," she said, rushing the interview along, "you said you were tired of blowing things up—"

"Of destroying things," David corrected.

"Destroying things," she repeated. "What's the difference between shredding things or destroying things, or leaving people behind whose lives you crushed..." She stared down at the sharp tip of her pencil, embarrassed at her outburst.

The room went dead. Julia took a deep breath, and when she glanced up again, the barber was toweling the last remnants of shaving cream from Ryan's face. Then he began sweeping hair up from the floor.

In the stilted silence, while the cornhusk broom scratched back and forth on the floorboards, Ryan answered. "My rank is inspector. I'm a field surgeon."

Although he spoke quietly, he couldn't have shocked her more if he'd jumped up and screamed.

"A doctor," said David. "Healing instead of stab—"

Ryan scowled.

David tilted his plaid cap and scratched his forehead. "But you need special training for that. And equipment."

"Does five years' training with the Royal Military Surgeons qualify? And if you lean back any farther on that bed, you're going to crush my medical bag."

"Hell," David muttered, twisting around to straighten the leather grip behind him. When three heads turned to stare at David, his freckles deepened with color. "Pardon me for the bad language, Jul—Miss O'Shea, but don't you see the irony? He was good with a blade before, and now he's still good with a blade."

Ryan winced. "That was the whole idea."

The barber packed his things and dashed to the door. Just before he reached it, he nodded at Julia.

Please don't say it, she silently begged him.

But Todd did. "I'd be most honored to petition as your man, the one in your ad, Miss O'Shea." He always tried to impress her by increasing his vocabulary, whether his sentences made sense or not. "I do reckon the contingency would be how much I have to offer. I imagine you'll have a proliferation of candidates—"

"Please, Todd, can we talk about this later?"

"At your decree, my lady."

When he left the room, Ryan glanced at the pile of newspapers. "What's he talking about?"

"Nothing important. Some—some help I need at the shop."

She didn't bother peering over at David, but she could well imagine his frown.

To her relief, he returned to the interview. "This'll make great copy. A field surgeon, no less, the most difficult type of medicine. Right in the heat of battle you tend to the bloodiest wounds."

"I prefer not to talk about that aspect."

"Sure, sure." David grabbed his camera from atop the pillow and jumped to his feet. "For the record, we should get the exact date you left Calgary." He scowled at Julia, as if wondering why she hadn't asked that question.

She already knew the date: the last day of September, 1885. It had been a Wednesday evening. Her grandpa, as much as he hated Ryan and all the other Reids, had been the one to gently tell her that Ryan had left.

Ryan didn't meet her eyes, but hoisted himself to his feet. "Ten years ago is all the answer you need."

He clutched the towel around his neck, his face now clean-shaven, his hair trimmed short. Although he no longer looked like a grizzly bear, the wild edge to him couldn't be erased with a simple haircut. No one could erase that brutal scar on his face, and there was something crude about his stance and the way he assessed them. Yet time had changed him in other ways. His cheeks were thinner, his eyes more focused.

David scanned the room, peering at the duffel bag, then the shirt on the armoire. "Is there a Mrs. Reid?"

Julia looked hastily to the floor, but felt Ryan's gaze scorching her face.

"No," he answered. "I never married."

She didn't care, she told herself. She didn't give a hoot.

"Hmm," replied David. "Look at all those scars." He stepped backward and pointed his camera at Ryan. "It would be very helpful to the story if you'd describe how it came to be that you lost part of your ear. Did it happen in a bloody siege? That would make the most marvelous—"

Ryan growled.

David persisted. "This photograph would look splendid put next to the one I took earlier with your dirty hair and long beard."

"What photograph?" Ryan demanded.

"I took some pictures of the wagon trains. That's where I first saw you—riding on the back of a wagon."

"I don't want any pictures printed. This interview is over." Ryan strode to the door and opened it wide.

"But, sir," David pleaded. "Miss O'Shea, tell him."

Ryan turned his attention to her.

She felt a small artery pulsing at her collarbone. Her temples had somehow become drenched with moisture. "We would need more details to make this article exciting. Perhaps something adventurous from your travels."

Ryan slid the towel from behind his neck and dropped it to his thigh. His guns, strapped to his hips, swayed. "I'm a private man. If you'd like me to answer any more questions, only one of you can stay. The less irritating one. The one without the camera." He looked directly at her. "Miss O'Shea."

Her pulse bounded.

David stammered in protest. "A single woman shouldn't be left alone with a—a man in his hotel room."

When Julia didn't answer, David stepped backward through the door and into the hallway. "I really think, Julia, you should return with me."

She couldn't budge, reeling with thoughts of what she'd dare say to Ryan if they were trapped alone.

"I'll be fine," she said. "To get a story, I've been caged in the jailhouse with worse criminals."

She meant it as an insult, and Ryan flinched as though he'd taken it as such.

David's further protests ceased when Ryan closed the door in his face.

Julia jumped at the loud click. Ryan sauntered toward her. Overwhelmed by his size, she craned her neck to look up, and willed herself to remain steady.

Inhaling deeply, she filled her lungs with dusty air and the scent of him.

Surprising her, he reached out with a rough hand and untied the satin ribbon from beneath her chin. His fingers grazed her flesh and she shuddered at the warm contact. How dare he lay his hands on her.

Slowly, he slid the hat from her head, then tossed it to the mattress. Her braid shifted along her spine and the fresh breeze stirred her loosened hair. Her lace-edged blouse rose up and down with her breathing and caught his eye.

Once again, she felt exposed beneath his stare.

"Julia…" When he whispered her name in that same craving tone he had once used while kissing her temple and throat and breasts, she knew she should run.

Chapter Three

Breathless, Julia bolted for the closed door. "The rest of this interview won't take long." She rattled on, aware that her words were garbled. "I suspect only ten minutes or—or so, and I would prefer to keep this door—this door *open*."

Ryan beat her to it. Their shoulders bumped, setting her body aflame. Sunshine washed through the room and reflected in his eyes. The scars on his torso glistened.

Julia squared her shoulders and grabbed the metal doorknob, yanking hard. The pine door collided with his boot. He wouldn't let it open more than a crack.

"Do you mind?" she huffed, keeping her eyes on the knob, where they wouldn't get her into trouble. Her notebook pressed against her bosom. "It's not entirely appropriate, as David said, that a woman remain alone with a man in his hotel room."

"David's an idiot."

"He's a smart man who writes wonderful prose."

"Leave the door closed."

The blood rushed to her head but she forced herself to take a calming breath. She was a writer, a competent businesswoman who usually had no trouble expressing herself. "I prefer some circulating air."

Ryan took three steps into the room, thus unblocking the door. "All right, I'll leave it up to you. You can open it if you like, but I'm going to say exactly what's on my mind, and you may not want the whole world to hear."

She snapped the door closed. For heaven's sake, she wished he would don some clothing.

"Say my name," he murmured.

She whirled around to face him, her skirt brushing the tops of her high-heeled boots. "What?"

"I want to hear you say it."

"I'll do no such thing."

"Then you're not leaving this room. Even if it takes us a week. I'll call for the Scottish maid to bring us food and change our sheets."

Julia gasped. "How *dare* you."

"Say it," he commanded.

"*Mr.* Reid."

"Not that one."

"*Inspector* Reid."

"Keep going."

"*Dr.* Reid."

"That's not the right one, either."

Julia swallowed, thinking how stupid it was to argue. She was prolonging the agony instead of ending it. "Ryan," she finally said, staring down at her notepad.

"Look at me when you say it."

Hesitantly, she lifted her head. "Ryan."

The light caught his good cheek, newly shaved and paler than the dark planes that had been touched by the sun. His lips curled upward into a grin she half remembered. Then he exhaled one of the sighs she wished she could forget.

She was not the girl he'd left behind, nor did she want to be. He had accomplished a lot. He'd become a doctor. But she wasn't here to do his bidding. Ryan had forced her to say his name because he was bigger and more powerful.

She glared at his smug expression. Because he'd left her all those years ago, she had learned to cope on her own, and she was quite good at coping now. Maybe she should thank him.

"You're an ass," she said. "That's the name I'd give you."

He raised an eyebrow in mock response but seemed more amused than indignant. "How've you been, Julia?"

So he *did* remember her. She stepped back, dismayed by his gall. "You son of a…"

"You still have a colorful way with words."

"Yes, but now I'm paid for them." It was sorrow, this time, that caused a lump in her throat. "A man with any amount of honor wouldn't have pretended he didn't know me. You haven't changed one bit."

She wasn't sure whether it was her words or the sincerity with which she'd said them that caused Ryan to pale.

He retreated to the window, poured himself another shot of bourbon and drank. "I wasn't sure if you'd want me to acknowledge that I knew you, with Todd and your reporter listening. I wasn't sure how much they already knew about us, or how to protect you from gossip."

His reasoning surprised her.

"Don't worry," she scoffed. "I didn't brag about knowing you to anyone."

When he turned around again, the fire was back in his eyes.

"Still drinking? As a surgeon, yet?"

"I usually take a shot before surgery. To keep my hands steady."

He must be joking! But not a smile cracked his face. She disliked this conversation. He wasn't being straightforward about his feelings, or about acknowledging her.

"Aren't you going to tell me how you've been?" he asked.

"This interview is about you," she reminded him, "and we won't be discussing me." She raised her notebook and walked to the window. A puff of wind blew the muslin curtains aside. Sounds from the street below echoed upward—the thump of oxen, the calls of children. "Now please tell me, for the article, exactly where you went after you left Calgary ten years ago. What happened in the months before you joined the British Army?"

She heard him move closer, then felt his bare elbow brush against her sleeve. He positioned himself to look out at the boardwalk below. "Why do you want this interview?"

"Because if I don't do this story, another paper will."

"This is such a minor story. Would it be so bad if a rival paper ran it?"

"We've had nothing but bad news to write about for two months straight, and folks are getting tired of reading about the drought. We need something social, more cheerful, to sell papers."

"You look far from cheerful, Julia."

"I'm good with words, and that's all that matters. On paper, I can turn my resentment of you into joy."

If he thought that statement was ludicrous, he didn't respond. "Then we'll compromise. A question for a question."

"What do you mean?"

"I'll answer one of your questions for each one of mine you answer."

"I can't agree to that. *I'm* the reporter."

Ryan persisted. "How long ago did Brandon pass away?"

"*Stop it.*" She struggled for composure. "There'll be a lot written about you in other papers, rumors about why you left. Maybe you'd like to explain your version so that we'll know the truth. What is it you'd like folks in town to know?"

He stared at her. "I imagine that soft approach works well on most people."

"It always works."

He yanked the pencil from her fingers. "A question for a question. How long ago did he pass?"

She snatched the pencil back. "Five years."

"Five years is a long time. I'm sorry." Ryan hesitated. "What did he die from?"

She steeled herself. "No, you don't. That's two in a row. It's my turn. I'll ask again. Why did you leave town the way you did?"

He ignored her question. *Again.* "Brandon was in the prime of his life. It must have been traumatic, something accidental, something sudden."

The curtain beside them lifted, in a swirl of hot wind, which ruffled the pages of her notebook and stirred the hairs on his muscled forearms. "We don't have anything to discuss about our past. I've got nothing to say to you, do you understand?"

This time he snatched her notebook. "Then you'll listen."

She clicked her tongue in agitation. "When it comes to my private life, I don't listen to liars."

"An ass and a liar? That's a powerful combination," he said, his eyes lighting with laughter. "Is that how you'll describe me in your article?"

She took her notebook from his fingers. "I have a mind to. I should expose you as you really are."

His humor faded. Regret flitted across his features. "I suspect...I suspect most folks here know the hard truths about me already."

The sadness in his voice tugged at a corner of her heart.

"Once upon a time," he said softly, "you would have been impressed that I'd come back a Mountie."

"Once upon a time...you never would have left."

Ryan stiffened.

"I answered your question about Brandon. Now tell me why you left Calgary."

"To seek my great fortune."

"Oh, come now, that's so feeble."

"You don't think anyone will believe it?"

"Most folks in town will remember that you killed a man. Am I supposed to overlook that in my article? None of the other papers will, I assure you."

"Yes, you're supposed to overlook it. Time for another one of my questions. What did Brandon die of?"

"Cancer of the stomach."

Ryan winced.

Julia looked away, toying with her pencil, trying not to

succumb to the hot sting of tears. At least it had gotten to the point where she could say it aloud without weeping.

She volleyed another question. "Did you miss Calgary while you were gone?"

"Yes," he answered, then tossed out a question of his own. "When did you marry Brandon?"

Persistent talk of Brandon made her edgy. She wanted to let him rest in peace. What had happened between the three of them was over. She blurted the truth and didn't care if it hurt Ryan. "Nearly ten years ago."

Ryan swayed. Then he struck back with his own cutting remark. "Didn't wait long, did you?"

Her muscles tightened and she spoke before she thought. "Brandon loved me. There was no one else worth waiting for."

She didn't need to see Ryan's face to know her words had shaken him. His fist grew taut on the sill. "I was different then. More boy than man."

"If you suspect that time has stood still while you've been gone, you're mistaken."

"So I see."

"My next question. Why did you come back?"

He paused for a long time. "Because someone gave me an old violin."

She turned and looked past his shoulder to the marred violin case nestled in the bedsheets. Its buckles were weathered and scratched from years of use. "What does that mean? Who gave it to you?"

He shrugged.

When he didn't explain further, she continued to pry. "I didn't know you played."

"I don't. At least, not very well."

She blinked. "Maybe you came back to make amends."

"You think so?"

"To your family. To those who cherished you." She swallowed and turned to glance out the window again, at the busy street below, so he couldn't see her face.

"They didn't all cherish me."

"You have the poorest vision of any man I know."

"What do you care about my family? I don't recall you admiring anyone in it."

"What do you expect? What did they ever do for mine, except lock the prison cell when they had us in it?"

"What happened in Ireland in debtors' prison never mattered to me," Ryan said with a strained voice.

"It didn't matter that my father was broke and had no way to pay his debts? That your father was our jailer? Well, while you've been gone, the almighty Joseph Reid has never forgotten it."

"What does that mean?"

"Never mind. I…" Hiking her skirts, she stepped toward the door. "For the sake of my business, I'd like to continue this interview, but we can do it tomorrow." She needed time to recover.

The Reids had always turned up their noses at her and hers, even back in Dublin. Even on the ship crossing to Canada. There was one ship that sailed every September, filled with immigrants to Canada, and one year when Canada had widely advertised for homesteaders to settle their West, her family and Ryan's had been on it.

"Do I have your word you won't tell your story to a rival paper?"

"My word," he agreed after a moment. "However much that's worth to you."

"Then tomorrow—"

"I'll drop by your shop later today."

She recoiled. No. She didn't want him there. "My shop?"

Ryan parted the shabby curtains and nodded toward the building. "It looks prosperous. You've done well."

Yes, she had, thanks to the fury he'd roused in her—a deep, rich burn that had spurred her to fight against the low standards people had set for her because of who she was and where she'd come from. It was the same fire that fueled her determination to make her newspaper the best in town, that made her refuse to fall into debt as her father had. She'd never feel that shame again.

Like most debtors in the days before the new Irish laws had come into effect—laws that banned the practice of jailing people who were unable to repay their debts—her father had had to shelter his family in the cold brick building of the debtors' prison. No one else would take them in. He and Grandpa had owed money to the bank in trying to make their general store survive, so they'd all gone to jail: her father, mother, herself and Grandpa. Julia would never forget the damp scent of spring coming through the bricks, the humiliation of attending a makeshift school in the prison yard with two other ragged children, or the clang of keys on Officer Joseph Reid's belt as he patrolled the building.

"I'm busy later," she said to Ryan now. "I've got papers to deliver and accounts to call upon."

"I'll try, anyway. If you're there, you're there." Peering out the window, he frowned. "Is that your grandfather?"

Swiveling to look, Julia gasped when she saw Pete holding the door for Grandpa. Her folks had long since passed away—her father shortly after he'd served his jail term, her mother from being heartsick. *These* were the two men in Julia's life now. An awkward seven-and-a-half-year-old boy who was a legacy of his proud father, Brandon, a mirror image with sandy brown hair and dimpled cheeks. And a scrappy old man who would beat the world to a pulp on her behalf. But they were not for Ryan's eyes.

"Who's that with him?" asked Ryan.

"Someone passing by on the boardwalk."

"No, I mean the young fellow holding the door open."

"I don't see—" she swallowed firmly "—who you mean."

"They've gone inside."

Thank goodness. Maybe it was silly to try to shield her son from Ryan, but everything and everyone she'd ever loved in this life had sooner or later been hurt by a Reid. It was instinct to protect those she loved from those she distrusted.

Ryan let the curtain fall back into place. "As soon as I get a shirt pressed and make a short business detour, I'll be joining you in your shop."

The terror of his words caused her to trip toward the door. As well as protecting her son from Ryan's eyes, she wanted Ryan to keep from discovering that her newspaper was close to bankruptcy, and that she was blatantly seeking a husband. She knew it was wrong to be conscious of outward appearances, but she wanted him to think she'd done so much better.

Ryan reached out to steady her.

With his hands on her shoulders, the air between them softened for a moment.

He took advantage of that moment, removing her note-book and pencil from her hands to lay them on the bed, then reaching out to touch her neck. She wavered at his strength. Gently, with his thumb, he lifted her chin so they were eye to eye. Then he moved his thumb down the center of her jaw, her throat, over her velvet choker to the base of her neck.

Her sense of touch deepened, her body heated, the rush of sounds from the open window doubled. He had always made her more aware of life around her. At one time, she had felt thrilled to face the future standing at his side. But there had been no future with Ryan.

"I've come to say hello, Julia. There's no need to be afraid."

"Take your hands off me," Julia demanded, wrenching free of his grasp. When she looked at him as if he had the plague, Ryan struggled with uncertainty. It had been a long time since he'd felt such misery around a woman.

He'd once been in an earthquake on the northern border of India, and that was how it now felt, watching Julia. While he stared at her upturned mouth, the straight nose and crystal-blue eyes, he felt as if the shaking ground couldn't hold him, that no matter where he ran, he wouldn't be safe.

After ten years, the curves of her body had softened, but they still made *his* body ache. He wished he could say that she hadn't changed, but she had weariness in her eyes now, harsh lines on her forehead and, at times, a hollow-ness to her voice. Still, her olive-hued skin was beautifully taut, and her eyes dazzled him with her intelligence.

For a brief time when they'd been lovers, she had been

so receptive to his conversation, so giving in her nature. And how had he repaid her? By taking something from her she could never regain: her virginity. He'd taken it as callously as someone asking for a cup of coffee. He should have known better. He should have done better. Then she'd fled back into Brandon's arms. Many a night in Africa, Ryan had lain awake wondering whether Brandon had ever discovered she'd lost her innocence. Since she'd married Brandon, Ryan's competitor must have known.

Julia snatched her hat off the bed. She took her newspaper, too.

"Hey," he said, "that's mine."

"I'll give you next week's paper for free." With skirts whirling, she grabbed her notebook off the bed and stretched to reach her pencil, which had rolled under the pillow.

"But I want this one."

She refused to return it.

He twisted forward to help locate the missing pencil, his bare shoulder brushing her clothed one. Her touch could still shake him. "I can try and explain about my absence, Julia, but—"

"You had ten years. Not a word, not a letter."

"That's why you're so angry—"

"You have no right to tell me why I'm angry!" She jammed her straw hat onto her head. The blue feathers shook.

"I didn't write because I thought you hated me."

"I do!" She extracted her pencil. "Aha, here it is!"

"Thanks for the homecoming."

"What did you expect? All you Reids are nothing but spoiled men. You always seem to get what you want."

How much more of this did he have to swallow? He

grabbed her by the upper arm and wheeled her around. "How the hell do you know what I want?"

"You want whatever pleases you this instant, with no regard for consequences!"

Struggling to keep his breathing even, he grabbed her other arm and thrust her backward until she was pressed against the door. "If you didn't still feel something for me, your face wouldn't be so red."

"What a vain thing to say. Just as high-and-mighty as pretending you didn't know me when I walked through that door!" Her hand came up to slap him, but he pinned it at her side.

The blue satin ribbons from her hat fell down her shoulders, intertwining with her auburn braid. His gaze traveled the length of them, lingering where the outline of her corset strained against the cotton fabric of her blouse. Her hair was longer than it used to be, and the color had changed to something indescribable. It sparkled red in sunlight but turned a deep brown-chestnut when she stood in shadow. Her breasts looked just as tempting as they always had. He had half a mind to place his lips on one.

Glancing lower, he caught sight of the newspaper that had fallen to the floor. An ad in the bottom corner caught his attention because her name was written at the top. "'Wanted, one gentleman husband.' What is this?" He laughed heartily as he read further. "'Seeking a refined man of quality. If you have a respectable steady occupation and enjoy family life, please schedule an appointment with Miss Julia O'Shea at your earliest convenience.'"

Julia was after a husband, and the poor thing had to advertise for one. "That's what you're hiding."

He looked at her, still trapped in his arms. The deep crimson of her face and the icy gleam in her eyes telegraphed what she thought of him in a way that no words could.

Goddamn her and those eyes.

Boldly, he loosened his grip on her hands, dipped his mouth and covered hers.

He tried to evoke a response, but she didn't move. He pressed harder, but still nothing. Then ever so gently, he withdrew the pressure on her mouth, until he'd coaxed her lips to respond.

So she did feel something. When he stroked the back of her neck, every part of his body tingled.

So potent was her draw that he inhaled her. Her scent filled his senses, waking a long-dormant memory of clean skin and fresh breath. When Ryan yanked Julia closer, she allowed it. He moaned softly and swore he could hear the thudding of his heart.

Pressing forward for more, plastering his body against hers, he released her arms and slid his hands along her waist.

She broke free and slapped him.

Ryan staggered back, rubbing a sore cheek.

She turned the knob behind her and flung the door wide. As she tore out, she left the newspaper at his feet and the sting of her slap on his face.

"I suppose I deserved that, for pretending that I didn't know you."

"No," she said, pivoting back around, her cheeks flushed and her lips swollen from his kiss. "You deserved that for assuming you still do!"

Chapter Four

Julia hoped her shop might provide a safe haven for a few hours, or even a few precious moments to collect her wits after that horrendous kiss, but she was mistaken. Chaos reigned.

Grandpa, Pete and David were handing out the remaining newspapers to half a dozen distributors, while David's monkey, Willy, scurried across the counters. Willy had been left behind years ago by a traveling circus, and now, whenever David allowed, spent hours with young Pete. She was used to the sight of a monkey, but most strangers weren't. Monkeys were uncommon on the prairies. Adding to the commotion, three of the most unlikely men looked up from the counter to nod at Julia as she burst into the shop. She felt a nervous twitch in her chest. Perhaps they were here about her ad.

At the counter stood Todd the barber in his shiny brown vest, plus Mr. Shapiro, one of the town's newest barristers, and Mr. Rossman, the mercantile owner.

"Good afternoon, gentlemen." Julia flew behind the

counter, shoved her straw hat onto a lower shelf and faced the three men.

"Ma!" Pete raced up from behind. "Is lunch ready?"

"Haven't you already eaten?" She glanced at Grandpa.

"We thought we'd wait for you. Where were you just now?" Grandpa rolled up his sleeves and stared at the three men.

She didn't have the heart to tell him she'd just seen Ryan Reid. She had to break it to him gently, alone. She feared his reaction.

"I—I already had a bite to eat while you were collecting Pete from his cousins'." It was just a little white lie. There was so little food to go around, and only two pickled eggs left. She'd been counting on payment from her two suppliers this morning to stock her pantry shelf with several cans of beans, but it would be difficult to do now, since they'd paid her with rags and tin.

Grandpa eyed her. "Are you sure?"

Julia nodded toward the back hallway that led to the rooms where she, Pete and Grandpa lived. "You two go on ahead. The boy's hungry."

As they walked away, Julia scanned the shop and noticed that David's picnic basket had already been delivered by his two elderly aunts, who took good care of him. He bit into a huge yellow apple as Julia spun back to the three men at the counter. The heavenly scent of the apple—even if she only imagined it—made her stomach growl.

But she heaved in a breath and smiled at the lineup. "Now then. What can I help you gentlemen with?"

Todd wasn't shy. "About this here advertisement you

placed, Miss O'Shea. I can tell you with undisguised candor that I'm interested."

If only he were forty years younger. Julia was somehow pleased that he was showing an interest, and didn't want to embarrass him by turning him away in front of the others. "Drop by tomorrow, Mr. Mead, around eleven forty-five. We can speak then." That was roughly the same time David's elderly aunts, both unattached, came in to deliver their picnic basket, and Julia would introduce them to Todd. They were more compatible in age.

"That makes me…utterly rhapsodic."

"Pardon me?" asked Julia, amused by his language.

"I'm pleased." The barber smiled, revealing a straight row of teeth. He did take meticulous care of himself. Julia had never seen such lovely teeth on a person his age.

When he left, Mr. Shapiro, heavyset and wearing a wool plaid suit, stepped up with hat in hand. "I'm here to ask you out for dinner tonight, Miss O'Shea, at the fancy hotel. Just this morning, they received a shipment of frozen lobster on the eastern train. Their seafood never lasts long."

"My goodness." Julia fanned herself. This quest to find a husband might prove to be exciting. "I've never tried lobster." A full meal sent from heaven.

"Then you must. If I come back at six o'clock, would that be suitable?"

"Yes, quite. Thank you." Her mouth watered at the thought of ordering anything off a menu. How many years had it been?

He tipped his hat goodbye.

Sharp and to the point. She liked that. He did breathe a little too loudly, and his gait was a bit lazy, but she reckoned it was due to the hot spell and having to wear such heavy suits in his line of work. *Lobster!* Instinctively, she wondered if she could bring home a portion of her meal for Pete and Grandpa. Maybe if she brought a square of linen in her bag this evening…

Glancing through her front windows, she watched Mr. Shapiro walk by on the boardwalk. Fancy that. An accomplished man like him interested in her. And why not? She glanced beyond his rounded shoulders to the Prairie Hotel. No sign of anyone at the front doors. No Ryan Reid. Irritated with herself for looking, she brought her attention back to Mr. Rossman.

He leaned over the counter. "I'm here for the ad, too."

"Why, Mr. Rossman, you're already married!"

"It was my wife who sent me."

"Good grief! What on earth are you two thinking?"

"The missus has a nephew who's new to town."

Julia wilted with relief. "Oh, it's your nephew." She eyed the old man. Mr. Rossman's wife was twenty years his junior, which would make her nephew even younger. "How old is he?"

"Don't know for certain. Twenty-five. Twenty-six."

Good heavens. Julia was thirty-two. That would put him possibly seven years younger. She'd heard stories of younger men marrying older women, but had never witnessed such a thing herself. Certainly, she didn't want to become a town spectacle.

Mr. Rossman seemed to notice her hesitation. "He's a fine young man with steady employment."

She lowered her voice. "May I be candid, sir?"

"It's the only way to be."

"Why does he need you and your wife to speak for him?"

"Because he doesn't know about the ad yet. He's been out of town for two days as a scout for the wildfires."

"A scout?"

"He's a sergeant with the Mounties. Sergeant Holt MacAllister."

"*Oh.*" On the whole, Mounties were hardworking men devoted to the community. Of course, not all of them were desirable. She gazed again through the dusty windowpanes toward the Prairie Hotel. This time, Ryan burst out of the doors.

The sight of him startled her. Dressed in a black shirt and brown Stetson, he didn't bother to glance toward her shop before sauntering down the street in that self-important manner that David had so aptly described. She found it painful to watch Ryan. Painful to acknowledge that a part of her heart was still so shaken at seeing him again. Painful to realize that the chasm between them had widened into an insurmountable valley. Painful that at the age of thirty-two she hadn't been able to overcome the hurt and sorrow she'd felt so vividly the night he'd left her.

She swallowed against the big ball in her throat. She had other dreams now. Spectacular dreams for herself and her son. And land's sake, she was eating lobster tonight. Turning back to Mr. Rossman, she smoothed her lace collar. "Do tell me more about this sergeant."

Ryan headed to the bank to make a small deposit of gold. He'd suspected the sight of his scarred jaw and missing earlobe would garner the attention of a few folks, but by the time he reached the bank's front doors, irritation had set in. Three barefooted boys, roughly twelve years old, were following him along the sagging boardwalk.

"Go on," he said. "Run along."

"What happened to you, mister?"

"Nothing special. Go on!"

They shrieked and dashed away, dirty feet flying.

Indoors, it was cooler and darker. Ryan's eyes adjusted to the light as he headed to the teller's cage, deposited his gold, then asked to speak to the bank manager.

"Well, well, well. The Edge is back in town."

Ryan wheeled around to face an old acquaintance. It surprised him that this man with a gray beard and ramrod spine was the bank manager. The friendly teller left abruptly while the two men assessed each other.

"Cleveland Bosley." Ryan extended his hand, but Bosley declined the handshake, which left Ryan feeling stupid. "Bank manager, are you? And how's your wife?"

Through gold-rimmed spectacles, Bosley's eyes flickered over Ryan's face, then settled on the slashed earlobe. The banker grimaced. "Still heartbroken that you made our Johnny skip town."

"He wanted to be a boxer. I didn't give him that skill."

"You showed him how to use it."

They wouldn't settle anything by talking. They never could. "How's he doing?"

"Heavyweight champion of New York."

Not bad. It was what Johnny had always wanted. "I'm here on business, Bosley. Can you help me or not?"

Bosley raised his hand. There was an envelope in it. "I suppose this is why you're here. It came two days ago."

Ryan accepted the letter. When he had passed through

Toronto, he'd asked a teller at a branch of this bank to forward his mail. Judging by the return address, Worldwide Antiquities, this was the letter he'd been expecting. "Mighty obliged. My regards to Mary."

At first, the manager didn't respond. Ryan knew no kind words would be said about him at their dinner table tonight.

The man adjusted his stiff tie. "I'd like you to take your business elsewhere."

"But I just deposited—"

"There's a savings and loan across the street, and the Imperial Bank around the corner."

Son of a bitch. Fighting humiliation, Ryan felt heat wash up his face. "All right."

When Ryan turned back to the teller's cage, the handful of people in the room—three customers in line, plus two other tellers—grew uncomfortably silent. To top off his disgrace, Ryan waited twenty minutes before he was served again, pretending he didn't hear the whispering, didn't see the awkward shift in people's postures. His original teller no longer smiled as she served him.

It took another forty-five minutes to open a new account at the Imperial Bank. Thank God no one in there knew him. But as soon as he walked out, he bumped into Val Zefield and his brother.

"Hell," said Val. "Look what the snakes dragged in."

"Good to see you again, too, Val." Ryan crossed the road in an attempt to keep the peace. There were women and children passing in the streets and they didn't need to witness anything nasty.

"I've been waitin' a long time, Reid."

Ryan pressed on, but felt an unexpected hand on his shoulder. Turning, he raised his arm to protect himself, but Val slugged him in the jaw. A jolt of pain crackled down Ryan's back teeth. The force smashed him to the ground.

"I've been picturin' you like that for nearly ten years. I lost a lotta money the night you ran out. A hundred and fifty dollars. My whole goddamn house because you lost that fight!"

Ryan cradled his mouth. Nothing broken. "You should have bet on someone better." As much as he wanted to pound the life out of Val, Ryan rose slowly to his feet and backed away instead.

Val and his brother glared, then spat in the dirt. "Some Edge." They laughed and sauntered away.

Ryan dusted off the seat of his pants, picked up his hat and the envelope that had fallen to the ground, and nodded to a group of women that he'd be all right.

Once on the battlefield in Africa, when the wounded men on stretchers, dozens of them, had overflowed beyond the walls of the medical tent, and the flies had created a constant hum, Ryan had run out of suturing material. He'd made himself a promise as he looked at his assistant, Adam Willeby, the young man who'd bequeathed Ryan his violin—just before rebels shot him in the head. No matter how bad things got in the future, no matter how miserable Ryan might feel, he knew that nothing could ever be as desperate as that moment. He'd bargained with God. Not that he really believed in the Almighty, but he didn't disbelieve, either. He'd promised never to complain about his own life again, if God could just see fit to send him more suturing material to stitch the wounded. Just as soon as he'd voiced the thought, Adam's violin came to mind. It had been the best use of violin strings Ryan could imagine. Adam had died nonetheless. But two other men were walking on the planet at this very moment who still had violin strings holding their joints together.

Being slugged by Val was nowhere near as bad as sewing up men with violin gut strings. Ryan folded his letter and tucked it in his shirt pocket, deciding to read it later. Right now he had unfinished business. He swallowed a trickle of blood and headed for O'Shea's Printing Shop.

Ryan spotted Julia the moment he walked through her shop door. Removing his cowboy hat, he acknowledged to himself that he didn't have to answer any more of her newspaper questions. But in all the time he'd known her, this was the only thing she'd ever asked of him. Even strangers on his journey had asked more of him than she had.

The place looked like one of those traveling fairs Ryan had seen once in England, with Julia standing in the middle. A monkey, yes, a *monkey*, was squealing from the rafters and zipping above everyone's heads. The thin, blond scarecrow in a plaid cap who called himself a reporter was seated at a desk in the far corner, taking down dictation from an old gent sitting with his back to Ryan.

Julia stood behind the counter facing a group of six men, some hollering for stacks of newspapers to distribute. Two or three others, judging by their pointed comments, seemed more interested in her as a potential wife.

The hair around her face was moist from the afternoon heat. The vertical pleats of her blouse billowed over her breasts and tapered softly into her waistband.

It wasn't Ryan's fault that Julia had fallen so hard for him in her youth. They'd never talked about their sentiments. She had always just been there, like a comfortable chair in her grandpa's saloon, whenever Ryan needed a drink or a friendly ear. He had figured she listened in that same attentive way to all the men she'd served. Hell, he'd witnessed it with his own eyes. She had a way of noticing what every person in the room said, then coming back with a sentence or two of encouragement precisely when a man needed it. Those were the same qualities that likely made her a good reporter.

Ryan had never considered her for marriage back then, and his past behavior shamed him. Now, marriage didn't even enter his thoughts.

When he'd been younger, he'd thought that barmaids were…well, just barmaids. There for the taking. It had surprised him that she'd been a virgin before they'd met. Quite frankly, he hadn't known how to handle it. Later, after he'd bedded her, he had done what he'd always done when things scared him: he ran.

Well, he was back to face all his shortcomings, in all their blazing glory. As a promise to the late Adam Willeby.

Julia glanced up from the notepaper she was writing on and finally noticed Ryan. As her eyes met his, he thought of that burning kiss back in his hotel room, and vowed he wouldn't do it again.

She excused herself from the other men, slid out from behind the counter and approached Ryan.

He was the first to speak. His words were honest. "I hope you pick out a good man."

Her eyebrows pinched together. "There do seem to be plenty to choose from."

There was a fight in her voice and it rankled him. Years ago, she'd been more carefree, easy to bring to laughter, never uttering a harsh word.

What had happened to the quiet Julia Adare? She was now Julia O'Shea. Ryan wondered how much of her current anger had to do with him and how much with her circumstances. Because of their family history, he'd tried to keep his visits to the bar a secret from his own family. That is, until that night when it'd blown up in his face.

He hoped that as Julia aged, she wouldn't turn into one of those bitter old women. He had a mind to tell her so, but didn't want to be shown the door. After his run-in with the banker and the two Zefield brothers, Ryan was thinking that explaining his side of things in her newspaper might soothe some ruffled feathers in town. It couldn't hurt. And so he would wait patiently while she finished with her suitors.

She planted her hands on her hips. "I'm surprised you're here, after our last discussion."

"The slap in the face, you mean?" He expected her to look away in embarrassment, or tell him to hush his voice, or do anything to indicate she was as troubled by her own reaction to the kiss as he'd been by his, but she didn't flick an eyelash.

"It was well warranted, don't you think?"

He grumbled silently to himself. She was so much tougher than she used to be.

"If you don't mind having a seat," Julia said, pointing to the two empty chairs by the open door, "David should be right with you. He's working on an advertisement for the preacher and should be finished soon."

"The preacher?" The man had his back turned, so Ryan couldn't see his face.

"He has some hogs he'd like to sell."

Ryan lowered his gaze to his hands, fingering the brim of his cowboy hat, feeling oddly disappointed that David, not Julia, would be finishing his interview. Seeing her again was as comforting as it was painful. "I'll sit right here like a good schoolboy."

"You were never a good schoolboy."

Amused, he sauntered to the chairs and sank onto one. "I'll try my hardest. Good luck with your own—" Ryan glanced past her hips to the lineup "—endeavors. If you need any help choosing someone, I'd be glad to assist."

Pursing her lips, Julia returned to the counter as Ryan crossed one booted foot over the other. He was glad he wasn't in the running. It was ridiculous, really, for these men to have to stand in line as if they were ordering sausages at a fair.

The minutes passed slowly. Two of her would-be suitors—ranchers, it seemed—left, while one remained. He was dressed in a clean business suit, so he obviously worked in town as opposed to on a farm. Ryan didn't recognize any of them and was happy no one recognized him.

He stretched his legs again, trying to get comfortable on the wooden seat. No sir, he wasn't interested in marriage. He enjoyed his life unsettled. In his travels, he'd witnessed a lot of marriages, and the bad ones all had one thing in common—two terribly unhappy people forced to stay together for the sake of appearances. Ryan, in contrast, thrived on constant change. Always had. His ability to deal with evolving circumstances, a changing battlefront, life-and-death decisions, had toughened him to the point that very little could get beneath his skin to hurt. He'd be utterly bored staying put for too long.

When the preacher walked by, Ryan stood up and nodded. He recognized the old guy.

"Reverend Dickens, how are you?"

The white-haired gent in a clean blue shirt stooped forward. "Ryan, my boy? Goodness, is that you?"

Praise the stars, a friendly reaction from *someone*.

"Yes, sir."

"When did you get back into town?"

"A few hours ago."

"That means you've missed your folks."

"Yes, sir."

"Well, we need to catch up, don't we? Cleanse your soul, so to speak." The reverend laughed. Ryan didn't. The man had always had a talkative nature. Frankly, he talked too much. "What say we have supper one evening and I can fill you in on your mother's illness—"

"My mother?" Ryan's heart nearly stopped.

"Isn't that why you're home?"

"No, I haven't heard. What's wrong with my mother?"

"She had a stroke five months ago, but is near to full recovery."

Ryan couldn't speak for the sorrow that gripped him.

"Tell you what," said the reverend. "Why don't we make it supper tonight? The owner of the fancy hotel, the Picadilly, keeps inviting me for a complimentary meal on account of a favor I did for his daughter. Why, just this morning at breakfast service, he was telling me he got in his annual shipment of lobster. It goes fast. It always does. Why don't we meet at the Picadilly, say around five-thirty?"

Ryan nodded in agreement, still unable to speak, but the minister didn't seem to notice as he left the shop.

Slumping in his chair, Ryan took several moments to compose himself. He had lived life to the fullest while he'd been away, but so had everyone else in town. Life had gone on without him. If his mother had passed away…God forbid…Ryan wouldn't even have known.

He was brought out of his trance by the sight of a little boy moving around the shop—the kid he'd seen earlier from the hotel window. Ryan watched the boy weave in and out between David's desk and the chairs. The child started playing with some pencils and ink pads as David rose from his seat and looked at Ryan.

"I'll fetch us each a glass of cool water and be right back to talk to you," the reporter said. He also mumbled something to the kid, so Ryan assumed he was his son.

The boy was just as skinny, with a similar ruddy complexion. About seven or eight years old, he was barefoot, wearing overalls, with shaggy brown hair and protruding ears. But when he stepped back and glanced up, Ryan was nearly blown out of his seat. The boy was a young duplicate of Brandon O'Shea. He had the same lopsided dimple, the same large ears, the same clump of brown hair, the same hesitant way of sizing up a stranger.

Struggling with the sight of his dead friend's child, Ryan cast a look in Julia's direction. Her son. Hers and Brandon's.

Life *had* gone on without Ryan. He'd never been struck by such a pang of emptiness. It was more than he could handle. It was just…a shock. Rising to his feet, he took an unsteady step toward the door.

"Hey, Doc," David called from behind him. "Where you going?"

"We can finish up another time. You can find me tomorrow morning at the fort. I'm headed there now to check in."

Ryan didn't turn, but he heard a quick shuffling of feet behind him. "But I brought you a glass—"

He swung around at the same instant that a fist cracked his already sore jaw. It normally wouldn't have decked him, but it hit the exact spot where Zefield had punched him. The painful force landed Ryan on his back, on the floor.

"Back for more, are you, you son of a bitch?" Flanagan Adare, Julia's grandfather, of medium height but as thick and gnarled as an old pine tree, stood panting above Ryan. "Couldn't get enough the first time 'round?"

"Grandpa!" Julia hollered from behind the counter. Her sole remaining suitor stared.

Ryan rubbed his sore mouth. "Damn it, Flanagan, hold your horses. I'm not back to cause trouble." He tasted blood again. The old goat had got in a lucky punch.

"I don't care why you're back. *Get out.*" Flanagan stared at Ryan's missing earlobe. "I see that other folks feel the same way I do about you."

"Some."

"The bright ones."

Ryan attempted to rise, but fell back down when the room started spinning. "Good to see you, too, old man."

"Some women might be easy to fool, but you're never going to bullshit your way past these old eyes again."

"I give you my word, I'll keep my distance."

"Your word is worthless. You left her to die. She was ill with scarlet fever for three months. Jesus Christ, she was all I had left in the world, and you left her to die."

Ryan felt as though someone had kicked him in the ribs. She'd had scarlet fever? Still dizzy from the fall, but clawing his way to a sitting position, he reeled toward Julia. By the trembling of her mouth, he knew it was the truth. He moaned. God, he'd had no idea.

"Sir, sir!" David said to the old man, setting down his water glasses and racing to Ryan's side. "I invited him here. This man is a surgeon. He served in the British Army and is now an officer with the Mounted Police!"

Flanagan stared down at Ryan, his white hair and whiskers stark against his suntanned skin. "It doesn't make him a better man. He is what he's always been. A selfish bastard."

Ryan stumbled to his feet. The haunting brown eyes of Brandon O'Shea's boy followed him. Shame of a kind Ryan had never felt before permeated every inch of him.

How was a man supposed to catch up with ten years of regret?

Flanagan didn't relent. He kicked his foot in the direction of the door. "You've had your look. Now get up and get out. You're not even good enough to crawl on her floor."

Chapter Five

Humiliated. That's how Julia felt all afternoon as she finished up in the print shop. Folks in town who weren't supposed to know that she and the black sheep of the mighty Reid family were connected—or rather, had been in the past—now detected something worthy of gossip.

The fact that Grandpa had punched out the new surgeon was somewhat of a bonus for the wagging tongues, the news tearing through town faster than the wildfires taking root in the foothills. Julia heard the whispering at the bank when she delivered her newspapers, felt the stares at the market when she traded in her crate of tin scraps for two turnips, and dodged questions from her neighbor, old Mrs. Perkins, in the backyard while she pegged her laundry on the line. Julia refused to tell them a blessed thing. As for Grandpa's unexpected punch, she silently gave a big hurrah.

But her son was someone she'd never dodge, so when Pete started asking questions while she prepared for her evening out with Mr. Shapiro, Julia found herself struggling to answer.

"Who was the man Grandpa hit?" Pete glanced up at her while she brushed her long hair at the hallway mirror. He was short for his age, and sometimes it concerned her whether he was getting enough to eat.

"Someone we knew a long time ago."

Pete scooped one of her shiny hairpins off the rickety wooden stand. He spoke matter-of-factly, but Julia heard the masked curiosity in his voice. "Grandpa hates him."

"I know." Hoping to distract Pete, Julia asked him to hand her the tortoiseshell comb. It had been her mother's in Ireland, something she'd said brought her luck whenever she'd worn it. Julia hoped for luck tonight with Mr. Shapiro. She'd decided on her newly washed navy skirt and navy blouse. The color was as subdued as the dark colors Mr. Shapiro usually wore. Yet, set against her skin, gave life to her complexion.

Pete placed the comb in her palm. "What did the man do?"

How could she explain it to a child? She shifted her weight to her other leg, suddenly aware how constricting her corset felt. Before she left this evening, she must remember to loosen it. "He was very rude to me when we knew each other."

"Then I hate him, too."

Pete's protective nature always brought out her tender side. "Don't say *hate*…it's an awful word."

"But he's an awful man." Pete's gaze deepened. "Isn't he?"

She brushed her hair harder. The sound of bristles running through it swished in her ears.

"Isn't he, Ma?"

She yanked her hair back so tightly that it hurt. "Yes."

"Is it true he's a doctor?"

Julia anchored the comb then lowered her arms. "It's true."

"How come a doctor treated you so bad—"

"Listen to me, Pete." She placed the brush on the stand and sank down to her son's level. "Just because someone holds a high position, or dresses well, or has a pocketful of money to show you, doesn't mean that person is nice. You have to be careful around people like that. Sometimes the folks who seem to have everything can...can treat you the worst."

Pete absorbed her words.

"And," she added, "just because someone else has tattered clothes or can't afford a fancy haircut, or was born with poor looks, doesn't mean they're bad. Do you understand?"

"I guess so."

Julia's stomach growled, reminding her how hungry she was, and making Pete giggle.

"Let's forget about all this gloom and go find Grandpa. He promised you a game of checkers, while I get to see what it looks like behind the fancy brass doors of the Picadilly."

Julia hugged her son close, then kissed his cheek and rose to her feet. He'd always be her top priority.

She gave herself one last inspection in the mirror. She hadn't had a lot of time to pull herself together—no fancy braiding of hair or soaking in the tub—but she was presentable. She marveled at how effective her advertisement for a husband had already been, bringing in four possible suitors, and wondered what this evening would hold. Her life had certainly come a long way since her first disastrous involvement with Ryan Reid.

* * *

They entered the crowded dining room at precisely five minutes past six. Mr. Shapiro was wearing one of his dark navy suits, and Julia took it as a sign of good luck that they were both wearing the same color. A perfect match, in her happy opinion. He'd been right on time, and she appreciated a man who didn't make her wait. Ryan had never thought it important to tell anyone when he was coming or going.

Julia swept the dull thought of Ryan Reid out of her mind, vowing to concentrate on the more intelligent man standing beside her.

"A table for two, Stewart," Mr. Shapiro said to the head waiter. "Something intimate and quiet where we can talk."

His talk of intimacy caused a ripple to roll right up Julia's spine. She took the opportunity to boldly tuck her arm under his elbow, indicating her approval. Looking a bit shocked at her forthright gesture, Mr. Shapiro grinned awkwardly and patted her hand. Then he quickly disentangled himself, sweeping the air in front of him to indicate she should walk ahead, following the waiter.

Feeling somewhat rebuffed, Julia tiptoed across the plush Oriental carpeting, around the seated customers, past candlelit tables, imported English cutlery and the piano player in the corner, to reach their secluded booth. Fine-grain leather met her fingertips as she slid to the window.

She was hoping Mr. Shapiro would eagerly slide in beside her, perhaps finding himself uncontrollably attracted to her, but he preferred to sit across the table at a distance.

"A bottle of your finest French red," he said to the waiter, just as Julia glanced two tables over and spotted a familiar dark head. Ryan.

Her stomach, spine and throat all seemed to seize at once. What was he doing here? Had he come to spy on her?

The ape!

She tried to calm her thumping heart while accepting a menu from the waiter. She would darn well enjoy this meal. *Her* evening out with the distinguished barrister who was interested in marriage. She skimmed the page. Beetroot, cream of chicken soup, Russian dumplings. She started again, concentrating this time. Beetroot, cream of chicken soup, Russian dumplings, cornmeal—

"We could start with a platter of pickled peppers," Mr. Shapiro said. "By golly, that's a tongue twister. Peter Piper picked a platter of pickled peppers. How many platters of pickled peppers did Peter Piper pick?"

Julia looked up and smiled graciously. For a barrister, he had an odd sense of humor.

"If Peter picked his so-called platter, and the poor person peering past his pot of porridge stole one, then I'd have me a potentially powerful lawsuit of peppers. Ha ha ha…"

"Hmm." Julia didn't know how to respond. His laughter was attracting some attention in the room. She glanced down at her menu. *Cornmeal! Wild rice and greens!*

The waiter returned with two wineglasses and a bottle. "Bordeaux," he exclaimed, as if she was supposed to recognize the name. She nodded weakly as he poured the wine. "The lobster's going fast this evening. I highly recommend it."

Julia was no longer sure of her choice. The platefuls of red skeletons scattered throughout the room didn't look appetizing. How on earth was she supposed to eat one of those complicated things?

"Perhaps a rare steak," she said, her mouth watering.

"We'll both have lobster," Mr. Shapiro declared. "My dear, you must try it."

She smiled at his determination to take care of her. Oh, she missed those days. "All right. Thank you."

"Wild rice and greens, and a basket of rye bread," said Mr. Shapiro. When the waiter left, the barrister added in a hushed tone, "I almost asked for pickled peppers." He giggled.

Stealing a glance past his reddened ears and the couple at the table beside them, Julia took note that Ryan hadn't caught sight of her.

His face was a mask of seriousness as he listened to the preacher sitting across from him. Ryan looked striking in his boxy black shirt. It deepened the color of his skin and balanced the deep, rich black of his hair.

A minister was an odd choice of company. And she noticed that every time the waiter came up behind him, Ryan reached for his gun, as if expecting to be ambushed. She supposed she couldn't blame him, after Grandpa's attack.

As long as she sat here minding her own business, surely Ryan wouldn't see—

Without warning, the couple sitting between them rose and departed, having finished their meal. This left a large gap between her booth and Ryan's table. Sure enough, he glanced up at the departing woman and her floppy shawl, and spotted Julia.

She wanted to melt in her seat. Ryan raised his eyebrows in dismay upon seeing her, glanced at her giggling partner and the bottle of Bordeaux, and then let his gaze linger on her buttoned blouse and the full length of her skirt. He didn't bother to nod in a civil manner.

With his face turned directly toward hers, the bruise on his lower lip from Grandpa's blow became noticeable.

As he stared at her, her corset felt tight. She realized she'd forgotten to loosen it before leaving the house.

She pursed her lips in irritation and turned back to Mr. Shapiro, pressing her hand over his on the table. "I do wish to thank you for this invitation."

"My pleasure." He extracted his fingers from beneath hers. Goodness, the man was shy. "We have a matter of great importance to discuss. The possibility of matrimony."

Julia sighed in contentment. She would *not* look at Ryan again. "Yes, please go on. What did you have in mind?"

"Well, you know I'm rather new to town. Just three weeks here. It's been rather difficult these past two months."

"Why difficult?"

"Because my Elizabeth passed away."

"Elizabeth?"

"My late wife."

"Oh, dear, I'm so sorry. I didn't know you were married."

"Fifteen happy years."

"Two months ago, you say?"

"Yes." He leaned over the table. "I wouldn't be looking for someone to share…everything just yet. Her death has taken such a toll. To be forthright, I'm not looking yet for anyone to share my—" he lowered his voice to an almost inaudible tone "—bedroom."

He didn't want a wife to share his bedroom?

"You see, it's the cooking and the cleaning I need help with. Why, it's a disgrace that I spend more time in restaurants than at my own dining table. Elizabeth would be appalled that there's no one to look after me…"

Julia groaned as he went on and on about what his Elizabeth used to do for him. He needn't say anything more, for Julia's answer to his proposal would be no. She wasn't looking for another child to take care of. She already had one.

Sometimes, in an instant, a person just knew when another person wasn't suited to them. This was that instant. It was similar to the moment earlier this year when David had shown a surprising interest in courting Julia. She simply wasn't attracted to the blond reporter. Besides, she knew someone else who had taken a terrible fancy to him.

"Well, then." Julia spoke to Mr. Shapiro in her most cheerful tone. There was no reason to ruin the evening. They could still enjoy the meal, and he could certainly afford it.

"She used to shine my shoes every morning, whether they needed it or not. Take a look, my dear Miss O'Shea, at the condition of my shoes today." He stuck his foot out from beneath the table.

Not wanting to be rude, and understanding the poor man's misery at the loss of his beloved wife, Julia poked her head over the edge of the table.

"True enough, they are dusty."

"Do you see? Do you see how the dust has settled into the fine cracks along the edges?"

"Yes, I—I see that. If I might be frank, they could use a good polish."

"You are indeed a remarkably insightful woman."

He tucked his shoe back beneath the table as Julia glowed at his silly compliment. She was smiling more at the predicament she found herself in than at anything else, when she raised her head and met Ryan's gaze across the empty table.

His smirk completely wiped out her good humor. Ryan glanced in amusement in the direction of the barrister's shoe and then the manner in which Julia had pressed herself over the edge of the table.

She felt a tide of heat rise up her neck. She would *not* let this evening go to waste or allow Ryan to assume that the man she was dining with was an idiot. And so she smiled at Mr. Shapiro and pretended they were having the most fascinating conversation.

Across the room, Ryan was enjoying his cream of chicken soup, but finding Julia's choice of men perplexing.

Shapiro was a weak-looking man—a lawyer, Ryan had heard—who was frumpy around the edges and who seemed focused on his own troubles. The whole time Julia had been sitting with him, she'd been doing most of the listening, not the talking. That would eventually lead to one thing: complete boredom with the conversation. How long before her eyes began to glaze? Ryan would give her two more minutes before her pleasant smile became a forced one.

In the meantime, the preacher finished his summary of the Reid family news, for which Ryan was grateful. The man's kindness, on a day when Ryan had been attacked by nearly everyone who'd recognized him, gave him a thimbleful of hope that coming home hadn't been a completely lost cause. But when Ryan thought about Julia nearly dying from scarlet fever, he felt nauseated again.

The preacher was saying, "And your sister, Shawna, married the fella who owns Quigley's Irish Pub. Grizzly sort of man, used to be a Mountie himself up until his accident with a damaged knee. His permanent inability to ride a horse cut that career short."

It was hard to imagine little Shawna all grown up, let alone with two sons of her own. All of his siblings, including Travis and Mitch, had married while Ryan had been gone. They all had kids. Ryan had no wife or kids to offer up for his time away, despite the fact that he was the eldest.

"And the owner of the brewery passed away just last year…don't know if you recall him…."

Births, deaths, strokes. The more the preacher talked, the more isolated Ryan felt. The man took a break to chomp on his overflowing lettuce salad while Ryan took a bite of bread, wincing at the pain of his newly swollen lip, and thinking about how his afternoon had gone.

Reporting to Superintendent Ridgeway at the fort had gone smoothly, even though Ryan felt displaced there, too. He was relieved that things were quiet in Calgary— no tension with the Indians, no outlaw gangs on the loose, no outbreaks of disease. But it also meant there was no use for his medical skills. The fort already had one surgeon, Dr. John Calloway, and despite John's warm greeting to Ryan, he didn't need a hand with anything.

The town had another doctor, a civilian—Dr. Virginia Waters. Ryan had never worked with a female doctor before, but he paid her a visit. He introduced himself to her and her old blind uncle, who'd also been the town doctor at one time. Things were slow with them, too. All that Ryan had really accomplished today was moving his clothes and possessions from the Prairie Hotel into the officers' barracks at the fort.

There was only one thing that troubled the Mounties at

the moment. Something everyone in town was talking about: the drought and the wildfires. The drought was already responsible for the death of dozens of cattle and sheep, and the wheat fields were suffering from lack of rain.

Controlling fires was the Mounties' responsibility. It was a natural extension of their duties, since they were all relatively young, healthy men committed to helping the community. Just an hour ago, Ryan had volunteered his services to Superintendent Ridgeway, not only in a medical capacity, but to help the fort and town in any way he could.

And then there was that troubling letter Ryan had picked up at the bank. It was a major disappointment, since it was filled with inaccuracies. When Ryan had passed through Toronto and gotten Adam's violin restrung, something had made him decide to get an assessment of the instrument. But the letter from the antiquities dealer was full of errors. First they'd misspelled his name—Dr. Reed, not Reid—which annoyed him. Then they'd made an error by inserting a comma where there should have been a period in a sequence of numbers, and finally they'd stated that they had dispatched a dealer from their western office to contact Ryan. Without his approval!

He felt more confused about the value of the violin after the professional assessment than he had before.

Ryan's gaze returned to Julia and settled on her soft complexion. The navy fabric against her throat looked oddly formal, a starched style Ryan had never seen her wear. It contrasted with her girlish figure and the warmth in her eyes as she listened to the lawyer droning on and on.

There was only one thing Ryan knew for sure after having met her today. She and Flanagan both hated his guts.

"Why, it's Mr. Shapiro." The preacher slurped his tea and glanced across the room to the booth where Julia sat with the lawyer. The piano man played a lively tune in the background. "We must go and join them."

"What?" Ryan bolted upright in his chair. "What on earth for?"

"Why, the poor fellow recently lost his wife. He's forlorn and could use a blessing at the table."

"If he wants a blessing, perhaps it can wait—"

"*Dr.* Reid." The preacher lifted his checkered napkin from his lap and slapped it on the table. "These folks may one day be your patients. It's important you get to know them. Is it not?"

Ryan felt a flush of shame. "Yes, I realize that and I don't mean to be hasty, but I believe…I believe Miss O'Shea is seeking a husband, and who are we to intrude—"

"Nonsense. What young women today think is totally appropriate, I'll never understand. Imagine meeting a fellow who lost his wife only two months ago, and jumping into his arms. No sir, it's not the same world I grew up in. What on earth has gotten into her fickle—"

"Two months?"

The preacher clicked his tongue with disapproval. "Writing it down in an advertisement as if she were buying a rooster at the market. 'Gentleman husband. Steady occupation.' Why didn't she write down his required height and weight as well? She needs us to steer her in the right direction—"

"I don't think so, Reverend."

But the minister was already rising and speaking to the waiter. "Please bring the rest of our meal to that booth over there. We'll finish dining with our acquaintances."

Ryan knew the minister hadn't witnessed Flanagan's punch earlier today, so Ryan assumed the holy man was unaware of the tension between him and Julia. Ryan had blamed his bruised lip on an overzealous mustang that wasn't fully broken, and now he felt ashamed of the lie.

Rising to his feet in total embarrassment, Ryan knew he had two choices. Make a quick excuse to the preacher and run out the door, or follow the man.

Why did he feel like a delinquent schoolboy as he decided on the latter course, trudging behind the man in the weathered old suit?

"Miss O'Shea, Mr. Shapiro," said the preacher. "Allow me to introduce my dinner partner, Dr. Ryan Reid. I believe you and he have already met in your shop, Miss O'Shea."

The lawyer rose and extended his hand as Julia sat agape. She clamped her mouth shut again, then brushed imaginary strands of hair from her cheeks, all the while looking at Ryan with barely concealed animosity.

"Nice to see you," she finally said to the minister. "Have a pleasant evening."

If she'd hoped that the minister would be so easily dismissed, she was mistaken. He plunked down next to her and waved Ryan to the other seat. "We're here to share the hour with you. I understand you two are thinking of holy matrimony, and I thought I might give my best advice. The doctor here has just arrived in town and, of course, everything said to a doctor stays in the strictest confidence."

"Listen," said Ryan, still standing and attempting to make a getaway. "I feel that I'm intruding, so I'll—"

"Nonsense." Mr. Shapiro patted the leather bench beside him. "I do have some foot problems and it might be good to get to know a doctor. And Miss O'Shea was telling me she's experiencing a bit of indiges—"

"I'm fine. It went away."

The scowl Julia gave Ryan was enough to goad him to stay. He wasn't a piece of dirt on someone's shoe that she could find so stinking offensive.

Ryan squeezed in beside Shapiro, then leaned back in alarm. Sitting across from Julia like this gave him a direct view of her eyes. Cold blue eyes that looked as if they carried venom.

With a great deal of ceremony and amusement, Ryan lifted the fresh napkin the waiter had delivered, and settled it on his knee. "Where does it hurt exactly, Miss O'Shea?" he asked her.

There was no answer.

"When you swallow?"

Again no answer.

"Do you find your blood pounding a bit too fast at the moment?"

"Yes…I'm sickened by something and I'm not sure I can disclose it in mixed company."

"Please don't be delicate on our account. Tell us, what is it that doesn't sit well with you?"

Her lips thinned.

"I'm sure Mr. Shapiro, as your potential husband, would want to know what's bothering his fiancée."

"Yes, my dear, yes," cooed the lawyer.

"Rooster," the preacher mumbled to Ryan. "Rooster to market."

"Whatever it was," she said hastily, "it seems to have passed."

"Dr. Reid is with the Mounties," said the preacher as they waited for their main dishes to arrive. Shapiro and Julia continued eating their wild rice and greens, although Ryan noticed the lawyer wasn't leaving her much of a share on the plate.

"You don't say." Shapiro chewed loudly while talking. He glanced at Ryan's slashed earlobe. "How're things at the fort?"

"Slow."

"What are you doing about the wildfires?"

"We're still assessing the situation. Two scouts are due back tomorrow morning. We'll get more information then."

Ryan noticed Julia's interest pick up at the mention of scouts.

"I see," said Shapiro. "Are you worried?"

Ryan felt all gazes upon him as he repeated what the superintendent had told him earlier today. "We have a lot of men available to do whatever it takes. Sometimes these brush fires die down on their own. Sometimes they meet up with a river and that's that."

"Yes," said Julia, "but the drought has dried up so many of the little riverbeds…"

Shapiro nodded at her in between bites. "Like the doctor says, there's no sense worrying about things until we get a proper assessment."

Ryan wasn't quite so sure, but he didn't comment.

The waiter waltzed up, juggling four plates of food—three filled with lobster, one with beef.

Julia peered at her red-shelled creature, then glanced at Ryan. "You're not eating lobster?"

"Nah. Too messy for my taste. I much prefer a rare steak. But you folks go right ahead."

Ryan waited for the others to start. The preacher pried open his lobster tail, while Shapiro tore off a claw and cracked it with his bare hands. Julia reached for a slice of dark rye bread from a central bowl, buttered it and watched the others.

If she wasn't hungry, she wasn't hungry, thought Ryan. He cut off a piece of grilled steak and popped it into his mouth. The texture soothed the sting in his lip. "My, this is superb."

When he glanced up, Julia was watching him chew. She practically mimicked his up and down motion with her own jaw. Then she turned and slathered more butter on her bread.

"I hope," said the preacher to Julia and Shapiro, "that if the two of you decide to get married, you'll give yourselves an appropriate length of time in your engagement to get to know one another."

Julia began coughing. Ryan poured her a glass of water.

"Please, Reverend, may we discuss this later?" she squeaked.

"Many times, folks like yourselves tell me they'll drop by later to discuss a troubling matter and then never return. There's no time like the present, young lady. Now then, Mr. Shapiro, would you be moving into the back of Miss O'Shea's store, or would she be moving into your home?"

Julia, turning pink with embarrassment, ripped off another piece of bread, chewed it as though she were starving, and stared at her lobster.

While Shapiro answered, Ryan caught her eye. *Like this*, he motioned with his cutlery, indicating she should pry open the tail. She shot him a look of exasperation, then proceeded to do as he suggested, exposing a tender piece of white meat. Julia looked thin to him, and he was pleased she had a full platter in front of her.

"I've got much more room in my house than Julia does," said the lawyer. "I wouldn't call it a home yet, because it lacks a woman's touch. Why, there are ancestral curtains that still need to be hung, fine china that needs to come out of its case—I haven't thrown out anything that was Elizabeth's, you know—and I dare say my sheets need a good wash."

After that disclosure, Shapiro tore off a long thin claw from his lobster, then slurped the juices until they dribbled down his chin. Ryan thought he looked like a walrus gorging himself on his prey.

The preacher was just as noisy, but not as sloppy. "A fine meal. Fine meal."

Julia kept her head bowed over her plate. She finally took a bite of lobster tail and began to chew. And chew.

"How is it?" Ryan asked, since no one else seemed to notice this was her first time eating this exotic dish.

The preacher and lawyer turned their heads while cracking open the guts of their lobster.

Julia paled. "Very good. The texture is a little strange. Sort of like a rubber boot."

Ryan tried to suppress a smile.

"Now then," continued the preacher. "Let's get right to the heart of the matter. The sanctity of marriage includes the intimate privilege of man and wife. Do you two intend to have children?"

Julia gasped, brought her napkin to her mouth and struggled to rise. "Please excuse me. I'm not feeling well and must return home."

The preacher rose from the booth to let her out. She leaped to her feet and made her excuses. "Please, gentlemen, finish your dinner. I'll be fine and I'll—I'll see you another time, Mr. Shapiro. Thank you for dinner."

All three men were on their feet as they watched Julia run through the crowd, dodging seated customers. Shapiro had his checkered napkin tucked neatly inside his collar. It draped over his suit like a bib. "What on earth is troubling her?"

The preacher continued to suck on a claw, but winked at Ryan. The son of a gun had scared her away on purpose.

Ryan felt a trifle sorry about what had just happened. "I'll go see if her indigestion has gotten the better of her."

"Yes, thank you, Doctor," Shapiro called after him. "Do go and see what ails my future wife."

Chapter Six

"The first time I ate lobster was when I watched them drag some out of the Indian Ocean. I couldn't believe we actually boiled those beautiful creatures." Ryan caught up to Julia on the boardwalk as the setting sun moved across store rooftops. The rays cast a rich orange glow over her skin and turned her hair that deep auburn shade that mesmerized him. Behind her shoulders, eighty miles to the west, the snowy peaks of the Rocky Mountains formed a rugged ridge.

"I don't care when you first ate lobster. Please stop bothering me."

Julia's paisley bag bulged in her arms. It looked heavier than it had appeared in the restaurant. Could she have taken…? No. Ryan banished the thought.

He adjusted the brim of his hat low over his eyes and ignored the pounding in his swollen lip. "Is your indigestion acting up? Perhaps you have an aversion to seafood. That can be dangerous. I once saw a man in India choke—"

"It was very rude of you to join us at our table."

"Yes, I noticed that you're quite taken with Shapiro. The way he sucks on those little claws must be very appealing—"

"You have no business judging him."

"On the contrary, I was just observing."

"I shall—I shall be seeing him tomorrow."

"Do you have many like him in the running?"

"That's none of your concern."

"If I were you, I'd go for a stronger man. One who can chop a cord of wood while knee-deep in snow."

"Really? Is that the type of man you'd fall for, if you were a woman?"

Ryan cast his eyes over her, all dressed in navy as if she'd just come from church. He ran a hand across his black shirt. "I can honestly say no one's ever asked me that before. Let's see…if I were a woman, what type of man would I fall for?"

He tilted back his Stetson and laughed softly. "I don't rightly know what women see in men. In my opinion, we're a bunch of ugly mules."

"You only like things your way."

"I'd agree with that as well."

"Only want us when you need something."

"I told you, we're mules."

"Most of you have only one thing on your mind." When she gave him a pointed scowl, Ryan knew she meant the bedroom.

"Unlike Mr. Shapiro," she added. "Why, maybe I should take him up on his offer, if only to have time away from the bed—"

She stopped herself from finishing, squeezing her lips together.

Her admission was unbelievable. "He doesn't want you in his bed?"

"Never mind." The wind mingled with her hair. "It's an inappropriate topic."

"Between who? You and me? Or you and your future husband?"

She huffed in response and increased the length of her strides.

He laughed. "My God. There haven't been any men in the last five years, have there?"

"None of your business!"

"Intimacy is important. It's not healthy for a woman your age to be totally inactive. You're suppressing—"

"And you're an ugly mule!"

"We've already established that. What you don't seem to see is that you'd be willing to give up that part of yourself that makes you human, that makes you whole. I may not believe in marriage, but I believe the passion between a man and woman is sacred—"

"I do *not* wish to discuss this with you."

She accidentally hit his thigh with her bag. He thought he detected the scent of fresh baked rye bread.

"Sorry," she snarled, as if not the least bit contrite that she'd smacked him.

"Don't marry that man. You and everything beautiful about you would go to waste. Pick someone smarter. Pick someone who makes your heart speed at the thought of making love."

The way that his had on their night together. "Remember?" he whispered.

"Yes, I remember how it was with Brandon."

Ryan was unprepared for the wallop to his heart that her words brought.

They continued along the boardwalk. Golden light glittered across the hemline of Julia's navy skirt as she walked. The same light washed across her face and cast shadows along her throat. He noticed she'd removed her velvet choker for the evening.

Ryan thought he heard a strange sound and wheeled around, hand on his gun.

"Why do you do that?"

"What?"

"Put your hand on your gun at every sound?"

"I guess I'm jittery at the thought of being punched in the face again."

"Grandpa was never able to mask how he feels."

"Unlike his granddaughter."

"What's that supposed to mean?"

"It's...it's hard to read you, Julia. I used to be able to tell how you felt just by the way you moved. Now I'm not sure what you're thinking even when you speak."

"Good."

"Why didn't you tell me about your son?"

She kept walking, silent.

They turned down a dim alleyway toward her back porch.

"Do you have any other children?"

"Only Pete."

"He looks just like Brandon."

"Yes. I'm very proud."

"Why didn't you tell me about your boy?"

"Maybe...I didn't want you to hurt him, too."

Ryan sighed. "I had no idea you were ill when I left

town," he said as gently as he knew how. "The thought of that tears me apart. I'm sorry."

"It happened a long time ago."

"Scarlet fever is one of those illnesses that wracks your body."

"As a doctor, you would know that, but—"

"Did you get the high fever? The painful throat?"

She nodded but didn't add more.

"There's a danger of it spreading to your heart. Was there any problem—"

"I'm fine, Ryan."

"Did you have much pain? The vomiting and abdominal pain—"

"It worked through its course," she said, hushing him. "I have no idea where I picked it up, and to rest your physician's concern, it didn't spread to anyone else. And let me assure you," she added, "the past is no longer important."

Her meaning was clear. *He* was no longer important.

They reached her back porch and she leaped up the stairs.

"I'd like to ask you something." Ryan felt uncomfortable being on her property, especially since she wanted to escape him so badly. He pushed back his Stetson so that he could see all of her, standing two feet above him in the beaten-up alcove. "Supposing you were gone for a long time, separated from your family and friends. Maybe you felt a bit of shame at how you might have left things with them. Supposing they wouldn't accept your apologies. What do you think would be the best way to approach the people you feel you might have…might have hurt badly?"

She pressed her heavy bag against her chest and studied him. "That would depend on them. If they felt that my word had been untrustworthy, then I would have to rebuild my integrity in their eyes. But for some folks, integrity can't be rebuilt. Once you've lost it, you've lost it." Her words were softly spoken, but their sting was sharp. "I suppose I would take my cue from how they reacted upon seeing me again. If they…they slapped me across the face, or punched me, or told me point-blank to stop bothering them…then I would show my respect to those people for once in my life, and keep my distance."

With that wretched announcement, she disappeared into the dark shadows of her home, allowing the screen door to slam in his face.

Julia arose to the early morning sun streaming through her bedroom window, wondering what her meeting with Sergeant Holt MacAllister would bring today, and hoping not to see Ryan again for quite some time.

Her conversation with him last night on the back porch had unnerved her. Afterward, she'd tossed in her bed for hours, churning with all sorts of unwelcome feelings. She was angry that Ryan assumed a simple apology could make up for what he'd taken from her, and she was disappointed in herself for letting it matter so much.

At the breakfast table, she deflected Grandpa's questions about her dinner with Mr. Shapiro, saying only that the loss of his first wife was too recent to go forward with another marriage. Grandpa seemed satisfied with that, but Pete wanted to know more. As he inquired about the men, she passed her son two slices of the rye bread she'd saved from her dinner at the Picadilly last night.

"Who do you think's gonna win?" Pete asked.

"It's not a matter of winning or losing," she replied. "I'd like to find a friend we can both count on when we need him."

"You mean like when we need someone to lift the heavy crates of ink?"

"More than physical strength."

"You mean like when there's a dance and you wanna go?"

"That's part of it. Mostly what I mean is that I'd like someone who'll be on our side, just like Grandpa always is, if there's a storm outside, or one of us gets sick, or for fun things like going swimming in the river with us on a beautiful sunny day."

Julia kissed her son on the cheek, helped him rinse his teeth with cleansing powder, then walked him to his cousins' house. The little boy, Max, was already waiting with a game of checkers set up. Brandon's eldest sister, Anna, always smothered Pete with love. She greeted him fondly as soon as she saw him, allowing Julia to run her errand with just a trace of guilt at leaving Pete behind.

Julia met Mr. and Mrs. Rossman at their mercantile, and the three of them set out for a walk to the depot. Holt's train from the Rockies was scheduled to arrive at nine o'clock.

Grandpa had agreed to introduce the barber to David's elderly aunts in the print shop later this morning, thereby relieving Julia of that duty. Grandpa had also agreed to hand-deliver letters of rejection to three other would-be suitors. One had been rude to Pete. One was a widower with seven children of his own and seemed interested only in a nanny. The third was a miner who surely hadn't bathed in months.

Counting Mr. Shapiro—whom Julia was avoiding at the moment—Holt would be her sixth candidate. She wasn't hoping for much, but the Rossmans were decent people and perhaps their nephew, if, God forbid, he didn't look *too* young, would be an interesting choice. At least at his age, the odds were in his favor that he could keep up with the vigor of seven-year-old Pete.

Mrs. Rossman, a short round woman with a ruddy complexion and friendly manner, waved to her nephew as he stepped off the train. Mr. Rossman remained silent beside Julia.

Julia felt a tingle of heat race up her skin at the sight of Holt MacAllister in uniform. Due to the crowd, he didn't spot his aunt and uncle immediately. He leaped off the train with a duffel bag slamming against his broad back, and curly light hair skimming the collar of his red tunic. He looked a bit worn at the edges, perhaps from having been stuck in the woods for a week and unable to properly shave or bathe. Julia found the tiny imperfections attractive. Hardworking men had always appealed to her; they showed strength of character and dependability. The Mountie uniform and half-grown beard made Holt look strong, but she had to admit, with some discomfort, that he seemed a bit young. Younger than her.

Holt peered down the platform at a group of two or three other Mounties. To Julia, they were a blur of red uniforms and dark breeches. Her eyes were on him.

The other scout accompanying Holt, a red-haired, youthful man, jumped off the train and headed toward the troops.

"Come this way," Mrs. Rossman urged her. "We'll catch up with him at the end of the platform and I'll introduce you."

Julia fell into step behind the buxom woman, while Mr. Rossman followed. Julia was careful not to allow her newly pressed beige skirt and lace blouse to scrape against anything dirty. She adjusted her velvet choker and swung her loose hair over her shoulder.

With a sigh of pleasure, Julia bounced to Mrs. Rossman's side as Holt reached the waiting group of Mounties.

"Holt, it's so wonderful to see you've come back without harm." Mrs. Rossman reached up on tiptoe to give her well-built nephew a hug. "Your uncle and I would like to introduce you to someone special."

A nervous smile touched Julia's face as Holt stepped back to take a good look at her. Appreciation sparkled in his eyes.

"Sergeant," one of the Mounties said, stepping through the crowd. "Good to see you back. We're here for your report on the wildfires."

Julia turned toward the Mounties. She recognized the voice. Her heart fluttered. Ryan. Also dressed in full uniform, he was several inches taller than the other brawny men, and was staring, perplexed, at Julia.

Lord, why did he have to be here? Was it some sort of cruel joke that he always appeared when she was conversing with potential husbands?

"I'll be right with you," Holt replied to Ryan with an easy nod.

Julia sent Ryan a well-deserved scowl. He glanced from her to Holt. His expression turned from curious to a smug grin.

She wanted to kick him. What did he know of her or her dreams?

Ryan gave her a covert signal with his hand, indicating that her choice was not bad. As the others introduced themselves to Holt and his family, he leaned in close to Julia's ear and whispered, "A little young, isn't he?"

"Button your lip," she whispered back, vexed beyond belief. "Perhaps his youth could coax me out of my so-called suppression."

"In the bedroom, experience is better than youth."

Ohhh! He knew just the thing to say to make the tide of crimson rush up her cheeks.

"And now," said Mrs. Rossman with the poorest of timing, standing aside to clear a direct path from her nephew to Julia, "we'd like to introduce you to Miss Julia O'Shea."

Julia uttered a flustered hello, stepped forward with an outstretched hand and prayed to God that the Rossmans would not announce to everyone here that she had placed an ad for a husband. Surely, they would sense the need for privacy.

"Pleased to meet you," said Holt, enveloping her hand in both of his. His smile was warm and gracious. He glanced at his aunt but said nothing more, as if *he*, at least, could sense the need for a private conversation.

Why had Julia agreed to meet him at the station?

Falling behind the Mounties as they walked beside the boxcars, Julia supposed she was enthusiastic to meet him because of her dismal failure with Mr. Shapiro. Or perhaps she was eager to prove to Ryan that she could find a match who suited her just fine. Or maybe there was a secret desire to meet the man who might be interested in a woman seven years his senior.

Weaving along the platform's edge and questioning the two scouts on the status of the wildfires, Ryan found Julia's choice of Holt MacAllister amusing. What could a mature woman find appealing in such a young man?

It would fizzle to nothing, Ryan was certain.

He preferred to concentrate on his task. Since his medical skills weren't needed at the fort for the moment, Ryan had requested active duty, so that he could get to know some of the Mounties beneath his command and dive right into police work. The superintendent had asked Ryan to meet and question these Mounties.

Everyone followed the two men to the boxcar that held their horses. While Holt and the other scout, Evan, retrieved their bays, Ryan noticed across the crowded platform that another train had arrived, this one from the East. A strange-looking fellow caught Ryan's attention.

He was a short, heavyset man in a gold plaid suit, with a bushy ponytail. Ryan overheard him ask the porter carrying his bags to direct him to the nearest hotel.

The porter mumbled something Ryan couldn't make out.

"Yes," the newcomer declared. "From Worldwide Antiquities."

Ryan moaned in disappointment. So the fellow had arrived. Ryan supposed he could simplify things and walk across the platform to introduce himself.

But he had little patience with incompetent people. Still annoyed that the company had dispatched a dealer without his permission, when he wished to keep his affairs private, and that the spelling in their letter had been so poor, Ryan decided more pressing things needed his attention.

The Mounties reassembled at the end of the platform, close to the exit doors. Holt and Evan held their horses' bridles, and Julia and the Rossmans stood at Holt's side.

"How fast are the fires spreading?" Ryan asked.

"Sir, they're beyond our worst fears," said Evan.

Ryan stopped. The entire group hushed and listened.

"How so?" asked Ryan.

"Some of the fires have merged. One of them is huge," said Holt. "It started out with a few acres of scrub, and it's now up to a couple hundred. The winds and the drought are working in its favor. Folks in the area believe it started with a lightning storm."

"How close were you able to get to it?"

"With our horses, we rode for a full day out of Canmore," said Holt. "Fifty or sixty miles, or thereabouts. What makes it so troublesome is that the winds are conspiring against us, always blowing straight down the mountains toward Calgary."

A chill of warning raced up Ryan's spine. It was coming this way.

Chapter Seven

The waiting began at sunrise. Ryan hated waiting, yet the following day, that's what everyone's advice seemed to be: wait.

Right after breakfast, Ryan approached Superintendent Ridgeway in the fort's courtyard.

"Sir, I think we should reconsider our options. According to the scouts, one of the fires is spreading. The rail line leads more or less in that direction. We could fill up a water car and take a team of men and horses to contain it." Ryan knew they couldn't douse a fire that size, but they might be able to prevent it from expanding by digging trenches across its path and dousing the ground with water. The British had accomplished something similar once in Africa.

Listening closely, the superintendent chomped on an unlit cigar. Behind him to the east, the rising sun met the prairie grassland. A warm wind stirred Ryan's shirt and pressed his breeches to his legs. Rocky peaks spanned the landscape to the west.

"Listen, son, every summer it's the same thing. Brush fires come and go. They'll die down on their own when the rain comes. There've been two others that have already died."

"But there's a severe drought."

"This is prairie land. There's always a drought. I'll admit, this year it's lasted longer than most, but what you're suggesting is a major operation. Wait. Wait just a few more days and you'll see the fires fade. In the meantime, get acquainted with the other surgeon. John's delighted that headquarters finally sent him another doctor."

Still uneasy thirty minutes later, cloistered in the fort's small hospital, Ryan found himself bandaging the twisted ankle of a constable, as Dr. John Calloway looked on.

"Most of the gauze and supplies you'll need are in the overhead cupboards." John, tall and eager, opened one of the doors. "Ointments and tonics are stored along the north wall, the coolest area of the wing. Dammit, it's good to have another set of hands around here."

"I'm not complaining that the hospital is empty, but I wish there was more for me to do."

"Wait. Just you wait and see how busy it can get."

Their patient limped out of the room on crutches.

John peered at Ryan. "You look a lot like your brothers, though you're older and bigger, and half your ear's missing." He laughed. "But I never knew Mitch and Travis had another brother."

Which meant they didn't talk about him, thought Ryan with a twinge of loneliness. Why would they? He'd deserted them along with everyone else. "When do you figure they'll be back from the cattle drive?"

"Wait a few more days."

With nothing better to do, Ryan headed to the jailhouse to acquaint himself with the Mounties on guard. As he crossed the courtyard, his boots skimming the short, parched grass, he heard a voice call out behind him.

"Wait! Sir, wait!"

Ryan's hand fell to his holster. On instinct, he spun around and pointed his revolver, just in case the voice belonged to someone who had a grudge.

It was the short man in the gold plaid suit Ryan had seen yesterday at the train depot. Coughing, he adjusted his gold-rimmed spectacles. "Sir, I meant no harm. My name is Harrison Hobbs."

The antiquities dealer was accompanied by David Fitzgibbon and his monkey. Ryan groaned and put away his gun. "You shouldn't sneak up on people. You could get your head blown off."

David tilted his portable camera toward the ground with one hand, and touched his cap in greeting with the other. "Good morning."

Ryan nodded. At the sight of the reporter, he wondered what Julia was doing this fine day, but didn't bother to ask.

"Mr. Fitzgibbon here was kind enough to bring me," said Hobbs. "You're Dr. Ryan Reid, are you not?"

"Would that be Reid with an *e* or an *i?*"

"Huh?"

"Your company, Worldwide Antiquities, misspelled it."

"How do you know I'm from Worldwide Antiquities?"

"Wild guess." Ryan peered down at the gent's suit coat. "You've got a card sticking out of your pocket that says so."

When Hobbs laughed, he looked like a friendly rodent. His long brown hair was tied at the back and sat curled between his shoulder blades like a squirrel's tail. His top teeth were long and sharp. Still, he was a cheerful-looking sort.

"Sorry about the misspelling, sir, but surely you're impressed with the violin's value—" Hobbs stopped abruptly. He turned sharply toward David, as if realizing he shouldn't be discussing price in front of anyone else.

"What violin?" asked David. He stepped back, centered Ryan in the camera's view and snapped a photograph. The magnesium flashlamp ignited, covering Ryan's boots with soot and ash.

Ryan held up his hand. "Enough pictures." Then he told Hobbs, "You made a mistake in the value. One too many zeroes. And the comma should have been a period."

"I received a duplicate of your letter, and I don't believe any mistakes have been made. But that's why I'm here. I'd like to see the violin. My specialty is string instruments. Why, just last month, a monk who'd emigrated from the Swiss Alps brought in a cello I couldn't believe…"

The man continued talking while Ryan stood in total dismay. One hundred and eighty-eight thousand dollars?

Surely they meant $188.00, and had printed one too many zeroes. Or had mistaken a comma for a period. After all, they'd misspelled his name, and it was reasonable to assume they'd made a mistake in the price, too. Even at $188.00 it equaled the cost of an entire house!

Hobbs continued rambling. "…finest tonewood materials, I believe from the Carpathian Mountains in Romania, true to one of Amati's apprentices, perhaps made in Italy as we suspect. On the other hand, there's the possibility of a German master…"

One hundred and eighty-eight thousand dollars!

Had Adam known how much his violin was worth? He'd taken the bloody thing into battle, for cryin' out loud!

Hobbs was in his own world. "The rich, mature sound of the tonewood penetrates to the back of the concert hall—"

Chaos interrupted them. The monkey squawked and jumped off David's shoulder as a woman visiting with the superintendent's wife waved to them from the raised boardwalk of the office buildings. "Yoo-hoo, David, good morning!"

David groaned. "Not now. Please, not now."

The woman wouldn't be dismissed. She stuck out her arm so the monkey could jump up on it. "I've got another question for you, David, regarding photography. I was wondering about the chemical composition of the processing agents. Just a minute and I'll come down there to speak with you!"

"Who's that?" asked Hobbs, studying the woman's pretty face and the mass of chestnut-brown hair spilling over her shoulders.

"She won the pleasure of my company for twenty-four hours in a raffle last year," said David. "Now she thinks she owns me. Miss Clarissa Ashford. The jeweler's spoiled daughter."

"She's beautiful," whispered Hobbs.

"Have you ever heard of the tiny South American tree frog? It's got brilliant red and green colors but is filled with poison." David gripped his camera. "I've gotta run."

"Wait!" Miss Ashford shouted after him. "Wait!"

The monkey chirped and raced to catch up with David as he clattered away with his rickety camera. The lady kept hollering, while Hobbs turned back to Ryan as if nothing extraordinary was happening.

One hundred and eighty-eight thousand.

"Now, sir, may I please see that violin? Let's not wait any longer. I hate waiting. Don't you?"

Julia found Sergeant MacAllister more appealing as the days wore on. She discovered he was precisely twenty-six, which thankfully made him closer to thirty than twenty. He was now only six years her junior. And his birthday was in the spring, while hers was in the fall, so at certain times of the year he was only five years younger.

Oh, it was no use.

After three tumultuous days of justifying their age difference in her mind, Julia finally tried to ignore it. If only Ryan would allow her to forget.

Holt came for her on Saturday evening. They took a stroll along the boardwalk after dinner and he answered questions about his family back East. She found herself thrilled when he told her he admired a woman with so much intelligence that she published her own newspaper. On Sunday morning, he met her and Pete by the church doors after service and included her son in a lively conversation about bullfrogs and horses on the walk home. She'd been touched by Holt's sincerity. Then, on Monday at high noon, in between his duties at the fort, he took the time to call at her shop to deliver a basket of handpicked wild roses.

Unfortunately, she wasn't there to receive them in person because she was calling on customers to collect advertising fees, and interviewing the Sweeney family to include the birth of their third son on the society page. Later, she visited the livery to find out about the theft of three saddles that had occurred the night before.

That evening, Holt showed her more kindness by having a lovely dinner delivered from the diner next door. The roast beef and vegetables went a long way to feeding her, Pete and Grandpa. There'd even be enough left over for another dinner for Pete. Holt hadn't left a card or anything, but she knew it was from him.

Holt's gifts were proof that he was a considerate, even-tempered man worth getting to know. As for Mr. Shapiro, he came calling again. Julia told him gently but quite directly that they weren't suited. He was disappointed, saying he was counting on her to iron his shirts later that day. She told him he would have to wear them wrinkled.

Everything would have gone smoothly with Holt if Julia hadn't bumped into Ryan at the fort the following day, Tuesday, in her attempt to drop by and thank Holt for his roses.

"Does he have your knickers in a knot?" Ryan eyed the single rose she'd taken from Holt's bouquet and slipped into her hatband.

Julia sent him a cool glare.

"I mean, when he kisses you," Ryan continued. "Does he get your knickers twisted?"

"That's a crass and vulgar thing to say. But I half expect it from you."

"I see. So the answer is no."

"What he does and doesn't do to my knickers is none of your concern!"

"Don't get so upset. If he hasn't kissed you yet, he might work up the steam by the end of the week. Some younger men get a little shy around mature women."

"Uhh!" Julia yelled in exasperation before tugging on the lines of her horse to get her buggy moving.

"I'll let him know you stopped by!" Ryan hollered, laughing after her.

The man's head was too big for his hat. And the most maddening thing of all was that Ryan was right—Holt hadn't worked up the courage to kiss her yet.

"Please tell Holt I was here to thank him for the roses and roast beef!" she hollered smugly.

"I'll tell him thanks for the roses, but the dinner was on me!"

Julia stopped her buggy with a soft jolt and turned around. "What do you mean? Why would—would you send me a meal?"

Ryan glanced at her worn clothes before answering. "Just my way of saying sorry you didn't enjoy the lobster."

Her cheeks prickled as though stung with tiny needles. "Why didn't you leave a note?"

"Because I wanted you to enjoy the meal, no strings attached. Did you?"

Slowly, she nodded. "Thank you."

He sighed with such contentment that her embarrassment set in. Perhaps he'd noticed that she wasn't doing as well as she was letting on. She turned back to her horse, slapped the reins and left Ryan behind.

By Wednesday, the newspaper article about Ryan's return to town was almost complete and ready to run. Thank goodness. She would hand the entire project over to David and wash her hands of Ryan. He was getting too close for her comfort.

She had a notion at the back of her mind to run a continuing a series about the Reid family. Despite her personal distaste for Ryan, he was the third son to enlist with the Mounties. Folks found that sort of thing interesting.

Maybe the society page could use an infusion of encouraging articles about men and women who contributed to the town. She could start with the new schoolteacher who'd just arrived from Vancouver and knew how to speak four different languages, or the boot maker who'd lost one hand in a hay baling accident when he was a boy, but still made the best pair of cowboy boots this side of the Rockies.

But, thought Julia, glancing down at the final draft of her article about Ryan, this story wasn't nearly as inspirational as those pieces would be. This one leaned toward the negative.

A soft afternoon breeze rolled through the front window and stirred her hair. It was ten degrees cooler in the shade than in the blazing sun today, and everyone was staying indoors if they could help it. She'd worn her thinnest blouse because of the heat, the one with the open neckline that didn't reach right to her chin like most of her others.

"You were right about the article about the black sheep." David rose from behind his desk and joined her at the counter. "It's going to sell a lot of papers."

Julia felt a twinge of guilt. She wasn't sure she should run the article on Ryan the way it was written. "Let me work with this a bit. It still—"

"It's fine the way it is."

"But the first paragraph is so harsh—"

"It's the truth. Every word of it."

"But it's not the way I wish to sell—"

"You've been reworking this article for three days. I've never seen you this torn up about a piece. What is it that you want to say in the article that hasn't been said?"

She sighed. "I'm not sure."

"Then please leave it alone. It's fine."

If it was fine, why did holding it between her fingers make her hands quiver? If it was honest, why did she weigh every word and wonder whether she was being fair?

"You know, it's too bad we don't know more about that violin of his." David watched a wagon roll by the front window. "We might include mention of it."

"What's special about his violin?"

"There's an antiquities dealer chasing him around town. I just saw him slip into the pub behind Ryan." David nodded in the direction of Quigley's Irish Pub down the street. "I get the feeling that the instrument is worth a lot of cash."

"Really?" That was odd. But perhaps it was an angle she could include in her article. Something optimistic. Julia grabbed her straw hat from beneath the counter, adjusted the scooped neckline of her blouse and headed toward the door. "Then I need to see Ryan."

Quigley's Irish Pub wasn't the sort of establishment Julia frequented. Normally she would never go there alone, but she was desperate. If she didn't change something about Ryan's story, then she'd have to live with it the way it was written.

The pub was owned by Ryan's sister, Shawna, and her husband Tom Quigley. Since both of them were still out of town—Shawna visiting relatives to the south, and Quigley on the cattle drive—Julia figured it was safe to enter. There would be no other family members looking down their noses at her as she questioned Ryan.

Julia pushed through the stained-glass doors and stepped into the noisy space. Her eyes moved over the line of Mounties seated along the bar. They were off duty, of course, wearing denim pants and light-colored shirts, but she recognized their faces. What she didn't expect to see, at a table in a far corner, was a most unlikely pair.

Holt MacAllister laughing and drinking with Ryan Reid.

Dismayed, Julia turned on her heel and headed for the exit and the sunlight.

"Julia!" Holt called out.

She moaned, stopped and slowly turned around to face them.

"Over here!"

Both Holt and Ryan stood up as she approached. Judging by the way Ryan's shoulders stiffened, he disapproved of seeing her here. His eyes skimmed the neckline of her low-cut blouse.

"The surgeon and I were just having a drink." Holt stepped to another table and got her a chair. "Here. Join us. Dr. Reid's been telling me about England. Did you know he's been to Africa?"

For one second, the eagerness in Holt's voice reminded her of her son. Were all young men impressed by tales of adventure?

Julia's stomach tightened as she sat down. Ryan was dressed in a freshly ironed white shirt that tapered into the narrow waist of well-worn blue jeans. The shirt made his skin look browner and his shoulders broader. It was diffi-

cult to think around him. Cigar smoke drifted over from
the next table. The soft glow of the wall lantern behind
Ryan made her strain to see the subtle expression in his
dark eyes.

She gave him a cool smile, as if to say, *I'm here to speak
to you, but it's for work, not pleasure.*

While Holt flagged down a barmaid to ask for a glass
of apple cider for Julia and another round of Guinness
for the men, Ryan dipped close to her ear, his proximity
making her shiver. "You've got a strange way of looking
at a fellow."

"Do I? I—I get that way around Holt."

Ryan's mouth thinned. He sank into his chair, tilting it
as far away from her and the table as possible. Well, she
was glad. She wanted him to keep his distance.

Julia glanced around. The pub attracted an odd mix of
people, from Mountie officers and ranch hands to high-
society folks. She wasn't the only woman here. There was
another room beyond this one, a dining room draped with
velvet curtains and paneled with highly polished mahog-
any. It was packed with couples enjoying a late lunch, no
doubt cooked by the French-Canadian chef the Quigleys
had hired several years ago.

But Julia was the only woman in the bar itself.

How strange, she thought. At one time, she'd managed
a bar twice this size. Several years had passed; she felt out
of place. To add to her discomfort, two of the couples
from the dining room were glancing in her direction and
whispering. They were likely gossiping about her and
Ryan, perhaps talking about the punch Grandpa had delivered. Or, blazes, it might be fresh gossip about her and

Holt, and his answer to her ad for a husband. She looked away from the dining room.

Focusing on the folks in the bar, she searched for a man who might be the antiquities dealer, the one David had mentioned, but didn't see anyone who seemed interested in Ryan.

Holt finished talking to the barmaid and, surprising Julia, leaned over her and planted a small kiss on her cheek.

She felt a tide of embarrassment race up her skin. Holt had never kissed her before. To do so openly like this…it had to be the Guinness affecting him.

Their first kiss and Ryan had to witness it. When her breathing slowed, and Holt settled into his chair, she glanced at Ryan. He was staring at her again, in that direct, methodical way that usually started somewhere around her bosom and worked its way up to her eyes. His stare made her angry. *He* made her angry.

"Well, then, what brings you by?" asked Holt.

Her answer was long and convoluted. "I came by because I heard that you…that you and some other people I need to speak to were in here."

Why had she come? Oh, right, the violin and her article.

Holt seemed puzzled by her rambling response. "It's always good to see you. The doctor and I were just discussing the wildfires and what we're going to do about them."

"Honestly," she said, "please tell me. Do you think the fires are getting worse?"

"It seems so," said Ryan. "From the watchtower ten miles out, it seems as though the fires have combined into one. And it's growing."

She didn't like the sound of that. "What *are* you going to do about it?"

Holt nodded toward his senior. "The doctor here is organizing a group of volunteers to go and fight it."

"You are?" she asked. "But you're a doctor. Don't you have other things to do, things that doctors handle? Shouldn't you be working with patients?"

"No patient will have him." Holt chuckled. "The men at the fort have Doc Calloway, and the women and children in town are too scared of his looks and his repu—" Holt lifted his glass. "There I go again. Don't seem to know when to keep my mouth shut." He gulped his beer. Although Holt obviously found Ryan's situation amusing, there was no humor in Ryan's own expression.

"There's more to fighting fires than attacking the flames," he explained to her. "We'll need a large assembly of men. I'm afraid they'll need a doctor to attend to any burns."

Julia shivered. She hadn't thought of that.

"He was a commander in the British Army," Holt added, "before he became a doctor. So he's got both talents. First commanding men in battle, then working as a surgeon. After he studied medicine, he set up the medical tents on the front lines of the rebellions in Africa. Leading the firefighters seems right up his alley."

"Oh," she said. Holt was impressed by Ryan's background, but Julia was struck with fear. She feared for the safety of the townsmen who might go to fight this fire, possibly both Holt and Ryan.

Ryan seemed ill at ease as Holt gushed on about Africa.

The barmaid plunked a glass of apple cider on the table. Julia murmured a soft thank-you and took a sip.

"I've got to be going," said Ryan in the awkward lull that followed. "I'll…I'll leave you two alone."

"No, please," said Julia, jumping out of her seat.

"Julia?" Holt glanced from her to Ryan.

Ryan said nothing, but simply stared in that aggravating way. His eyes started at her waistline this time.

"Holt," she said, "I'm here on business. I'm doing an interview with Dr. Reid for tomorrow's paper, precisely on the topic of his travels. Excuse me, but I've got to ask him a few more questions about the firefighting and about his violin."

The gentleman sitting at the next table, smoking the smelly cigar and wearing a gold plaid suit, turned his head in their direction at the mention of a violin. She wondered if he was the antiquities dealer.

"I don't have time for more questions, Julia. I've got things that need doing and have no interest in discussing my private life." Ryan walked away. The sound of his spurs faded.

Julia murmured an apologetic goodbye to Holt without asking his permission to leave. Her work was her work, and he would have to understand that. She needed to make a living. Never again would she or her family be in debt.

"Shall I escort you out?" Holt called after her.

"There's no need."

She followed Ryan through the back door and out into the alleyway. It was one of those hot afternoons where the shadows hit razor-sharp against the walls, and the birds chirped loudly on the rooftops.

Ryan must have heard her shoes crunching on the pebbles behind him. He didn't bother to look, only spoke. "MacAllister allowed you to come after me?"

"Certainly. I explained—"

"No explanation would be good enough if the woman I was courting got up to follow another man. I guess that's where he and I differ."

"Holt may be a lot younger than you," she blurted. She halted in her footsteps. "But he's certainly the more mature one. There's not a jealous bone in his body."

Ryan pivoted on his boot heel to face her, spurs jangling. "I would never let you chase after another man while I stood and watched."

What an absurd thing to say! She was not chasing after Ryan! And why was he so easily roused to anger?

She'd had enough.

"Oh, wouldn't you? You let Brandon chase after me while you stood and watched."

At her accusation, Ryan flinched as if he'd been struck. He sank back on his heels.

Tingles of warning erupted on her skin. She didn't wish to get into this, she really didn't.

He stepped forward, unable to control a spasm in his voice. "And do you know what that makes you? Do you know what they call women like you who flirt with two men at the same time?"

She gasped. He might as well have called her a teasing whore aloud. She felt her eyes water with humiliation, but pulled her shoulders back as she measured every word. "Yes, I do. They call women like me, who are able to see right through the men who hurt them, smart."

She no longer cared how cutting her article about him might be. She didn't care how much she hurt this man. "You always had the ability to cut me to my knees," she whispered, backing up toward the door she'd come through. "You inflict pain on those around you as often and as quickly as others smile. You're a bastard."

He stared at her long and hard, the pulse at his throat throbbing in time to her own. Then Ryan leaped toward her so fast that she sucked in her breath.

He towered over her. Then, as if he were a puppeteer pulling invisible strings, he walked her backward until she was pressed against a wall, in the shadows. His body was so close he nearly crushed her. "That man in there, who may be your lover soon, couldn't protect you from the wolves."

"I can do my own protecting."

"Really? You think if MacAllister saw me standing here in the shadows with you, my fingers dancing along your neckline, he would flinch?"

"Your hand is nowhere near my neckline. Step away from me before I take your gun and shoot you."

But there he was. His long cool fingers sweeping along the lace, grazing the top of her bare bosom, causing goose-flesh to rise on her skin and her heart to pound like an African drum.

With an indignant gasp, she pushed his hand away.

But his face lowered toward hers, and she saw the kiss coming. Too shocked to move, she felt his mouth on hers.

He had an iron grip on her waist, but he removed his palms as if willing her, goading her, to walk away from him and this.

It was so painful to be around this man. Whenever he was gone, all she did was wonder where he might be, who he might be talking to. When he was near, all they did was argue or…or do this.

Something about this kiss was different. It was softer

than the one he'd snatched in his hotel room. It was more of an equal kiss between a man and woman than a stolen one. This kiss was more like the ones they'd shared ten years ago. Warm, caring and seductive. Making her think of the pleasures of making love to him.

The feelings scared her. She struggled to move out of his embrace.

"No," she said. "No."

Clasping her loosely, Ryan groaned and pressed his forehead against the wall, trying to recover from the kiss himself. He didn't have much time, for the pub's back door burst open. The person who stepped outside surprised them both.

Chapter Eight

~~~~~~~~~~

At the sound of the door opening, Julia tried again to spring from Ryan's grip. The shock of being caught caused her to slam against his hard chest. Her auburn plait rippled along her shoulder and swung over her bosom, while her skirts swirled around his boots. Quickly gathering her composure, she stepped away from Ryan and the door, brushing fallen strands of hair off her forehead and trying not to look as though she'd just been caught in the arms of a scoundrel.

The man in the golden suit she recognized from the pub stepped out. "Dr. Reid, I would really like to negotiate for that Italian violin. I think what I offered you was quite reas—" Julia's fumbling hands drew his attention and made him stop.

She pretended nothing was amiss, although his stare was forthright as he glanced at her gaping neckline and the way she twisted her fingers.

"Never mind, Hobbs," said Ryan. He ran a hand through his dark hair and didn't glance at Julia. "You took a look at it, and I told you I'd think about your offer. Now, if you don't mind," he said to them both, "I've got a lot of things to do before my train rolls out. The volunteers need to be organized." With a curt nod, he headed down the deserted alleyway toward the crowded boardwalk.

Julia and the dealer gaped after him. She was still spinning from their encounter. The man had no sensitivity. He'd just kissed her!

He'd kissed her in an alley and, with no explanation or apology, gone on his merry way. His arrogant stride alone made her want to throttle him.

Mr. Hobbs peered past her at Ryan's departing figure.

"It's no use," she said. "The man's got a mind of his own. You'll never be able to change it."

Mr. Hobbs studied her for a second. He motioned down the same path Ryan was taking toward the boardwalk. "Care to discuss the matter?"

Maybe there was something this man could tell her about the violin. She ran a hand over her hair and tucked her loose blouse back into her waistband. The straw hat that she'd tied around her throat flopped against her back. It was likely crushed from her encounter from Ryan. "Why not?"

Hobbs extended his arm as a courtesy, and she slid her hand in the crook of his elbow.

While they headed toward the boardwalk, the gent introduced himself. "Harrison Hobbs from Worldwide Antiquities."

He passed her a business card.

He was an odd-looking man, short and stocky, with long teeth, but he exuded charm when he smiled. Something about his manner was relaxing.

"Confidentially speaking, miss, do you have any pull with Dr. Reid in regard to the sale of his violin?"

Julia laughed and slid his card into her skirt pocket. "Mr. Hobbs, I have no pull with him whatsoever."

The man adjusted his gold-rimmed spectacles, swept his view over her low neckline and joined her in laughter. "Well, then, we are equally powerless."

Never one to pass up an opportunity to get confidential information on one of her subjects, Julia let the man keep talking. By the time they reached the boardwalk, she'd learned several new things about Ryan's violin. Things that might be helpful for her story.

Although, truthfully, she should publish the scathing article as it was, for every word of it was truth. After Ryan's insults to her, he didn't deserve to be shielded.

On the boardwalk, Julia disengaged her hand from Mr. Hobbs's arm, ready to walk home on her own, but the sight of Ryan standing in the middle of a crowd of young men stopped her. The commotion drew Hobbs's attention as well.

"We're leaving tomorrow morning on the 8:00 a.m. train. Who'll go with us?" Ryan looked around as several hands shot into the air.

So soon? thought Julia.

"Are the Mounties going?" asked a cautious farmer from the back.

"Yes, sir, they are," said Ryan. His wide shoulders cut a square profile in the crowd. "But the more men we have, the easier it'll be on everyone. We've got thirty constables and I'd like to see at least that many civilian men join us. Will you come?"

The farmer squinted. "I don't know. A thing like this—"

"The answer's no! He's needed here," said the very pregnant young woman in a thin calico dress standing beside him. She slipped her arm through his and tugged him toward the mercantile.

Julia didn't blame the woman for refusing to let her husband go. The town had fought two or three fires in the past five years that she could remember—some that had consumed single homes, some larger blazes that the Mounties could barely control—and there had always been casualties. Everyone knew the risks involved, especially a pregnant wife.

Getting volunteers together was a problem in itself, since the town couldn't afford the latest firefighting wagons and watering equipment. The Mounties always had to work so hard, scrounging for donated linen hoses, and running them through riverbeds, or wells, or whatever water source was at hand.

The crowd's murmuring got louder and the questions more direct. Julia's gaze flew back to Ryan, who stood at the center of the commotion, cool, steady, calm.

Her pulse began a faster beat. How long would he and the rest of his men be gone?

It was Julia's duty to listen closely, for she could include the information in tomorrow's paper. It meant a very late night ahead, writing columns, setting type and running the presses, but her usual late hours this close to deadline made her paper the town's most up-to-date.

Creating a firefighting camp was a huge undertaking on Ryan's part. Luckily, they'd be traveling by train, so they could bring lots of supplies. She listened to him organizing whose horses they would take, who would handle the tenting, and who would volunteer for cooking. He coordinated it with a list he drew from his pocket, matching what the Mounted Police were bringing to what ranchers and businessmen would add.

Julia didn't notice her reporter coming up the road, until she heard the flash of David's lamp when he took a photograph. Beyond David's right shoulder she saw half a dozen riders galloping toward them.

Her heart contracted when she recognized their faces.

Joseph, Travis and Mitchell Reid.

Ryan's family had returned from their cattle drive. Ryan hadn't spotted them yet because they were approaching him from behind. They were headed for Quigley's, likely to get a drink and to catch up on news before they headed to their ranches. It was highly unlikely they knew Ryan was back in town.

She saw the wagons driving by in the distance as the drovers made their way home. Tom Quigley, riding on a wagon due to his damaged knee, turned the corner at the bank, heading down the alley to the livery where he boarded his horses.

Catching her breath, Julia turned to Ryan. He was finalizing details, saying goodbye to some of the men, when he finally looked up at the riders.

Tall, dark and dusty, wearing chaps and cowboy hats, Joseph, Travis and Mitchell slid off their horses and hitched them to the post in front of the pub, oblivious to the fact that ten feet away stood their long-lost Donovan Ryan.

But the paleness of Ryan's face and the tug of his Adam's apple were enough to tell Julia how important this moment was.

* * *

His father had aged. Ryan couldn't get the sorrowful thought out of his head as he stared at Joseph. The man looked old.

Joseph used to be extremely heavy, but he'd lost some weight since Ryan had last seen him. He was still on the heavy side, and over six feet tall, but the hair at his temples was completely gray and his face creased with wrinkles. He hadn't shaved in a few days, so his jaw had a light coating of white whiskers.

Ryan's younger brothers, on the other hand, looked to be in their prime. They were taller than their father, both muscular, both with charcoal features and stern gazes. Most people could barely tell them apart, but Ryan knew. He knew them well. He wished he'd been a stronger man when he'd left this town, wished he hadn't left things the way he had, wished he could spin the clock back to regain the ten years he'd lost with these good men.

As Joseph removed his Stetson and murmured a few hellos to folks he knew in the dispersing crowd, he glanced in Ryan's direction. His face turned glum as recognition glimmered in his eyes. His hat dropped to the planks of the boardwalk. "Holy Jesus."

Ryan gritted his teeth and held back ten years of emotion. It was so damn good to see them. "Pa."

Travis turned toward his older brother and stared in disbelief.

Mitch, the youngest—who'd always been the most affectionate, a boy who wasn't afraid to laugh aloud or spend hours trailing his older brother in the forest while they searched for imaginary vultures—stepped back, cold-sober, to assess Ryan.

"Good to see you all," said Ryan. He smiled gently, hoping to break the chill.

Mitch was the first to recover. His eyes watered, but with rigid determination, he scooped Pa's hat off the boardwalk, gave it to the old man and stared at the pub doors as if nothing unusual were happening. "Didn't we come here for a drink?"

Ryan felt as though he'd been slugged in the gut. Mitch was turning his back.

Hell, thought Ryan, the kid hates me.

Except that Mitch wasn't a kid. He was a fully grown man with perspectives of his own on what might have made his hero, his older brother, leave town the way he had.

Ryan had hurt them all.

"It's good to see you," he repeated. His voice grew hoarse with sentiment as he peered from Mitch to Travis to his father.

"Where were you?" said Travis, as reserved and cool as a Rocky Mountain lake. "We tried to get ahold of you. Five months ago when Ma suffered a—"

"I heard about that," said Ryan with shame, "and I'm sorry."

"No, let me finish," said Travis. He held up his hand. "Ma had a stroke months ago and we searched from here to the Arctic for you. Her sole wish was to see her oldest son. We couldn't find you." Travis pointed his finger in the air for emphasis, his body stiff.

"I'm sorry." It was all Ryan could offer. But he witnessed the raw pain that still simmered in their eyes. They must have been tortured trying to fulfill Ma's wish and being unable to locate him.

Joseph lowered his hat to his side. His hand trembled. "I don't think you know the meaning of the word."

"I do, Pa. And I'm especially sorry for how I left things with you."

"I told them they were wasting their breath, tryin' to find you. The last time I saw you, you gave me quite a memory. One to last a lifetime."

Ryan winced. He'd punched his father square in the jaw and had knocked all three hundred pounds of him to the floor. Ryan's mouth quivered. "Didn't we both say and do things we regretted that night?"

"He's your father, for God's sake," said Mitch. "Your father."

Ryan took a deep breath and wondered how he might possibly piece this back together. Or even if he could. "Where's Ma?"

"She's in the south, visiting with the Killarneys," said Travis. "Shawna, and our wives and children, went with her."

Even-tempered Travis. He was the boy in the middle and had always had a calm head on his shoulders. Ryan had heard from the preacher that Travis had married his childhood girlfriend in the time that Ryan had been away. Sadly, she had died in a horse accident, and Travis had remarried a good-hearted young woman with twins of her own.

So much living and dying while Ryan had been gone.

Even Mitch was married. To a woman who'd won him in a crazy Mountie raffle. That sounded more like the easy-going fella Ryan remembered, than the hardened man standing here gawking at him.

"Where've you been?" Travis asked.

"I joined the British Army."

"What the hell for?"

Ryan shrugged. "I suppose because they wanted me. Someone wanted me."

Travis glanced around at the staring faces. Ryan hadn't noticed that some townspeople had stuck around to witness this reunion. Even Julia was still watching from farther down the boardwalk, standing beside David. Ryan lowered his head. He felt no pride in what he'd done to these people. He was ashamed that strangers were watching his feeble attempt at apologizing, but he couldn't turn his back and walk away from his family.

"What's going on out here?" Travis eyed the crowd.

One of the ranchers answered. "Ryan's organizing a group of volunteers to go and stop the wildfires."

Travis, Mitch and Joseph scrutinized Ryan. He felt their eyes assessing him, staring hard at his missing earlobe.

The rancher added, "He's a Mountie just like you. And a surgeon."

"You're kiddin' me," said Travis.

"No, sir, it's the truth."

"Doesn't the United Kingdom have a postal system?" asked his father. "Don't you think your ma would have liked to know if you were alive or dead?"

Ryan winced.

"What do you want from us, Ryan?" his father asked.

"I…I wanted to see what you look like. I wanted to see how big the boys had grown." Ryan stared at his brothers. They were so tall. "And before it's too late, I wanted…I wanted to say hello to my ma and pa."

"Before we died, you mean?" His father rolled his hat between his fingers. "I got a lot of livin' left in me, and you can bloody well take a hike. When we needed you, when we really needed you because your mother was askin'…you didn't think we were important enough to let us know where you were. Now you've come home to get rid of some newfound guilt. I'm not interested."

Ryan felt the blow of each word.

His father continued, "And now you're a doctor. Is that supposed to make up for it all? What I remember is that you killed a man and then skipped town and left us to deal with it." With that, Joseph Reid pushed through the stained-glass doors of Quigley's Irish Pub and disappeared.

The lump in Ryan's throat made it difficult to swallow. The man he'd knifed had jumped him first, blade out, in the alleyway. Ryan hadn't intended to kill anyone. It just happened. The Mounties had declared it self-defense. The man had been a drifter with no family anyone recalled. Ryan hadn't been able to dig up any of his relatives. Joseph Reid had called Ryan useless and lots of other names, so Ryan had decked him. He should have controlled his rage, but looking back, he supposed the reason he couldn't was because his father had been right.

Mitch, with a heavy sigh, ran the back of his hand across his mouth. "When Ma asked, we telegraphed everyone we knew in Alberta District to see if they'd heard from you. I wrote letters to Ontario. Shawna went to the superintendent of the Mounties to see if there was anything he could do to find you. But you had disappeared off the face of the earth. I don't understand…how you could treat us like that." Mitch shook his head, then followed their father into the pub.

How many more times could Ryan say he was sorry?

Travis looked at Ryan with pity, as one might look at a sparrow with a broken wing. He, too, apparently had nothing more to say to his older brother.

"David!" Travis called the reporter. "Come into the pub with us for a drink. Tell us what we missed while we were gone. I want to know about the wildfires. What are the rest of the Mounties doing about it?"

"You could ask Ryan," said the reporter. "He's a North-West Mountie now."

"Yeah. I need a bit of time for that to sink in. Come on, I'll buy you a beer." They left Ryan standing there as they went inside the pub.

The entire group had turned away from him.

Ryan tried to blink back the sting. He glanced down at the hat in his hands and played with the brim. It was blurry from the water in his eyes.

Everywhere he went, he seemed to cause more anguish than cheer. Things were different than how he'd imagined them. In the quiet hours of a restless night, he'd often imagined that upon seeing him again, someone—maybe his affectionate younger brother—would shake his hand, or offer to take his hat and listen to the stories of where he'd been and what he'd done with his life.

"Ryan?" someone murmured.

"Ryan?" the soft voice repeated.

It was Julia.

He looked up. The crowd had dispersed, save for the two of them. "Will you be putting that in your pages tomorrow? I suppose it was quite a sight to witness."

She crossed her arms and rubbed them briskly. "What did you expect from them, Ryan?"

"I don't know. Maybe I expected compassion."

"I don't think you can expect compassion until you learn to give it."

"Oh, thank you. Thank you for those wise words."

"It's just like you to lash out at someone—at me—when you feel like a pile of dung."

He didn't wish to argue. He stepped beside her and leaned against the handrail of the boardwalk, absently watching the strangers walking by in the late-afternoon sun.

Her voice softened. "As a surgeon, you likely show some compassion to your patients, otherwise you wouldn't be a doctor. But you don't have that ability with your family, or the people closest to you. You've always been unable to share yourself, your heart, with those who love you."

He ran a hand along the splintered rail.

"They didn't notice I was here," she said, speaking almost to herself. A wagon, pulled by two heaving oxen and loaded with boulders, creaked by. "They didn't blink, they didn't nod in greeting. But then, I've always been invisible to them." She sighed. "It got worse after you left."

"Why would it get worse?"

"They blamed me for your leaving."

He felt the heat drain from his face. A few moments passed before he could speak. "Maybe there's another reason."

"Like what? I've known your father since I was a child, when he locked the cell doors every night, yet he never looks my way."

"Maybe he's ashamed of that fact." Leaning over, Ryan dug his elbows into the handrail. He wondered why this had never occurred to him before. "Maybe he can't bear to look you in the eyes. Jailing an innocent child must have been torture."

Julia raised her eyebrows and took some time to let that sink in.

"Since we're being honest, the problem you need to overcome," she said eventually, "is that you can't see how you affect the people around you. That's always been in your character. You leave town and never look back, and you think no one will notice or care."

He considered it. "That might be true. And your problem is your inability to forget when other people have wronged you."

He straightened to full height and turned to face her. She muttered an exclamation. He was reminded of the kiss they'd shared earlier, and wondered if she'd felt the same runaway danger he had. The same pounding in his chest he felt now at being this close to her.

"I'm not saying you're a vengeful person, Julia. I don't believe you are. But you harbor your pain and can't let go. I see the hurt in your eyes when you walk down the street, when you pass by the banker's wife, who makes unkind remarks about your printing shop—"

"How do you know that?"

"I also see the hurt when you walk by the society women and they don't glance your way. I saw it when the waiter at the Picadilly Hotel looked down his nose at you for not recognizing a bottle of Bordeaux wine. I saw it when you looked at my father. I see it when you look at me."

"Am I supposed to forget who left who?"

"All right. So you think I'm incapable of sharing details of my life with anyone. Then I'll tell you something. I was ill, too."

"What do you mean?"

"I came down with scarlet fever four days after I left town. We must have passed the illness between us that night."

She stumbled at the rail, and had to grab a post for support. "Oh, no…" She struggled with confusion. "That's so awful," she whispered.

"I think we picked it up from that couple who came through the bar, remember? As we were closing up that night, they were complaining about sore throats and headaches."

"Yes, I remember. They each ordered a shot of rum mixed with hot tea." Julia ran a hand along her throat. "Where did you go? Who helped you through the suffering?"

"There was really no one."

"But the burning fever…"

"I'm ashamed to say I had to pay a stranger to feed me. To change my sheets."

Ryan peered down the road at two settlers in a covered wagon, then at a young mother hurrying her children to the mercantile. "I've got to go. They're waiting for my report at the barracks." But he had one more thing to say. "I had no one, Julia, but I'm glad you had someone who cared about you…two people who loved you. Your grandfather and Brandon."

Julia stepped back into the shadows, so he had no way of knowing how she felt. Ryan stepped off the boardwalk and headed for the fort, with an overwhelming sense of grief that he'd lost something of great importance today.

He had no idea if the situation with his family could be fixed. And he had no idea what was going on between him and Julia. The pain between them was as raw and vivid as ever, yet he was losing the battle with his damn attraction to her.

Maybe they'd all be better off without him.

Chapter Nine

It was near midnight when Ryan lifted the violin out of its red leather case and placed it on his bed in the officers' quarters. "Why did you give this to me, Adam?" he mused aloud.

The question echoing off the plank walls went unanswered as always.

He removed the bow, lifted the violin to his shoulder and walked to the window. When he was settled in front of the windowpane, whose view over the river and iron bridge into town was now a sea of darkness rippled by moonlight, he ran the bow over the strings.

The soft sound filled the room. He was getting pretty good at scales. Nothing fancy, nothing complex, nowhere near Adam's beautiful ability to play the classics, but it was all Ryan knew.

You needed a lot more than inspiration to play beautifully. You needed to work hard to learn theory. Adam's bowing had been magnificent. He had a unique way of left-hand phrasing.

In truth, Ryan would make an awful violinist. He had no sense of timing, really, and his fingers always fumbled with positioning. He set down the bow on his small pine table, twirled the violin in his hand and fanned his fingers across the smooth wood.

"Violins have more than four hundred years of history," Harrison Hobbs had explained to Ryan earlier. "Like all classical violins, this one has a gorgeous slender neck. The fingerboard, bridge and tailpiece are made to perfection. It is as valuable as we suspected…from Italy, by the master Alessandro Baldassare. Look here, inside the body…"

Ryan ran his hand over the smooth scroll, enjoying the intricate carvings and wondering where Adam had got the violin.

"If anything ever happens to me, Captain," Adam had said to Ryan more than once as he'd played in the medical tent for the patients late at night, *"I want you to have my violin."*

They were too close to enemy fire to pretend that death wasn't a possibility. "But you'll want your family to have it."

"Don't have any. That's why I joined the army."

"None?"

"No, sir. My folks died in a fire in London when I was young, before they could have more kids. And the aunt who raised me couldn't have any. She passed away last year."

"You know I can't play. Why do you want me to have it?"

"Because…" and this was the part Ryan had to ask three times before Adam finally replied, *"…because, sir, I feel that…I wish you were my father."*

Gently, Ryan tucked the violin back into its case.

"Adam, if you only knew what a mess I've made of things with my own father."

Ryan wondered if Adam had known the violin's worth when he took such chances, bringing the instrument into battle.

Of course he knew its worth. Adam was only twenty himself, but he was a master player who knew every composer born since the year 1200. And yet the value of the violin hadn't seemed to matter to him, only the beauty it produced.

"I wish…Adam, I wish I could hear you play again."

Upon Adam's death, Ryan had made extensive inquiries with the British Army and the government to see if there was anyone left related to Adam. Ryan hadn't known the violin's worth back then, but figured that for sentimental reasons, someone in the family should have it. When he couldn't find anyone, Ryan got to thinking about Adam's final wish.

They *had* been like family. Adam had felt like a son to Ryan.

The violin had spurred him to return to Calgary, in the hope that he could mend things with his father. When Ryan reached Toronto, he'd had the violin restrung, since he'd used the original strings in surgery, and had inquired as to its value. The subsequent letter followed him to Calgary.

Ryan couldn't play the instrument. He would be the first to admit he had no talent. And now that he knew what it was worth, he was uneasy as he played. If he sold the violin, would Adam approve? What should Ryan do with the money? Give it to charity? Use it for upgrades to the town? He'd like to see his mother with a good portion of it. She'd be fair at dividing it amongst the family and needy organizations in Calgary. If he gave some to Julia, would she forgive him for the past? Would she think less of him for trying to sway her with money, or more of him for helping her to ease her struggle?

"What should I do with it, Adam? You led me back to Calgary, but being home hasn't helped solve a thing."

Ryan stared at the beautiful curves of the violin. If Adam could meet just one person, one person from Ryan's life, Ryan knew without a doubt he'd want that person to be Julia.

It was something he didn't want to think about. It was something he just felt.

"Have you all shut down the railway line, like I asked?" Standing in the center of the railway station the following morning, Ryan tried to keep the irritation out of his voice as he spoke to the engineer, but it crept in anyway. It wasn't the engineer's fault that Ryan had woken up angry. Now that he'd had a good sleep and had overcome his sentimentality of last night, he was rightly sore at the way everyone was treating him. Julia, her grandfather, half the town, plus his father and brothers.

"Yeah," said the youthful engineer, "we shut 'er down."

"In both directions from here to the Rockies? Both east and west?"

"Yeah, but there's a lot of griping."

"I'm getting used to it. Griping is all I've heard since I got back to town." Ryan tossed his brown, wide-brimmed Mountie's hat, a Stetson, onto his pile of baggage sitting in the center of the busy platform. He had some decisions to make about his violin, buried in the pile, but the noisy packing of supplies and troops kept him occupied. "What's the problem?"

"The vice president of the railway arrived in town late last night, fully expecting to take the train into the Rockies tomorrow. You know how much he loves relaxing at the Banff Springs Hotel. He was thinking of those hot springs and the fishin' he was—"

"Tourists and visitors are the last thing on my mind. I'm trying to fight a fire. We closed the lines in both directions to keep everyone safe."

Ryan parted from the engineer and strode down the platform.

This was turning into a huge operation, with more than a dozen railcars set to go this morning. Behind the steam engine stood a coal car, a tank car filled with hundreds of gallons of water, passenger cars with third-class seating, where the men would also sleep at night, the cook's railcar, the food supply, a medical car, a command center, and two boxcars for the horses. On the other side of the platform sat another steam engine, ready to take more water and supplies out the following day, and to deliver messages back and forth between the fort and Ryan.

Ryan shouted advice to the men loading the horses, then the ones packing axes and shovels. He was in a testy mood. He wouldn't tolerate fools this morning, and knew it was because of what he'd been through yesterday.

If his family didn't want anything to do with him, then fine. He wouldn't trouble them. He wouldn't make them suffer another bead of sweat over his life.

When this wildfire was under control, he'd stay in

Calgary long enough to see his mother. He wanted to see her lovely face again and to apologize for his painful absence. In his heart, he knew she'd never turn him or his apologies away. Then after he'd spent some time with her, a month or two maybe, and if she was well enough, he'd explain that to keep peace within the family, he'd ask for a transfer north.

The fort in Edmonton was calling for men, and Ryan preferred to live in a town where he was respected. He'd still be close enough, within two to three days' travel, to visit his mother on occasion, but his constant presence wouldn't tear the family apart.

The sight of Julia on the train platform this morning didn't help his mood. Ryan stopped short for a second, to catch his breath at the surprise of seeing her, then continued walking.

She stood on tiptoe, with her assistant beside her. David was folding the tripod of his camera and packing it away, while she was leaning into an open railcar window, talking to her Holt. Ryan guessed she'd come to say goodbye to her suitor, but he could barely watch the two smiling at each other.

Ryan's eyes traveled over the loose cream blouse that billowed over her breasts and tucked neatly at her waist. The gray fabric of her skirt rolled over her shapely behind. His gaze lingered over that part of her—the womanly part, the part he hadn't seen or touched for ten years. The part he envisioned naked nearly every time he spoke to her.

The kiss from yesterday still lingered on his lips.

He was honest enough to admit he was still attracted to

Miss Julia O'Shea. As much as the admission bothered him, maybe it would be easier to deal with the anger he felt every time he spoke to her, if he understood why he felt it.

Why did he feel such betrayal?

Was it because he'd never really been able to control her, or how she felt, or who she chose as a lover? Or was it because, even after he'd worked long and hard these last few years to become a better man, it didn't seem to matter to anyone but him?

He tried to mask his sadness. When he got closer to Julia's group, he managed a carefree salute in Holt's direction, hoping to escape the scene, but Julia spotted him.

She spun around and dropped Holt's fingers as if they were hot coals.

"Sir, I'm coming out to help load the other supplies," Holt called from inside the car. He tucked his bags beneath a bench and disappeared down the aisle.

Before Julia could say anything to Ryan, a constable dashed across the platform toward them, hollering, "Commander!"

Julia looked past Ryan's shoulder, then turned around as if looking for someone else.

David nudged her, whispering, "He's the commander."

"Oh," she said softly, staring at Ryan. "The commander."

Ryan got a tiny bit of pleasure from her acknowledgment. He *was* the boss. He was running things here. He would do everything in his power to make this firefighting operation go smoothly.

Glancing down into her wide eyes, he knew he controlled the movements and actions of sixty men, yet in his heart knew he would never control this woman.

It was an irony to be the commanding officer, for he was about to work in close conjunction with his brothers.

Due to Ryan's experience in the British Army, he had the highest rank and seniority among these Mounties. He even outranked his brother Mitch, who was also an inspector, though a junior one, and his brother Travis, a sergeant major. However, on the superintendent's word, Ryan had subdivided the chain of command. Mitch was to lead the fireline, and Travis, a skilled horseman, was to attend to the horses. His brothers would report to Ryan, and take over command if he had to shift his focus to any wounded men. Working with his brothers so closely on duty, when they were estranged in their personal lives, seemed like a bitter twist of fate.

"Sir," said the constable approaching Ryan, interrupting the moment with Julia, "you wanted the newspaper as soon as it came out."

"Thanks, Jackson." Ryan grabbed the folded sheets of the *Calgary Town Crier* just as Julia moaned.

"You really don't need to read that now, when—"

"Why not?" Ryan flipped through the dozen pages, looking for the society page.

Julia blurted, "You've got so much else to do at the mo—"

"The paper's out early today, isn't it?"

She fidgeted, rubbed her neck and avoided his stare.

David spoke up. "Normally it's out around noon, but Julia stayed up till midnight finishing the writing. Since I'm leaving on the train this morning, I printed it early. Flanagan will take care of delivery the rest of the day."

"I see." Ryan took a hard look at Julia's face. Why was

she nervous? When he found the society page and read the headline, he knew why.

A Violin Worth Thousands. And there beside the article were two photographs. One of Ryan from last night, standing in the middle of town, shouting to be heard above the crowd of firefighting volunteers. Behind him, his father and brothers were walking into the pub, turned away from him. Ryan swallowed hard at seeing their disgust again, burned into a black-and-white image. The other photograph was one of Hobbs with the small collection of banjos he was selling at the mercantile.

The first sentence read, "Ryan Reid, absent without a trace for ten years, brings home a fortune." Ryan looked up slowly. "I thought you were going to explain my side of things, Julia. I thought you'd rise above all this—above mentioning the monetary worth of my violin, and then capitalizing on the way my family has reacted to my return."

Julia lowered her voice. "In the article, I barely mention your family's reaction."

"The photograph says it all."

"That's not what I see when I look at it. I see you in the midst of all these men, struggling to help—"

"And the violin? Why on earth did you focus on its cash value?"

"It's what folks…it's what makes everyone curious. People are interested in reading about uplifting news."

"Since I've known you, you have always focused on money."

Her eyes watered. Her chin quivered. "I beg your pardon?"

Ryan clenched his jaw. There were others around. As

much as he wanted to unleash the torrent of frustration he felt, he would keep it to himself. How could he blame her for what she valued in life? Her father had taken her to jail with him due to debts unpaid. She had always struggled for every cent she earned, in the bar, when Ryan had watched her work from sunrise to well beyond sunset, and even now as a mother.

He tossed the newspaper to David and strode away. He was afraid of saying one more blasted thing.

To his surprise, Julia raced behind him.

He headed straight for his luggage, refusing to answer her questions.

"What did you expect me to write?"

He didn't reply.

"What did you expect the town would like me to write?" she asked.

He still didn't answer.

Finally, she demanded, "Why the hell did you ever come back?"

Ryan reached his pile of leather bags and started digging for the ones he wanted. He knew exactly what he was going to do with his violin.

"No man can live up to a list," he said deliberately. "No man would want to."

"What list? *What list?*"

"The list you've created for your perfect husband. I'll bet Holt has a bit of money, doesn't he? That's on your list, I'll wager. Money. *Isn't it?*"

"So what if it is? So what if he does?"

Yeah, so what. Ryan found his bags and called out to Constable Jackson again, who was lifting a saddle off the ground.

"Yes, sir." Jackson tossed the saddle into the supply car and rushed to Ryan's side.

"I need you to deliver two bags this morning. Take very special care to do what I'm about to tell you."

Julia folded her arms across her chest.

Ryan thrust the violin case into Jackson's arms. Earlier this morning, he had looped two leather belts around it and attached a lock to the straps, to which only he had the key. "Take this and deliver it to Cleveland Bosley at his bank. Tell him to put it in the vault until I get back. No one is to touch it."

"Cleveland Bosley, sir?"

"That's right."

"Forgive me, but I thought the man—I mean I heard that you two had words."

"That's right, he hates my guts."

"Why would you send something of such value to him?"

"Here." Ryan unzipped another leather bag, of relatively the same size, and took out a wad of cash. "Tell Bosley to hire two extra guards around the clock to protect it. Tell him I want to buy as much insurance as I can in case this property is stolen."

"But to send it to the man who hates your guts, sir?"

"Oh, he'll be pissed as hell to get it. That's why I know he'll take extra special care that nothing happens to it while I'm gone."

The constable held tight to the battered case. Julia shook her head.

"And take this bag—" Ryan handed Jackson the one with his cash and valuables in it "—to the manager at the Imperial Bank. Tell him to hold it with the rest of my account, in the vault. It's not worth that much, so no extra guards needed."

Ryan cast a glance in Julia's direction when he added that, and she looked away with appropriate guilt. If she hadn't blabbed about the violin's worth in her paper, he wouldn't have to go to such extremes. What thief wouldn't want to steal it now?

"Yes, sir." The constable dashed away.

"Hold on," Ryan called. "You better take one more bag and deliver it to my mother. She's not there right now, but get it to the ranch. There's a dress in here that I bought for her overseas."

Julia stared down at the bag. Folds of blue linen and black satin piping protruded from between the clasps. Jackson nodded and took the three bags away.

"Julia!" called a woman. "Julia, there you are!"

Ryan and Julia spun around to see Clarissa Ashford, luggage in hand, dragging it toward them.

"Clarissa, good of you to come."

"Where does she think she's going?" Ryan asked Julia.

"With me." Julia slid her hand into her skirt pocket. "We're going with you."

"Like hell," Ryan boomed. "There's no room for women on this train."

Chapter Ten

It didn't surprise Julia that Ryan was forbidding her to go. What surprised her was that he thought she would take orders from him with no discussion.

Beside them, Clarissa set down her luggage and waited while they debated. Horses neighed, troops called to each other, old men sipped water from canteens. The scent of spices drifted past Julia as the cook wheeled his crates along the platform.

"Reporters need to go everywhere," she insisted.

"Then send David." With impatience, Ryan thrust his hand into his pocket.

"I'd like to say go ahead, David, do all the work that's the least bit dangerous. I'll stay behind and cover the easy stories. You talk to the men who robbed the bank, murdered the drovers, committed arson down the street. When there's a forest fire, you volunteer to go while I stay behind and—and fill up the ink wells in the shop."

"What's wrong with that? A man protecting a woman is—"

"This is the way I contribute to the world, Ryan. I own

a newspaper. What's wrong with it is telling me I can no
longer contribute in the way I wish to."

"What about your son?"

Her little boy was her only soft spot. "I've left Pete with
his aunt and cousins. He's completely safe and he loves
being there. Grandpa's at home if Pete needs him. I'll only
be gone for a day." But still, she would miss him.

Ryan's posture eased. "One day?"

"I know there's another train coming to the site tomorrow morning with more supplies, right?"

Ryan nodded.

"I was planning on taking it back. I'll have a look at the
camp tonight, write about what's going on, and print it up
as a one-page extra edition to the paper. It'll keep everyone
abreast of what's happening. On a daily basis, David will
send news back and forth on the alternating supply trains,
and photographs when he can."

"Your whole staff is covering only one story?"

"There *is* no other story in Calgary. No one will want
to read about anything else but this."

"And you might as well make a bit of money off the
fire, right?"

She glared up into his dark eyes. "Why do you say
things that make people instantly dislike you?"

"Why do you print things that affect how a person runs
his life? 'A Violin Worth Thousands.' Thanks for telling
everyone in the world it's worth stealing."

"I didn't think of it in those terms…it was so late last
night when I… No matter what I wrote, you wouldn't
have been happy."

"My happiness doesn't seem to be your priority."

Julia didn't know what overcame her then, but she laughed. "We agree on that point."

Ryan swore beneath his breath, causing Clarissa to turn away in embarrassment. "I can't handle much more of your honesty, Julia," he muttered. "For God's sake, can't you lie to me once in a while, if only to humor me?"

Lord help her, if she had to stand here for one more second and take this—

David strode up from behind. "I'm with you, Commander. Leave the women behind."

"David!" snapped Clarissa. She jumped into the discussion, dark hair flying about her face, leather gloves snapping the air. "You know how much I'd like to help. I'd be more than willing to hold your cameras, take dictation and do anything else a junior reporter does. There's no charge to either you or Julia. I'd simply like to be trained as someone's apprentice."

"Precisely." David turned to Ryan. "Forbid her to come, Commander."

Frustration seeped into Julia. David hadn't been able to accept how quickly and easily photography came to Clarissa. Last fall at the harvest fair, Clarissa had won David in a charity raffle for twenty-four hours. The town had expected her, as a woman with a questionable reputation for leading men astray and for creating havoc wherever she went, to use her time with David in the way the jeweler's daughter spent most of her days—going to social events where she could dress up and impress people with her looks and money. Even Julia was surprised when Clarissa had insisted David take her to the printing shop instead. Clarissa had learned as much about photography and reporting as she could jam into twenty-four hours. She and Julia were slowly becoming friends.

At first, David had been flattered that Clarissa had begged him to teach her, then a bit dismayed at how quickly she'd mastered the wet plate process of tintype photography. He then grew downright protective of his territory, annoyed that a woman could pick up his skills so quickly. If anyone asked Julia, and no one did, some men couldn't tolerate a woman being equal to them on the job.

Julia dropped her bag, took a giant step toward Ryan and David and waved her finger. "If either of you so much as consider sending us back to our dining tables where you think we belong, we'll organize a posse of women. Tomorrow morning on the supply train, hundreds of us will join you!"

David laughed, not accepting the bluff. "A posse of women." He elbowed Ryan. "Hundreds of them. Under normal circumstances, I wouldn't mind a posse of women chasing me."

Ryan didn't budge. "If you think I'm going to allow two women to blackmail me—"

"Two women are better than one," stated Julia in a softer, more compromising tone. "If Clarissa comes with me, we can stick together and keep an eye out for each other. There'd be—there'd be less for your men to do."

Ryan let out a low growl. He took a long moment to make his decision, and during that time, Julia didn't dare breathe.

"The women can come until tomorrow morning," he declared. "Then they both leave on the first train back." Ryan, dark and bulky, towered over David, who was fair and slim.

"But absolutely, under no circumstances, are you bringing your monkey. I absolutely draw the line at monkeys."

"No monkey, sir. I left him with Pete. No monkey, I promise."

With the small semblance of pride he had left, Ryan strode down the platform and continued barking orders.

"I would have liked to see your posse of women, Julia." Holt smiled at her from his crowded bench across the aisle. More than five hours had passed. The train jostled her to the point of discomfort. Her corset was looped too tightly. The windows were open, but the air was hot and dusty. It swirled around Julia, lifting the moistened hairs at her temples.

"Hear, hear!" shouted another Mountie. "I vote we go back and get the women!"

Laughter erupted around them. Now that she'd calmed down, Julia did see the humor of her threat. Some of the rowdier Mounties had caught wind of her words and wouldn't allow her to forget them.

"Nothing like a group of women galloping on horseback to light my fuse!"

"They don't even need to be galloping," another man hollered. "Just the beauty of a woman on horseback is all I need."

"Bareback?" called another.

"Yes, but do you mean the woman or the horse?"

At the stifled laughter, Julia looked to the plank floor and felt her face heat. Clarissa twitched beside her. From the corner of her eye, Julia saw Holt partially rise off his wooden bench, glaring in the direction of the man who'd made the indecent remark.

The men grew silent as the car continued rolling through the foothills, yellowed from lack of rain. The train chugged up along the valley of the Bow River. If Julia craned her neck she could see a wall of jagged mountain peaks tipped with snow and ice. Summer meltwater saturated the pines growing on the lower slopes of the mountains. She'd never seen anything so remarkably lush and green.

Inside the train, it wasn't so much the sight of Holt that quieted the men, but the sight of their commander at the front of the car. Ryan was equally disapproving of the off-color remark made in front of the women. Just one look into the black depth of his eyes was enough to silence the crowded railcar.

Ryan's two brothers were riding in the car behind them, Julia had noted. Ryan sat away from her and her group. He had allowed the women to come but obviously wasn't going to entertain them with conversation.

It was rather disheartening, Julia realized, being so ignored by him.

Up to this point, Ryan had been busy attending to a Mountie who'd injured his arm hoisting dozens of empty water pails to the roof. When the train had left the station the man had been clutching his forearm, but insisting he was fine. An hour into the ride, when he couldn't help twisting in pain at every bump of the train, Ryan demanded to inspect it.

She tapped her wrist, watching him attend to the injured Mountie. She had a clear view, straight down the aisle past three dozen men, to the surgeon crouching at the feet of the other Mounties—as if he were a servant rather than their commander. She'd never seen him care for a patient before, and there was something so giving in his expression, so natural in his posture, that she couldn't look away.

He was at ease with his men.

Ryan's shoulders lost their sharp edge. His face, normally creased with hard lines, softened around the mouth. He was generous with his words, although Julia couldn't make out what was said. The injured man, who'd begun the ordeal stiff with pain, had unwound so much in Ryan's presence that he was leaning forward and asking questions. Inconspicuously, his shirt had been removed. Ryan was bandaging his forearm.

Ryan's face echoed something from the past. His eyes glowed with understanding, and his touch seemed to soothe the man.

Julia remembered that touch. For the first time since Ryan's return, she allowed the memories, the good ones, to come flooding back.

The tilt of Ryan's dark head, the way the light skimmed his glossy black hair, reminded her of the way his face had been poised above hers on that one powerful night when they'd been alone in the bar. Ryan had locked the doors and offered to help clean up, carrying beer steins and shot glasses to the sink to be washed. Half an hour later, Julia had been completely undressed, lying on his long leather coat on top of the magnificent oak bar, beneath Ryan. He, equally naked, equally primitive and possessive, had slid his lips down across her throat to settle on her breast.

With her heart pounding from the memory, Julia reached into her satchel and removed her newly ironed handkerchief. It was cream linen and embroidered with neat, ladylike initials, J.O., so unblemished compared to the sensual thoughts racing through her brain. She dabbed the virginal handkerchief across her perspiring brow, thankful no one could read her mind.

Unable to stop herself, Julia stole another glance at Ryan. To her unease, he finished with the Mountie, took a seat across from the man, and looked directly down the aisle at her.

Their gazes met. Both looked away. Ryan coughed and glanced at his boots, while Julia studied the landscape speeding past the window. She ran her handkerchief across her moist throat. There had been a time when his eyes couldn't get enough of her.

He didn't kiss like a normal man. His kisses didn't start at her mouth or her face, but burned along her throat, then straight to her bosom. She'd never met a man so centered on a woman's breasts and thighs. So willing to spend hours pleasing her.

The train jerked and swayed, bouncing her off the seat for a second. Their eyes met again. This time, he didn't instantly look away. His gaze lowered to the lace blouse that draped across her chest, lingering for an indescribable moment, then flickered downward toward the floorboards. She felt a tingling in every muscle.

Julia wondered how much longer the trip would take. She felt the train straining beneath her boots as they climbed slowly but steadily upward in elevation. On flat prairie land, the train could travel up to forty miles per hour. But with the heavy load they were carrying up a slope, they were lucky to get five. She heard the soft neighing of horses several cars away. The wildfire was getting closer, and at times, ribbons of smoke drifted through the open windows. The earthy scent of aspens, cottonwoods and spruce was being smothered by its odor. But being in the same cramped quarters with Ryan affected her senses, too. How long would this torture last?

Ten minutes must have passed before she straightened her spine again. She didn't peer in his direction, but felt the burn of his eyes on her face. Perhaps it was only her imagination. Mustn't look, she warned herself. Mustn't look.

But she couldn't help it. Slowly, she lifted her chin. This time, he was staring at her directly, refusing to glance away. His temper, his impatience, seemed to pull her out of her complacency and leave her shaking.

Her question went unspoken, but it weighed heavily between them. *Do you remember what you did to me?*

Julia glanced down at her lap, then at the stitching on her satchel's handle. *You kissed my belly, my thighs, and a spot where I hadn't ever imagined that men and women would kiss.*

She'd kissed him there, too.

The revelation had caused problems between her and Brandon. Once, eager in her lovemaking, she'd whispered the same suggestion in Brandon's ear. He'd been so aghast, wondering where she'd even heard of such a thing, that it had spoiled the evening and she'd never brought it up with him again.

How very different it had been with Ryan. Anything she could have suggested—indeed, anything he could have— they would both have been eager to pursue. Not that Brandon had been a bad lover. He'd been caring and tender, but there were boundaries to what he thought appropriate. Unfortunately, something in Brandon had made *him* broach the subject of intimate kissing twice again, and each time, when she'd refused to answer where she'd learned of it, Brandon had gone mad with jealousy. *"It was Ryan. It was that bloody Reid!"*

"Are you all right, Julia?" Clarissa leaned in to whisper.

"Yes, thank you."

"You look awfully heated. Would you care for some water from my canteen?"

"No…I…" Julia ran the handkerchief along the back of her neck, which was sopping. "I'll manage till we get there."

Would she?

She looked up again to see Ryan watching her, without an ounce of shame or hesitation, his deep, mesmerizing brown eyes sparkling with life.

She stared back, caught in a tangle of emotions and sensations. *You promised me that night that you'd never fight again. You promised you'd never leave me. You vowed that it didn't matter what your family thought of me, you would never leave.*

The rumble of the train shifted; they were slowing down. The steam engine hissed and the brakes squealed. How wrong she'd been to listen to a liar.

And now that liar was commanding her what to do.

Julia looked out the window at the cloud of distant smoke. She was worried about her ability to cope with the fire and wondered how much more of him she could take.

Chapter Eleven

When the train came to an abrupt stop, Ryan leaped out of it, eager to escape Julia's eyes. Attending to his work seemed much easier than dealing with her unspoken accusations.

"Holt, come with me. The rest of you stay inside!" Ryan commanded from outside the train, standing in a field of wild grass and trees. It was past two. "Stay inside until I give the order to disembark!" He motioned for his brothers to join him, too.

With such a heavy cargo of livestock, water and equipment, it had taken them six hours, double the usual time, to get to this specific break in the river.

Three huge granite boulders, each fifty feet high, marked the spot that the scouts had told Ryan would be far enough away from the fire to group the men.

"Dammit," said Holt, whistling at the sight of heavy smoke in the distance. "The fire's traveled a hell of a lot farther than we scouted two days ago. The smoke's thicker and covers more acreage."

"The wind's been controlling the speed of the fire," said Ryan. "And it's been strong for the last two days. But it's died down a lot the last couple of hours. Did you notice how calm the trees were on the ride here?"

"Yeah," said Holt.

"All the wild animals have left. I haven't seen any birds for the past hour. Spotted some deer and antelope along the river ten miles back, but nothing since then."

"If the winds shift direction, we'll have nothing to worry about. The fire can burn in the wilderness if it heads north or northeast."

"How far do you think we are from the edge of it?" asked Ryan.

"Judging by the smoke, I'd say six or eight miles."

Mitch and Travis joined them in the tall grass.

"What do you think?" asked Mitch, staring at Ryan.

Ryan gave him a hard look.

"Sir," Mitch added. He didn't say it with warmth, but he wasn't rude, either. "What do you think, sir?"

However his brothers chose to act toward him personally, Ryan demanded complete respect in the field.

"What I think is that we're a bit far from the fire and incapable of containing it on all sides. But six or eight miles gives us enough leeway to dig some ditches to try and stop it from spreading toward town. We should take advantage of the calm winds while we can. Tell everyone we stop here. Travis, see to it that the horses get some exercise. Mitch, organize three groups to start the digging. Tell the cook the men will work for an hour, then eat. That should give him a good start."

Both his brothers hurried off to obey orders.

"I can smell the bacon frying already," said Holt. "He must have started on the way here."

"Commander?" Travis called to Ryan, pausing in his tracks. "I spotted another clearing when we passed, about five miles back. It would be another place to settle the horses if the fire chases us downhill."

Ryan nodded. "It's always good to have options. Keep your eyes open for fords in the river, too, in case we need to cross it in a hurry. Make sure everyone is aware of the safety concerns, especially if we get separated from the train and need to escape on horseback. Two men to one horse. Have everyone partner up."

Travis turned and signaled to the waiting men to disembark. Dozens jumped off the train as the youngest Reid brother rushed back toward Ryan.

Mitch pointed to a gully ahead. "See that creek? Half our ditch may be dug for us already if we use the gully to our advantage. We could extend it to create the first fireline."

Ryan peered out at the grassy slope. "I thought so, too. We could dig another long ditch a hundred yards behind it and clear all the burnable material in between, then douse it with water so the fire won't skip."

His brother agreed.

So at least their business arrangement would be amicable. Ryan felt more at ease knowing his brothers intended to focus on working together to beat the fire, while ignoring their troubling family situation.

"Inspector," Ryan said to Mitch. "You're the second in command."

"I'm aware of that."

"If anything should happen to me, or if I get sidetracked as a physician, you'll be in charge of the firefighting."

"Understood." Mitch wheeled around. "Let's start the unpacking," he hollered to the men. "The food stays on board with the cook. The medical car stays intact. We'll unload sleeping rolls and blankets at nightfall. For now, shovels and axes only!"

"Holt," Ryan instructed, "tell the engineer to choose two other crew members. The three of them should always stay within fifty feet of the engine. *At all times*, night and day. Their priority is to back up the train in an emergency, if and when I blow the whistle."

"Got it." Holt raced off toward the steam engine, stopping briefly to help Julia disembark with one of David's smaller cameras and her satchel.

When Holt left, Julia turned around to survey their surroundings. David and Clarissa soon joined her, and Ryan made his way toward the little group.

"Safety is a main concern," he told them in passing. "You'll need to double up on a horse, but since there are three of you, I could—"

"Holt's already partnered with us. With me." Julia raised a hand to her eyes to protect them from the sun's glare. "Clarissa's got David and I've got Holt."

"Good. That's good." But Ryan was caught unprepared for the remark. Holt had beat him to it. Then, with no time for hesitation, Ryan raced away to organize his men.

The men got to work immediately. At half past two, every shovel was entrenched in soil, every Mountie and volunteer digging a ten-foot-wide ditch that would serve as a fire-

break. Julia stopped writing and looked up from her journal. She stood in awe of the sight before her: sixty men lined beyond the gully, backs bent in the heat of the sun.

Ryan stood among them.

Dutiful and tough.

While Julia shooed the flies away from her face and tipped her bonnet to block the sun's rays, Ryan allowed the sweat to pour from his temples, to soak his white shirt. Other men removed their shirts to expose their skin, using their wide-brimmed brown Stetsons, the mark of a Mountie, to fan the dust, smoke and flies away from their faces.

When the cook clanged the bell for their meal, Ryan was the last to leave the ditch-digging to go and eat, and the first to step away when the meal was through. He had no problem facing the hard work ahead, lending a hand to a weaker man or offering praise for a job well done.

What Julia noticed most was the reaction of the men beneath his command. They were eager to do his bidding and did so with generosity. Julia wasn't an expert on Mounties, or on the army, but even in her ignorance she knew that Ryan had a gift for leadership.

At one point, while she studied him and wrote frantically, she noticed Holt staring at her. She smiled and stopped to fill his canteen with fresh water, but he said very little.

After a late dinner, one as plentiful and enjoyable as the first, the sun began to set and a new tension gripped the camp.

The wind was picking up. It snatched hats and blew them down the gully. It whipped the ties of Julia's bonnet and swept aside the black fabric draped over David's camera while he was taking photographs. Mostly, the strengthening wind created a wave of fear in the camp.

"Pack up your bedrolls and move them onto the train again," Ryan shouted to the assembly. "We're rolling back a few miles. The fire's advancing too fast for my comfort."

"But, sir, we're not finished with our double row of ditches!"

"We've got to go now! We'll roll farther away from the fire next time, about a dozen miles. That should give us enough time to dig two rows. The work we've done here already might be enough to stop it. Let's go!"

"What do you see, Ryan?" Julia closed her notebook and followed the direction of his gaze, over the curving Bow River toward the thick smoke up the valley.

"The fire's crowning."

"What does that mean?"

"It's jumping from treetop to treetop, over the forest canopy. The river's stopping it on one side, but it's uncontrollable on the other."

It was the quaver in his voice that unnerved her. Ryan placed a firm hand at her back and whisked Julia to the train.

Julia noticed the tension simmering between Holt and Ryan at their next stop. She felt uncomfortable that she was likely the cause.

It was more than an hour later when the troops disembarked at the new site. Everyone was giddy over the fact they'd completed the first firebreak, that it alone might stop the fire, that they'd all escaped immediate danger. Laughter filtered through the crowd, from all except Ryan and Holt. No matter how hard Julia tried to join the light-hearted conversations of the other men, her unease wouldn't subside.

She'd written steadily for her newspaper during daylight hours, but now that it was getting dark, she decided to rest her tired eyes.

She set aside her work. Tomorrow afternoon, on the train home, she could finish up whatever needed to be written before printing.

Around her in the camp, men lit coal oil lanterns and hung them from the branches of poplar trees and white spruce.

"We'll divide into two shifts," said Ryan. "Half of us will dig, while the other half sleeps. We'll rotate sometime around 3:00 a.m. and should finish up by dawn."

"Fires don't move as fast during the night," Mitch added. "They burn fastest during daylight hours, with the help of the sun and wind, so this should give us plenty of time to dig the trenches and get out of here."

It took ten minutes for the men to subdivide. Due to the pleasant evening weather, most grabbed their bedrolls from the train, intending to sleep outdoors on the far side of the tracks.

"What are you going to do?" Clarissa asked Julia. David stood beside them, wrestling with his large camera.

"I don't think I'll be able to get to sleep yet." She answered. "You two go ahead."

"It's a good idea for one of us to remain behind. That way, we can rotate our reporting with the change in shifts," said David. "Then we won't miss anything for the newspaper."

Clarissa disappeared onto the train. She headed for the commander's car, which Ryan had given up for the night to allow the ladies privacy. David would sleep outdoors.

Julia picked up a shovel and joined the group of men digging on the western slope of the river.

"What are you doing?" asked Ryan as she passed.

"I'm carrying a shovel."

"Why don't you join Clarissa and get some rest?"

"I will when I get tired. I thought I'd be more useful out here."

"Don't get in the way."

Her fingers tensed around the shovel. "I don't intend to. Why is it you object to everything I do?"

"Your safety is my responsibility."

"Ah, duty speaks. But I can look after myself from here to the train. It's only fifty yards. Holt is waiting for me over there. He doesn't seem to mind if I help with the digging."

Ryan scoffed, shook his head and stalked off in the other direction.

In all honesty, she didn't know why she'd said what she had, except that Ryan was always approving or disapproving of what she did. The way she saw it, they were in this firefight together.

Unfortunately, most of the other men saw it the way Ryan did. They stared at Julia as she trudged by, some openly suggesting she needn't work, that she should sleep and leave the labor to the men.

How could she sleep when there were thirty men beyond the cars, heaving and hoisting shovelfuls of dirt, sometimes overcome with smoke, sometimes parched for a drink of water with no one to supply them? She could make herself useful by at least carrying drinking water.

And so it began.

Ryan versus Holt.

The wise, older lion versus the brave young tiger.

When Holt made space for her in the lineup of men who were digging, Ryan stalked away to the other end with his shovel. When Holt raced to pull at tree roots, Ryan took a pickax and dug at bigger ones.

If Holt needed to rest, Ryan outlasted him before taking a break.

The evening wore on, and in the quiet forest, the sound of men grunting and straining mixed with the sound of metal tools scraping against stones and dirt.

Midnight arrived. At one unexpected moment, as Julia was catching her breath, trying to forget about the blisters smarting on her palms, Holt snatched a kiss.

She was carrying some canteens to the water tank to refill them, safely tucked out of view at a curve in the railcars, beneath a cottonwood, when he slipped up from behind and kissed her on the cheek, then lightly on her mouth. It was a pleasant sensation, and she felt oddly proud that he, perhaps, was appreciative of her work.

"Holt, do your muscles ache?" Julia twisted out of his reach. As much as she enjoyed Holt's kisses, she had to get this water to the men.

"Not really. I do a lot of lifting at my uncle's store, and pitch hay and straw at the fort's stables."

Standing in the moonlight, Holt looked young and healthy. He was eager to use the brawn God had given him.

If she married Holt, he'd be kind to her. He had a gentle, coaxing spirit that was soothing to be around. Holt was here to protect her, but allowed her the freedom to make her own choices.

Unlike Ryan.

When Julia heaved the straps of three canteens across

one shoulder and three over the other, Holt planted another kiss on her cheek. At that inopportune moment, the three Reid brothers walked by.

Ryan was speaking. "We've almost finished the first trench, and in another hour, we'll wake the other—" He stopped when he saw Julia.

Mortified at being caught, as if she and Holt were two adolescents sneaking around at a time when serious matters should be their concern, she pulled away.

Mitch and Travis turned to see what had halted their older brother.

"Good evening," said Mitch.

"We were filling the canteens," Holt muttered.

"So we see," said Travis, eyeing Holt's empty hands.

Ryan said nothing. Simply stared and judged. Then kept walking, finishing his sentence. "We'll wake the other men in about an hour."

Could he not give them some flicker of understanding? Julia fumed silently. She and Holt were likely to be married. It wasn't as if she was cavorting with every man who showed her interest.

Even amusement from the almighty commander would be better than that sullen look of disapproval. His brothers were no better. They'd been looking down their noses at her from across town for years.

Julia panted beneath the weight of the water as she made her way back to the trenches, telling herself that after all this time, she should be used to the Reids' reactions.

Yet the insult continued to hurt, working its way even deeper as she labored on.

She recalled what Ryan had said to her last night—that

she had an inability to forget when others wronged her. For the next hour, working on her knees, she thought about those words.

The muscles in Ryan's arms and legs ached as he stood with his brothers by the river. The strain of shoveling for hours made Ryan's biceps throb, reminding him that he wasn't as young as Holt MacAllister. Ryan would be damned if he'd admit his discomfort to anyone. He tried to bury the image of Holt and Julia kissing in the darkness.

"If these firebreaks don't work, what are we going to do?" asked Travis.

Ten minutes after passing Holt and Julia on the trail, Travis had led two horses to the riverbank and allowed them to drink. Mitch and Ryan had followed with four more. The horses now lapped at the running water as Ryan peered above the forest. Moonlight skimmed across everything in sight, giving him a decent picture of the trouble ahead.

"Then we'll pull back again and dig more trenches," Ryan answered.

Mitch rubbed the back of his neck. "We don't have a hell of a lot of leeway to keep doing that. Another pullback and grazing land and ranches start."

"I'm aware of that." Ryan stared long and hard at the smoke billowing above the treetops. "The fire skipped over the gully. Our first attempt didn't work."

Travis swore.

Mitch squinted toward the fire. "Are you sure?"

"Yeah." Ryan took a deep breath. "Once it reaches open prairie land and turns from a forest fire into a grass fire, it'll move faster. So I've decided on a different course of action. When the supply train comes in today, tell them to bring in dynamite tomorrow. Three barrels of it," he ordered Mitch.

"Dynamite? Dammit, three barrels? What do you intend to do with dynamite?"

"Nothing for now."

"Level with us, Ryan." Mitch's voice had a desperate edge. "I heard you were an expert with explosives. What's the dynamite for?"

"If these trenches don't work, we could blast bigger trenches to interrupt the blaze. Fire needs air to survive, right? Maybe we could snuff out the flames with a big enough blast. The exploding dirt and grass might smother them."

"I've never heard of using dynamite to smother a fire."

"I've been thinking about this for hours—in theory, it should work."

"Hell, you mean you've never seen it done?"

"I tried it once in Africa. I didn't use enough dynamite though. It had no effect. A large amount of explosives should suck the air out of the area, leaving none for the fire to feed on."

"I think we've got a wildman on our hands." Travis looked at Mitch. "A huge blast might *fuel* the fire," Travis argued. "The opposite of what you hope."

"No dynamite," Mitch insisted, shaking his head. "It might accidentally blow up the train. Or the track. We might trap ourselves getting out of here." Mitch tried to calm his horse at the water's edge, but his voice was impatient. "Ryan, you're being reckless. You used to suggest things like this when you were young and wild."

Travis added with a curt nod, "You might enjoy living on the edge, but the rest of us don't like taking chances. We've got wives and children we'd like to get back to."

They didn't seem to think much of his reasoning, but dammit, Ryan was in command. And this was different than anything crazy he'd done in his youth. Taking the reins of two horses, he headed back up the slope, wincing at the ache in his legs. "Maybe you're right," he said, buying himself more time to think. "We should wake the other men. You both get some sleep. I'll stay up for two more hours, then wake one of you to take over. Travis, send two scouts on horseback up the valley to report back on the current size and location of the fire."

The risks were high. But dammit, in theory it should work.

Ryan hitched the horses in a group of trees. Alone again, he walked alongside the silent train. As he passed the command car, he wondered if Julia was just going to sleep, whether she was lying in his bed or in a bedroll stretched out on the floor. He could picture her in the moonlight, her soft face turned upward, her body nestled in his cloak.

He wondered what she would think of his plan. It was times like these when he yearned to have a partner to confide in, someone who might see the logic in his thinking before dismissing what he had to say because of the type of man he used to be. He gave the railcar a soft tap and continued walking. Sometimes, the biggest rewards went to the people who took the most risk.

She couldn't make out his face. Inside the train, Julia was dreaming, and in her dream, he was kissing her body. She was seated in a chair while he stood behind her in the middle of the night, undoing the clasp that bound her hair, brushing the strands across her bare shoulders. Her hair, soft as early morning dew, slid down her arms and over the tips of her breasts. With brush in hand, he leaned over and took her puckered nipple in his warm mouth.

The warm sensation made her giddy, the heat of his breath sending pleasurable chills through her breasts and stomach. His moaning mingled with the moonlight and the hot, gentle breeze that stirred the bedroom curtains.

Who was he?

She strained to see his face, to see who could move her to such depths.

He was tempting. He was forbidden. He was lost and so was she.

"I think I smell smoke," she whispered as he lifted her, then laid her on a carpet of silk.

"It's the fireplace, my love," he whispered back.

"The horses…they're restless…I can hear them stomping outside."

"It's only the wind lifting the leaves."

His voice was low and familiar. Was it Brandon?

She sighed. It felt so good to be with him again.

When he straightened above her, she saw he was naked, too. Shadows concealed his face, and no matter how hard she stared, she couldn't be certain who he was. Moonlight glistened along the muscles of his chest, rippled softly over his smooth golden stomach, gilded the hairs below. Lowering his head, he kissed her shoulder, trailing his lips along her underarm, her elbow, her fingers.

Lifting herself up on her forearms, she struggled to see his face. A glimpse of his cheek reminded her of Holt.

Was it Holt making love to her?

Leaning back against the silken carpet, she allowed his lips to linger where they would. He chose her ankle, the inside of her calf, the top of her knee, and then upward along her thigh. She parted for him, eager to know how his lips might feel on her center.

But he surprised her by jumping to her abdomen, kissing the soft swell of flesh beneath her belly button, traveling up the line between her breasts. Kissing one breast, and then the other. When his lips found hers and he began a slow caress, she knew with shocking clarity it was Ryan.

With a loud exclamation, she woke up. Disconnected, she was clutching the pillow on Ryan's narrow cot.

"Julia, what's wrong?" Clarissa was standing above her, nudging her. "Your voice was filled with panic. What were you dreaming about?"

Chapter Twelve

Julia nodded weakly from under the bedcovers. "I don't remember…" But she did. She recalled every shameful detail. She was shocked at herself for the vivid nature of her imagination. Proper ladies didn't have such erotic dreams, and certainly not…not with three different men.

"Are you sure you're all right?" asked Clarissa. She was completely dressed to go outside and join the others in the digging, while Julia was trying to regain her composure.

"Yes, thank you. It must have been a nightmare." What did her dream mean? That she had an unshakable attraction to Ryan? *No.*

Clarissa sat down on the edge of the bed. Men's voices echoed outside. "I must have slept through the call for the second round to begin." She glanced at her pocket watch. "It's nearly four o'clock. David will be out there."

"Can you manage? With David, I mean?" Julia's sensibilities were returning. She was worried about Clarissa.

Clarissa lowered her hands from her blouse and hesitated. "Why does the sight of me repel him so much?"

"You're a threat to his abilities as a reporter. It took him many years to acquire his skills. He began years ago as a photographer, selling souvenir postcards. Then he worked his way up to journalism. It's taken you only months."

"Why are you giving me a chance, Julia? When everyone else in town dismisses me as spoiled and rich, why do you listen to my ideas?"

"Because I believe you have talent in the way you frame a photograph, and the way you phrase a story."

Clarissa was several years older than Julia, and used to be more flamboyant. It seemed to Julia that Clarissa was toning down her behavior, perhaps since developing an interest in reporting. She took her time answering questions, was thoughtful in replying and never giggled in a man's presence as some younger women did.

"Any other reason?" Clarissa asked.

"Because I know how it feels when no one believes in you."

"You're becoming a very good friend."

"I wish that others saw my presence here as a bridge to something better."

"You mean Ryan."

Julia nodded. Although Clarissa didn't know the full story, she had extracted some details from Julia over the course of the last week. Clarissa had been through her own share of pain, often creating squabbling between the men who vied for her. Once, she'd confided to Julia that it bothered her that she'd never married, that she'd never been able to sustain anyone's love. It was a matter of perspective, Julia had replied, and no one should need marriage to justify his or her existence. From others, Julia had heard that Clarissa had once sent a suitor to prison for a robbery he'd committed against his partner in a lumber mill, in order to impress her with the stolen money. It wasn't the same woman Julia knew now.

"How does Ryan see your presence?" Clarissa asked.

"Sometimes, the disappointed way he looks at me makes me want to weep."

"That's good."

Julia tucked the bedsheet beneath her chin. The scent of Ryan was everywhere, from an old leather coat hooked against the wall to the extra duffle bag on the floor. "How could it be good?"

"Feeling something is better than feeling nothing. Perhaps your heart is trying to tell you that."

When Clarissa left, Julia stared into the darkness, wondering what her heart was trying to tell her, wondering about the significance of her dream. At the beginning of her widowhood, she'd dreamed of Brandon every night. But what they'd once shared now felt as though it had occurred in another lifetime. Was it a blessing or a curse that such memories faded over years? She felt a twinge of guilt.

But Brandon had told her several times before he passed away that he didn't want her to be alone forever. "I'm sorry, Brandon," she whispered. "But I know you understand."

Holt was who she belonged with now—for the sake of their blossoming friendship, which she felt would sustain them through to old age, and for the sake of Pete's well-being. Holt was whom she should have dreamed about from beginning to end. Not Ryan.

"Not Ryan," she murmured, closing her eyes and hoping for sleep again. "Not Ryan."

* * *

Julia saw Ryan again shortly after waking.

The rising sun streamed through her windows, intertwined with a haze of smoke. The resulting cloudy light cascaded onto the brown wool blanket wrapped about her torso. A voice from outside, someone walking down the side of the train clanging a metal bell, called, "All awake! All awake now!"

Coughing, Julia scrambled out of bed into the cool morning air. She slid into a fresh skirt and blouse, washed her face and brushed her teeth with powder in the porcelain bowl, then grabbed her shawl and raced outside.

Mist from the river covered the forest floor. Heavy smoke from the wildfire engulfed the treetops and filled the air. Lord almighty, the fire was close. The scent of loam and moss from the freshly dug soil drifted around her.

Ryan came barreling around the end of the train, patting down his damp hair and clearing his throat. By his ruffled looks, he'd also just awoken.

"Good morning," he said to her. "Have you been up long?"

She shook her head. "Only five minutes."

When a group of men approached, Julia stepped aside to let Ryan do his work.

"Commander, the second trench has been dug and we've begun to strip the roots and leaves from between the two firebreaks."

"We've got no time to waste," said Ryan. "Have every available man strap a water can to his back and begin spraying."

"But we haven't dug up the soil in between."

Julia understood that fire could travel beneath the

ground, fueled by leaves and rotting vegetation. She'd been told of the danger several times. It could smolder for days before igniting, depending on how dry the area was. Everyone was concerned about the drought. She'd also been told that a forest fire had fingers. It didn't always move forward in a straight line, but sometimes advanced via long thin projections. The center of the fire might be hundreds of yards away, yet a finger could travel beneath the ground or leap from tree to tree.

"There's no time to strip the soil," said Ryan. "See how thick the smoke is? I want this area evacuated in fifteen minutes."

"But the cook has called for breakfast—"

"No time for breakfast. We'll eat on the train. Get the train crew to fire up the engine. *Now!*"

What this meant, Julia realized with despair, was that the fire had skipped over the first gully while she'd been sleeping, and was moving closer. To her eyes, there didn't appear to be an immediate threat, but Ryan's brisk orders made her nervous.

She found David and Clarissa by the water tank, running with buckets of water to douse the area. David's left forearm was weak due to certain muscles having been removed years ago in surgery to offset gangrene, but he was able to carry a bucket. He always wore long-sleeved shirts to conceal his arm. Julia was too small to strap a ten-gallon water can to her back, so she picked up a bucket and raced to the trenches.

Dozens of men carrying metal water cans pumped water onto the ground. The squeal of their pumping sounded like the squeal of swarming insects. On her third trip to the water tank, Julia recoiled at the sound of horse hooves pounding up the riverbank.

Travis galloped up to the train on a panting chestnut mare, shouting, "Everyone on board! All aboard now! The fire's moving fast!"

His brother Mitch helped secure the area. It took her by surprise how quickly everyone moved. They all seemed to know what they were doing, some racing to the train, others mounting horses to ride down the hill to safety.

Forty yards beyond the tracks, standing by the soaked, newly dug firebreak, David was lifting his camera from its tripod, and juggling two empty buckets at the same time. He clearly needed help.

Julia and Clarissa both reached him at the same time.

Holt arrived, too, whipping the camera to his shoulder in one easy swoop and encircling Julia's with a broad arm. "Come this way!"

At some point, the wind picked up, dispelling low-lying mist. A shaft of sunlight found its way through the smoke and Julia felt its warm rays on her face.

The beam of sunshine sent her spirits soaring. They'd made it. They'd accomplished what they set out to do. They'd dug two trenches and soaked the area between. Nearly everyone was on board the train, save for two Mounties spraying the last water from their cans on the ground.

Ryan appeared in her path. She wanted to say *good job* and *you've worked so hard,* but his stern demeanor kept her silent.

"Let's go!" he shouted to his men. "Leave it all behind!"

"Almost done, Commander!"

Julia turned toward the two Mounties. "But it doesn't look—"

Whoosh!

It was the sound that startled her. A loud sucking noise, one she'd never heard before, echoed off the trees. It showcased nature's violence and frightened her to her core.

And then the two remaining Mounties, running with water cans strapped to their backs, stirring the soil with their heavy boots and thus providing air to an invisible finger of fire beneath, went up in flames.

With a sickening twist in his stomach, Ryan watched the tragedy unfold, hollering "*No!*" at the top of his lungs and running toward the fallen men.

Ryan tackled one of the burning men to the ground, and their tumbling extinguished the flames.

He clutched Constable Luke Nolan by the shoulders and dragged him to the train, although Ryan knew with one sorrowful glance at the severity of the burns and the stillness of his face that this man was dead. Luke's heart had likely stopped beating from the shock.

Ryan confirmed it with a quick feel for his pulse. There was none. At least Luke had died instantly and hadn't suffered from his burns.

When Ryan looked up again, he saw Holt racing to the other injured man, Subconstable Franklin Pettigrew. A gust of wind caught the flames and they leaped higher, swirling over the men.

Holt was down, too.

Julia screamed—or maybe she was still screaming, for Ryan didn't recall when she'd started. But David had the presence of mind to drag her and Clarissa to the safety of the train.

Ryan's brothers seemed to come from nowhere, Mitch assisting Ryan, while Travis leaped into the fire after Holt.

"God, oh, God," said Mitch as they dragged Holt and Franklin from the blaze short moments later.

Holt's right leg was scorched, his boot charred, while Franklin's left arm and shoulder were blistered. The fire had burned clear through his red tunic. Both men, however, were breathing and conscious.

"You're out of danger," Ryan told them. "Don't fight us. We're taking you to the medical car."

They lifted the injured men aboard, plus the body of Luke Nolan, and placed them on the waiting beds. Ryan removed a whistle from his pocket and blasted it as loudly as he could, three times.

With a jolt, the train started moving, leaving behind flames shooting twelve feet above the forest canopy.

Ryan heard nothing but the steady rhythm of the two injured men breathing. Thank God for that. He swung around, quickly washed his hands in the tin bowl, ignoring his own cuts and scrapes. He searched for his surgical tray and found his scissors. Travis and Mitch, seated on another bed, watched him. His brothers said nothing.

"They'll need drinking water. Lots of it. It needs to be boiled water, from the canteen next door. Tell the cook to use his cleanest pot. Hand me some fresh towels from the cupboard behind you."

Mitch moved more quickly than Travis, who was coughing, but Ryan kept his focus on the injured. He filled two syringes with morphine and gave each man a hefty dose. It wouldn't completely remove the pain, but would dull its cruel edge. Ryan cut through the cloth of Franklin's uniform and pulled it gently away from the burned flesh, wincing when the man screeched. Ryan did the same for Holt's boot, getting Mitch to cut through the leather at the front and snip the pant leg. Holt was nearly unconscious from the pain, thus not as vocal as Franklin.

Cleaning debris from the burned flesh was foremost in Ryan's mind, to prevent inflammation and infection down the road. He picked away the loose material from the wounds—small sticks, chips of fallen leaves, loose dirt. The men groaned with every movement. Each man stared at Ryan's face while he cleaned their wounds, so he tried to hold steady. He tried not to flinch at the smell of scorched skin.

To keep the burns from moving deeper, Ryan pressed towels dipped in cool water around the edges, where the skin was still intact. There was no way he could put cloth on top of the wounds themselves, for he'd never be able to remove it later without tearing skin along with it.

He'd have to allow the wounds to settle, then surgically debride the damaged flesh a day at a time.

He forced the men to drink water. Fluids would be key to their recovery.

"This may seem cruel," said Ryan, "but the fact that you feel such pain is an optimistic sign. It means the burns weren't deep enough to destroy the nerves."

There was hope that Holt wouldn't lose his foot, since the burns were at his ankle and not too deep, and that Franklin wouldn't lose his arm. Ryan would know in a matter of days. Due to the dirty nature of the wounds, he was damn certain they would fester, but he wasn't sure how much.

When Holt's gaze strayed to the still man lying on the far bed, Ryan had Mitch cover the body with a clean white sheet. A deep sense of sadness pervaded the room. Ryan tried to keep his hands steady. It shouldn't have happened, and it shamed him that this had occurred during his command. Luke was too young to die. He was unmarried, but had a large family back East. It was too late to help him, but Ryan would do everything in his power to help the injured men remaining.

So he did what he'd always done on the battlefield—he focused on what he could do rather than on what he couldn't.

When Ryan finished attending to Holt and Franklin, roughly one hour after he'd started, he looked up at his brothers. He'd almost forgotten they were watching him.

"Ryan." Travis clutched his arm and rose from the bed. He was short of breath. "Do you…have time to take a look at me?"

To Ryan's horror, Travis uncovered a small burn hole on the underside of his arm, then on shaky legs, he took a step forward, and collapsed to the floor.

Fraught with concern for the wounded men, Julia was unable to sip the black tea that Clarissa offered her in the cook's car. Julia knew it would help calm her, but an hour had passed and she wanted to see Holt.

She sat with David and Clarissa at one of three pine tables screwed to the floor. Behind them, the cook and his assistants were busy working the stoves.

Mitch had been a godsend for the last hour, walking to and from the medical car, giving instructions to the cook and the Mounties, and information to Julia.

"The burn's not as deep as Ryan first imagined," he had told her thirty minutes ago. "The boot saved the bottom of Holt's foot from getting burned."

"How is Holt holding up?"

"In a lot of pain. Deeply troubled by the events." Mitch's voice had weakened, and she knew how hard it was for him, too.

"Please tell Holt I'll help him through this, that he won't be alone."

"You'll be able to tell him yourself, soon."

The word that Constable Nolan had died raced through the train. Julia's thoughts flew to Ryan. He'd done everything he could to stifle the flames, to drag the man to safety. She'd witnessed the anguish in Ryan's face at that awful moment when he'd realized Luke couldn't be saved, and it kept playing over and over in her mind's eye.

Who was helping Ryan?

Mitch had dispensed a lot of orders. He'd told the cook to feed the troops breakfast, and they'd eaten it on their benches. He'd done a roll call to ensure that all men and women were accounted for. He determined when and where they'd make their next stop. They still had an out-of-control fire to deal with, and it wasn't being sympathetic to their fallen.

They would bury Luke by the riverbank at the next stop. They'd send two men on horseback to signal the oncoming supply train that they were up ahead, then they'd continue as planned.

Now, with a shuffling at the door, Ryan himself stepped into the cook's car.

"Ryan." Julia rose to her feet.

Perspiration drenched the front of his shirt. His hair glistened with sweat, and smoke stains smudged his cheeks. Lord, he looked exhausted.

"Travis is down," he said.

"Travis is hurt? But how?"

"When he dragged Holt from the flames, he inhaled a lot of smoke. He's got a small burn, but that's not the problem. It's his lungs. I need help in here. Please, someone get Collins and Williams. They're skilled with their hands, and they might be useful."

Julia spun around to look at Clarissa. Julia didn't need to ask the question aloud, for the other woman understood. She nodded, rose and headed for the medical car.

"Where are you going?" David called after her.

Ryan stared as well.

"Ryan needs help, and we're volunteering," said Julia.

Nodding with gratitude, Ryan turned to David. "You could help me, too."

"How's that?" he asked. "I'm afraid I don't have the stomach for this sort of thing."

"I need your help with something else. I'd like to record these events," said Ryan, "but don't have time. I need to make notes in my journal for Dr. Calloway and the superintendent. Would you write up the course of events? I'll dictate my own thoughts later. Put the time in the left column, with a note to the right about what happened."

"Absolutely. I can do that."

Julia stood and made her way down the aisle, following Ryan. She flattened a palm against her queasy stomach and entered the medical car.

The three wounded men lay on the first three beds. She

tried not to look at the shroud of white cotton covering the body in the corner, but she heard Clarissa gasp.

The smell of seared skin made Julia nauseous. She ignored it and moved to Holt's side, averting her gaze from the open wound on his propped-up foot to focus on his face. He seemed to be sleeping, but then his eyes flickered open. She pressed her fingers to his and he squeezed tight.

When she looked to Ryan for explanation, the surgeon whispered, "I've given him a lot of morphine. He'll need steady injections, so he'll be drowsy like this for days."

"I'm glad there was something you could do for him."

Clarissa stood at Franklin's bedside, murmuring softly and adjusting his pillow.

Travis lay sprawled in the corner, breathing heavily in a deep sleep. Or was he unconscious?

"What I need most from you," Ryan said, addressing both women, "is to ensure these men get enough to drink. Their burns have depleted their reserves. They'll be in no mood to drink, but they need to be forced, every hour on the hour. They can survive a time without eating, but they won't survive long without water. Quite simply, it's life or death."

If Ryan intended to scare Julia into believing in the importance of drinking—if, indeed, he hoped the men themselves could hear him—he accomplished his goal. Holt's eyes flickered open, and Julia felt her stomach clamp with fear.

"I can do that," she said.

"One tin cup of water every hour. I'll leave my pocket watch here so you can both see it." Ryan looped the chain of his watch around a rafter by the window, securing it so it wouldn't swing too wildly with the jarring of the train.

The key to keeping her nausea under control, Julia realized, was never looking at the wounds. Since it was five minutes to the hour now, Julia filled Holt's cup and nudged him. His eyes opened and she tried to help him sit up, but he fell back in a trance.

"You've got to do it with or without his assistance," said Ryan. He slid a hand beneath Holt's back, lifted him slightly, then coaxed him to take a sip. Holt seemed to want to drink, but simply couldn't take large mouthfuls. "Small sips," Ryan advised. "Small sips and a lot of patience."

When he went to help Clarissa, Julia continued to help Holt drink. Lord almighty, it took nearly thirty minutes for him to finish his cup. The muscles along her spine strained with tension. Her lower back felt as though it was going to pop out of her hips.

"Ryan, do I wait now for a full hour to pass before the next cup?"

"No. You begin again at the top of the hour."

The second time went no faster than the first. But she was feeling better about Holt's condition. He wasn't as close to death as she had feared. A wave of loneliness for her son washed through Julia. More than anything, she wanted to see and hold Pete, but at least he was far away from the fire. He was eating well and sleeping well and laughing with his cousins.

Clarissa took care of Franklin while Ryan took care of his brother. Fortunately, Travis's injury didn't appear to reach too deeply into his lungs, so he was strong enough to sip water.

In between their rounds, when the train came to a stop, the women had a bite to eat. Ryan was so good at rousing

Travis to drink that he had time to tell constables Collins and Williams where to keep the water stocked in the medical car, how to draw up morphine injections and what to look for when checking the wounds.

On the third hour, close to eleven o'clock, Julia finally became aware of the stillness around them. She heard the supply train come to a rolling stop behind them, which meant it was time for her to leave.

A shameful part of her, one that she found difficult to acknowledge, wondered whether this would be her escape. It was difficult being here. Pete was expecting her at home, as was Grandpa. With much relief, she reasoned that Holt and the other injured men would be transferred to the awaiting train and taken home by the Mounties, where Dr. Calloway could continue to treat them. She would ride with Holt and ensure he received his full cup of water every hour on the hour.

Unfortunately, Ryan didn't see it that way.

"I'm not moving anybody unless it's directly to the care of Dr. Calloway. I won't load these men onto a boxcar as if they were livestock." Ryan refused to budge on this point. "Leave the men here with me. Take a message to Dr. Calloway to return on tomorrow's supply train. Or better yet, we'll have moved this train again by then, so we'll be very close to town. I'll make sure we're close enough for Calloway and his assistants to arrive on wagons for the injured."

Holt was staying behind, thought Julia with regret. How could she leave him while she fled to safety?

"Commander," called one of the newly arrived Mounties, Constable Jackson. Julia recognized him as the one from the train depot who'd delivered Ryan's bags to the bankers and Mrs. Reid. "Your mother's arrived home."

Ryan swallowed hard. "How is she?"

"Best I've seen her in several months."

"Did you give her the bag?"

"Yes, sir."

"Did she give you any messages?"

"No, sir."

Ryan's eyes flickered. He dismissed the constable and sought the solitude of the medical car.

It was obvious he'd hoped to hear more from his mother, maybe a kind word. Wishing there was something she could say or do for him, but knowing there wasn't, Julia went to pack her suitcase. She returned with it to the medical car, remaining silent as she and Clarissa made their patients drink.

For the next two hours, new supplies were transferred from one train to the other. Two dozen more Mounties had arrived. The sum total of police present was now above fifty, half the population of the fort. Some had remained in town to uphold the law and protect the settlers. Others were scattered throughout the territory on various duties.

"Julia?" a familiar voice called from outside the medical car. She jumped at the sound. "I'm having trouble finding you!"

She stepped to the open window. Grandpa stood peering up at her, chewing a wad of tobacco.

"What are you doing here?" she asked.

"They called for every available man. Since I'm a man, and still available, I thought I'd come."

"But at your age—"

"At my age, I don't want to die a predictable old man. But don't worry. I'm going right back on the supply train. I came to see for myself how you are and to accompany you home."

"I'm fine. Where's Pete?" Her heart leaped with concern. "You didn't bring him with you..." She looked up and down the path.

"Lordy, no. What do you take me for? Anna and her husband are taking the boys fishing today. They're real excited."

Julia smiled. Pete was just learning, but he loved the adventure of fishing. Anna was likely doing it to keep everyone's mind off the fire. If they headed out to their usual cabin east of town along the river, the family might not be back for a couple of days. Which meant Pete wouldn't be home even if she returned. And his belly would be full—eating fish was healthy.

"Are you getting enough to eat?" Grandpa asked her.

"I eat like one of the troops."

"Good."

The door to the canteen opened, and Ryan entered the medical car. The sight of his watchful eyes reminded her these men needed her help. Pete was well taken care of and didn't need her as urgently as Ryan did.

She waved goodbye to Grandpa. He set off toward a cluster of men saddling up some horses. Turning slowly, she looked at her suitcase standing by the door.

"Come, I'll help you carry that." Ryan went for her bag. "Your train's leaving shortly."

Julia ran her quivering palm down the front of her skirt. She looked past his broad shoulders to Clarissa, who was watching and listening. Biting her lip, Clarissa nodded to Julia, both understanding what they were about to do.

"Quickly," he repeated in a friendly tone. "You wouldn't want to miss the train."

"Actually, Ryan," said Julia, "I would. Clarissa and I both intend to stay."

Chapter Thirteen

Ryan bristled at how stubborn he was at times. Yesterday, he had almost refused to allow the women to board the train. Now they were offering their help, and he desperately wanted it.

"It's good of you to remain." He'd never been so impressed by Julia's warmth and eagerness to help. "And you, Clarissa. I can use your assistance. Thank you both."

The women murmured a reply and got back to work. There wasn't time to stand around and discuss it. Julia told her grandpa about her change in plans and asked him to take her report about the fire back with him to town on the supply train.

Later that afternoon Ryan had a heavier task to perform. Feeling sick from the duty ahead, he carried a shovel down to the river.

"Commander, let me do that," offered one of his men.

"Thank you, but I'd like to do it."

"Here, at least let me help."

They dug the grave in a pretty spot on the west bank.

Sunshine would always touch the grassy rim at dawn, and the view to the west, of dramatic mountain peaks, was breathtaking.

There were nearly a hundred people gathered for the ceremony, heads bowed in silence, hats removed in the hot sun. The closest thing they had to a minister was Dewey Binch, who'd studied the ministry for a year before finding a wife and settling down to become a farmer instead. Ryan added a few words to Dewey's, saying that he hadn't known Luke for long, but that he was a dedicated Mountie and one of the most hardworking Ryan had had the pleasure of meeting. The congregation said the Lord's Prayer. Half an hour later, Luke was buried and the men returned to camp.

Ryan hadn't had a chance to address Julia at the funeral, but he was always aware of her. It was comforting to see her at such a distressing time, to feel her presence in the medical car while they attended to the patients, to feel the fabric of her blouse swish against his arm in passing, to hear her quiet whispering with Clarissa.

The camp returned to digging trenches. This would be their third attempt to stop the fire, and Ryan prayed it would be their last.

Acres of woodland lined the Bow River, a funnel of fuel for the raging fire. To the east, the mountainous terrain changed to softly rolling foothills and flatter grasslands. Horse and cattle ranches sprawled on both sides of the river, although no herds were in sight. Ryan knew by instinct that the ranchers had corralled their animals out of the fire's reach, likely up north in the free-range pastures.

Ryan wasn't quite sure where the fire would go if it

jumped the firebreaks for the third time. It was difficult to guess whether it would die down on its own, speed through the woods along the river straight to Calgary, or ignite the prairie grassland.

Tilting his head to the sky, Ryan stared at the clouds. They were the first he'd seen in two weeks. Some seemed large enough to hold rain, but they were spread so far apart that it seemed unlikely resulting rainfall would stop a fire. Unfortunately, the wind was strong again today, which would once more stoke the flames. The best they could hope for was a shift in wind direction.

After dinner, the clouds grew bigger and closer together.

"Think it might rain?" the men asked each other.

"Hell, it just might."

The atmosphere around camp, as they began to dig the second trench, was one of hope and excitement.

At nightfall, with Julia's assistance, Ryan settled the patients with morphine, inspected their wounds and repositioned their limbs for better circulation. Constables Collins and Williams would take over, allowing Ryan, Julia and Clarissa a period of rest. They would rotate at dawn.

Ryan resisted giving Travis any morphine for the light burn to his arm because it would depress his breathing, which would hinder his recovery. Drinking water and resting for several more days would likely work their magic. Fortunately, the burn itself would heal quickly since it wasn't deep.

Julia remained quiet in Ryan's presence. He had a hard time knowing what to say to her, other than *please* and *thank you*. Her main concern seemed to be for Holt's comfort, which Ryan expected, but it made him wish she'd offer him one of her pleasant smiles or warmly touch his hand.

Soon it was time to retire for the evening. After bidding the ladies good-night, Ryan went to his tent, and invited David inside to discuss their journal keeping. The tent was tall enough for him to stand, and large enough to hold two folding chairs along with a foldaway table. Ryan had tossed his bedroll and duffel bag in the far corner.

"This is good," he said, reading over the details. "Please add to the list the number of men who arrived today to join the efforts. And where we laid Luke Nolan to rest."

They spent another half hour going over the records. Ryan initialed the pages.

Before he left, David removed a newsprint sheet from his leather dossier. "I debated whether to give this to you. But seeing how hard you came down on Julia for the article that appeared in the paper, I thought you should have a look at it."

"What is it?" Ryan held what appeared to be a faintly inked newspaper.

"The article about you that was originally slotted for the newspaper. Julia wrote it, but decided in the end that it was too harsh to print. I encouraged her not to change it, but she insisted it wouldn't be fair to you."

"Why are you giving it to me now?"

"Because I don't know what went on when you lived in Alberta before, but whatever you did to her, I think she needs to hear an apology."

"An apology? You have no idea what I've tried—"

"Try again." David suddenly seemed to realize to whom

he was speaking. "Sir. I think she needs to hear an apology from someone about something, sir. She's not herself."

Ryan creased the paper in his hands. "She's got an awful lot of friends who care about her."

"Yes, we do," David said on his way out. "Yes, we do."

Ryan took the paper, lowered himself onto his chair, brought the lantern forward to illuminate the ink, and read.

A crack of thunder roused Julia from the bed in Ryan's command car. She hadn't changed into nightclothes yet, simply closed her eyes for a moment from exhaustion. She must have fallen asleep on top of the blankets.

Disoriented, she heard another thunderclap and saw a vivid streak of lightning through the darkened windows.

With an exclamation of joy, she raced to the window to join Clarissa, who'd dragged herself out of bed, dressed in a cotton nightgown.

"Look at that," her friend breathed in wonder.

Drops of water hit the roof of the railcar and dribbled down the side. The window was slightly open at the top, and Julia stretched her hand out to capture some.

Laughing, she brought it to her lips and sipped. "It tastes like honey."

"Do you think this'll stop the fire?" asked Clarissa, doing the same.

"We can only hope. The rain is coming down softly now, but maybe it'll get stronger."

"I love the sound," said Clarissa. "Listen to how beautiful it is."

A sudden crackle of rain hit the leaves around them, increasing the flow of water as it hit the ground. A steady hum of what sounded like icicles bounced off the tin roof. Silence beyond that. Total silence in the woods and grasslands, as if every living creature stood in awe of the rain.

Another boom of thunder had the women in laughter. Lightning flashed, casting a glow over the spiral of dark hair spilling down Clarissa's back.

"I didn't know whether to wake you so you could change," said Clarissa. "You fell into such a deep sleep."

Julia smiled, grabbed the old leather duster from the hook on the wall and headed for the door. "It's all right. I'll change when I get back."

"Where are you going?"

"I've got to feel the rain on my skin."

The tan leather coat, soft and warm almost beyond recognition, and presumably Ryan's because it smelled like him, flapped against her shins.

A swarm of men, the ones who'd been digging the second line of trenches, were crowded together, seeking the tiny bit of protection the train's roof offered. One of them told her that the second trench was finished, and that Ryan had just ordered them to wait and see if the rain itself would be enough to soak the area. They'd already removed the dead branches and leaves from between the ditches.

So she'd just missed Ryan.

"What time is it?" she asked.

"One o'clock. Most of us are headin' to bed now, and I suggest you do the same, miss."

"I will in a moment, thank you," she said, hurrying off to a secluded part of the riverbank. It was nestled between a canopy of several aspen trees, and from it she could watch the rain undisturbed.

She got there along a deserted little path, but there was already someone standing by the river's edge. She recognized the wide brim of his Stetson, and the profile of his shoulders. Ryan.

Thunder boomed and seemed to roll straight down her spine to her toes.

She hadn't counted on meeting him, certainly not alone, so she swiveled away to find another spot.

"Hello," Ryan called softly. "Is something wrong? Do you need me in the medical car? Are the men—"

"They're fine." Bracing herself, Julia turned around. Gentle rain dampened her face. She could have turned away, or pulled the hood farther forward, but she loved the warm sensation of raindrops on her cheeks. "I came to hear the splash of rain on the river."

"You're getting soaked," Ryan called. "You should go back and sleep while you can."

"And I suppose you should, too."

Ryan pointed in the direction of another clump of trees to his left. "My tent's close enough if I need to run for cover."

Her gaze settled on the billowing gray fabric. The tent stood aloof from the train, but seemed somehow comforting, with the glow of yellow light coming from a lamp inside.

"Shouldn't you be sleeping inside the train tonight, like most of the other men?" she asked. "The tent might collapse."

"It's safe. It's rugged and made for times like these."

"Then why aren't you in it?"

Ryan laughed. The feel of rain dancing across their skin, after such a long drought, seemed to be making them both giddy. "I guess I wanted to enjoy Mother Nature, too."

A bolt of lightning skimmed the river behind Ryan.

There was danger in the air, and Julia knew it wouldn't be wise to stay here long. The lightning illuminated Ryan's height and massive body. He was wearing only his shirt and breeches, no oilskin cloak, no jacket. She wondered if he felt the chill of the night setting in.

Thunder cracked in the air, jolting her nerves and pushing her forward to join him at the river's edge.

"We shouldn't be out here," she whispered in between booms.

"It's lovely, though, isn't it?"

She sighed and listened to the flowing water bubble around the stones close to her feet. She could barely see the rainfall, it was so light, and there was no moon to aid her vision. After a few moments, Ryan's big hand and the square toe of his leather boot became clearer.

With trepidation, Julia turned around, trying to see past the tree trunks, but found only a wall of blackness. "It seems that everyone else has left the area."

"Most of them were sleeping under the stars, so moved to the train for cover. There are a couple of tents down yonder. The cook and his assistants set up close to the river after supper, so they could catch some fish for breakfast tomorrow."

"Do you think we have any hope, Ryan?" Julia sighed as she peered across the gurgling waters.

Ryan dipped a broad shoulder toward her. "What do you mean?"

"Do you think there's hope the rain will stop the wildfire?"

There was a long moment of silence, as if there was something else on his mind, before he answered. "There's always hope."

"But it's falling so softly."

"It might be raining harder where the fire is."

She hadn't considered that, and it brightened her spirits. She peered in the general direction of the fire, but it was so far away that she saw no light, no sparks. However, the heavy smell of smoke hung in the air despite the rain.

A rumble of thunder seemed to shake the very ground they stood on, causing her to yelp. Then, realizing she was safe, she giggled.

"That's the first time I've heard you laugh."

"You've heard me laugh before."

"Not since coming home."

Was that true? She thought about it for a minute. "Sometimes it's difficult to see the humor in life, when things are so against you."

"You used to laugh a lot. That's what I remembered most about you when I was away."

"You thought about me, when you were gone?"

"Often."

Now there was an admission she was totally unprepared for. "I'd rather set the past aside and not look back."

"But that's the point. We aren't able to set the past aside, are we, Julia? Every time we look at each other, we recall how it was that night between us."

"Ryan, please don't—"

"Remember that night in the bar, Julia? Remember lying on my coat and allowing me to touch—"

"It turns out that night was never very important to— to either one of us."

"It was important to me."

She nearly wept when he said it. "How could I

believe that, when you left the following day and never looked back?"

"I can prove how much the night meant to me."

"How? How could you possibly do that?"

"Because you're wearing the coat," he said softly.

Her hands flew to her shoulders. "What coat?"

"The one we made love on."

She looked down but could barely see it in the darkness. The leather duster felt wrinkled and weathered, and the flannel inside was nearly worn to shreds. "You kept it."

"Yeah."

"All these years?"

"Yeah. I took it with me to Africa."

"Why?"

"To remind me…to make me aspire to be something better than what I was."

She was unable to speak. Her throat clamped shut and she had to struggle to comprehend what he was saying.

"I'm so sorry for the way I made you feel when I left," he said. "It was wrong of me to walk out."

Tears sprang to Julia's eyes. "Thank you for saying that." Bursting with emotions she'd held in check for many years, many nights, she turned to walk away.

Lightning streaked the sky as Ryan reached out to grip her firmly by the wrist. "I'll walk you back."

Moved by his presence and his touch, she didn't have the will to shrug away his hand, but let it slide around hers. Their shared heat, beneath the drops of rain, connected them through all they'd suffered.

"Here," Ryan whispered at the path's junction, pulling her toward his tent rather than the train.

"What are you doing? I'm not going—"

"Come with me."

"No."

"I won't force you, but I do ask that you please come inside the tent for a moment. I've got to speak to you and we'll be out of the rain."

"What do you wish to talk about?"

"The article you wrote about me."

"You've already told me you disapprove of my mentioning the violin—"

"Not the one that was printed. The other one. The first one you wrote."

"How did you get your hands on that?"

"David cares a lot about you."

She dragged in a breath. "I'll have his hide in the morning."

"Don't you think you owe me an explanation? Five minutes of your time?"

He was right. She softened her stance, and he took hold of her wrist again. Searing her skin with the heat of his fingers, Ryan led her toward the soft glow of his tent.

Chapter Fourteen

He wouldn't take advantage of her, Ryan told himself. He wouldn't take advantage of the beautiful woman with water dripping from her auburn hair, who was standing nervously in the hazy lamplight.

After Julia removed the wet coat and hung it on a hook by the entry, Ryan offered her one of his two chairs. With hesitation, she moved deeper inside the tent and sank onto the seat.

The soft flapping of the tent canvas stirred the air, but the chill was absent. Here inside, the lantern warmed the air to a comfortable temperature.

"You're drenched," said Julia. "You should change your shirt before you catch a cold."

"Later." He realized he wouldn't be able to change without her watching, and he didn't want to escalate the growing intimacy between them.

"That's all this camp would need—a sick doctor."

"Women," Ryan said with exasperation. "Turn around and I'll find a clean shirt."

She did as she was told without a sound. Ryan fell to his knees and sorted through the clean clothes in his bag. He pulled out a soft blue cotton shirt, peeled off his wet one and replaced it.

It took less than two minutes. The sound of buttons unbuttoning and clasps unclasping mingled with the swishing of the rain.

The space felt suddenly hot and subdued.

Ryan was having second thoughts about this. If anyone should see Julia in here with him, the smear to her reputation might be insurmountable.

"You can turn around," he said.

When she turned her head and shoulders back to face him, her gaze lingered on his clean shirt. He watched the pulse flicker at her creamy throat.

His long shadow intertwined with hers on one wall. "Our shadows are falling on the tent," he said.

She frowned.

"It's visible to anyone passing that there's a woman in here—that you're with me."

"Oh, I see." She rose to her feet, understanding the implications. "Well, I won't stay, then."

Ryan walked to the table and dipped his face close to the lantern. The flame warmed his cheeks and brow. He turned a knob to extinguish the flame.

Julia let out a soft gasp.

It was so dark inside that they both needed a few seconds to allow their eyes to adjust.

She moved toward the entrance.

He tried to remember the headline of her article, and

spewed out the words. "Black Sheep Returns Ten Years After Killing Drifter."

She stammered. "It—it was an awful perspective."

He continued from memory. "Let's see if I've got this right. 'The man despised by the community and disowned by his family has reported back to Calgary, now a Mountie officer and surgeon.'"

She didn't respond.

"A hated man whom some still can't forgive."

He saw her flinch.

"It was harsh," she said.

"It was true. Why didn't you print it?"

Her voice wavered. "I don't know."

"When did you decide to change it?"

Her black silhouette shifted. "That night after your father and brothers came back from their cattle drive. After I heard the way your father talked to you."

"Why did that make you pull back?"

"I saw then…how much you'd suffered, too."

Stepping toward the exit, she brushed by him. His hand came out to clutch the soft flesh of her arm, above the elbow.

"Thank you for changing it. No one in town would ever come to me as a surgeon if I'd been depicted in that way."

"They don't come to you anyway." Julia's voice was soft and gruff and filled with sympathy. "Unless you're their only choice, as you are out here. But I've seen a side of you I didn't know existed."

Her words were like salve to a ten-year-old wound.

"The focus on my violin was…"

"Was stupid, too," she finished for him.

"It wasn't. It was honest, but much less harsh." He let

his hand drop. She stepped away, almost at the door flap, ready to vanish. But he had one more thing to say. "There are some extraordinary people in this world, Julia, who are a privilege to know. You are one of them."

She didn't move. The silence was overwhelming.

"I should check on Holt," she said in a voice filled with compassion.

Ryan closed his eyes. There was always someone between them. Brandon. Holt. "You should. And I should check on another constable, Gordon DeWitt."

"What's happened to him? Was he injured?"

"They tell me he's been Luke Nolan's best friend for two years. He's been taking Luke's death hard. Gordon's quiet, though. Doesn't say a word."

"I never noticed his difficulty, but I'm not surprised you did."

As casually as he could, but feeling far from casual as he thought about his men, Ryan tried to explain to her, a civilian, how it felt. He didn't wish to be gruesome, but there were things people who'd never seen war didn't understand. How could they?

"Sometimes in battle, the ones who aren't physically wounded, the ones who witness the wounds of others, are the ones who suffer the most. Sometimes the ones who insist they don't need help need it the most."

"Ryan," she whispered, almost at his back. The warmth of her breath penetrated his shirt between his shoulder blades, and he knew she was half an inch away. "Ryan, that's you."

"It is?"

She seemed to melt his heart. Perhaps she understood more than he did.

Julia wrapped her arms around him from behind, flattening her hands on his stomach, sliding them upward along his chest. Her chin sank into his back, and he'd never felt anything so wonderful in all his life.

The gesture took him so much by surprise that he stood frozen. She would finish hugging him, he thought, then step away. She felt sorry for him and simply wanted to tell him that, in a momentary flash of kindness. Then she'd continue on her way.

But her touch sizzled along his skin and set his flesh on fire. She caressed him as though she were cradling something very precious. He stiffened, unable to breathe lest she disappear in a puff of magic smoke.

"Am I dreaming?" he asked.

"If you are, then so am I, and it's a dream I've had so often and for so long that it's painful to awake and find you gone."

Shaken by her confession, alarmed at how potent her hold was on him, Ryan still couldn't move.

"Touch me, Ryan."

"I can't…I don't want to take advantage. Not another time."

"Touch me, please."

"When I was younger, I wouldn't have hesitated to turn around, to do everything I could imagine with you. But…I've learned my lesson about how selfish that is."

She disengaged her hands from his body but pressed her forehead into his back, saying nothing. With a soft moan of agony, she pushed away from him.

At that moment, he swung around and captured her in

his arms. It was a moment he savored, peering down into her shadowy face, seeing the rim of her lips, the vulnerability in her eyes. God, she felt good.

Lightning flashed, illuminating the curve of her cheeks and mouth. Ryan kissed her.

It was tender and warm, a kiss between two people who'd been lovers in a former life, who now, in circumstances beyond their control, yearned to connect again.

His hands went to either side of her face, caressing her cheeks.

With a soft groan, she parted her mouth, and their tempo surged.

He knew now that this was what he'd wanted since the moment he'd set eyes on her again. He'd taken—stolen—two kisses from her since, but they'd been nothing compared to this, when she gave herself willingly. Openly.

"I've missed you," he whispered into her temple, spreading soft kisses across her cheeks and lashes. He threaded his fingers through the damp mass of chestnut hair.

"It's good to hear you say it."

"I should have said it sooner."

"I wasn't ready to listen."

"And now?" He cupped her face and studied her expression. Thunder rolled through the tent, but neither of them budged.

"I'm not sure."

"Perhaps it's better to say nothing, and let our actions guide us."

"That's such a tempting proposition. But I think—"

"Shh...I want to feel you..." He kissed her again, on the mouth, then throat, then that hollow part at the base, where a simple gold chain draped itself across her skin and drove him mad.

She didn't fight him, didn't slap his face or push at his chest, simply melted into her own strength, losing inhibition. She unbuttoned the top of his shirt.

He was lost then.

Her silent invitation spoke louder than anything she could have said.

She wanted him as much as he wanted her, and there was nothing on this earth that would stop them.

Pulling away from her for a moment, but holding tight to her left hand, he scooped his duster from the hook and spread it out in the corner.

"Your coat?" she asked. "What are we to do with—"

She stopped short when she saw him unrolling another blanket, this one lined with fox fur, on top of it. His duster had been such a part of his inner life, his inner turmoil, for ten years, that he thought it only right to lie on it together once more.

Ryan lowered her to the floor.

She nestled into the flannel and fur.

"Oh," she exclaimed. "I don't think I've ever felt such luxury."

"In an old army tent?"

"Yes."

"In the middle of a storm?"

At her second, "Yes," Ryan laughed.

He would force himself, no matter how difficult it was, to take his time with Julia.

Stretched out beside her at full length, he rose on an

elbow and propped his head on his palm. He lowered his lips to her warm, awaiting mouth.

Her arms went up around his neck, and when she buried her fingers in the thick hair at the back of his head, his heart cried out.

He dipped his fingers along the V-neck of her blouse. It didn't take much dexterity to undo the buttons, and his fingers trailed lower, along her breastbone to the tilted curve of one breast.

The slow yearning in his body began to throb, aching in pleasure so vivid it wiped out all thoughts of right or wrong. All thoughts of tomorrow.

Soft rain drizzled down the outside of the tent, pattering on the leaves around them, enveloping them in a symphony that sounded better than anything he'd ever heard in Vienna.

In the darkness, he saw the outline of her face but couldn't make out her features. He traced the top of one breast, and then the other, reveling in the feel of her. Unable to wait any longer, he yanked at her stays.

Her fingers went still around his arm.

Thunder rippled; lightning filled the air. The flash gave him enough light to see her breasts tumble out of her corset as he tugged it downward. Two rosy circles beckoned for his touch. Her nipples, silky and generous, jiggled as she settled back onto the fur.

He swallowed hard, bringing his fingers up to her cheek, stroking her lightly. "Do you know how often this vision came to me, when I was away?"

"When you say such things—" her voice caught "—it makes me want to weep for what we lost."

He felt her sorrow. "I'm sorry. I don't want to make you feel that way. Not ever again."

"After you left and when I married…I tried to forget about us…about this…but—"

"Shh…don't think about the pain," he said. "Just feel the air on your skin and listen to the sound of the rain outside, and know that you made it through those hard times."

"Is that how you made it through, Ryan?"

"Every day of my life."

"Why didn't you come back to me, like you promised?"

"I was ashamed of who I was."

She was silent.

He pulled back then, but she grabbed his fingers, brought them to her lips and kissed them. "I always thought you would aspire to great things."

Julia had seen much more in him than he'd ever seen. Perhaps it was her silent faith in him, in what he could become that had driven him to prove his worth.

Tracing her fingers along his waist, unbuttoning his shirt and making him slide out of it, Julia brought his attention back to the need burning within him.

With tenderness, he outlined one rosy areola, careful not to brush her nipple until she ached for it. His touch had the effect he wanted, for her nipple sprang to life.

"Just one," he murmured with a smile. "The other one remains soft."

She laughed, then gasped as his mouth closed on her other breast, kneading the nipple into the shape of his lips. It pleased him that he had that effect on her. She seemed adrift in pleasure as he tongued one breast, then the other. He ran his warm hands up her ribs, beneath her arms, pressing her breasts together so that he could suck both at once. Oh, the joy of being with Julia.

She eased her palms along his stomach, making him quiver. He shivered as one hand trailed lower, nearer and nearer…. When he felt the soft stroke of her fingers outlining his rigid form, his touch on her fell still.

Closing his eyes, he allowed her to explore his shape through his pants, her finger outlining the shaft of his penis, lingering in sweet ecstasy near the sensitive tip. With a wordless murmur, he pressed his large hand over her slender one, intertwining their fingers.

"You know just the spot to touch," he said.

"It would be hard to miss."

Laughing with a depth he hadn't felt in years, Ryan rolled away from her. With deft fingers, he unbuttoned her skirt and slid it off her legs.

Moving to sit at her feet, he unrolled one stocking, then the other, holding her soft heels in his palms, kissing one foot and then the other. The ties at the front of her corset needed a good yank to come completely undone, but getting there was half the pleasure. He had to go more on feel than sight, due to the darkness of the tent.

Then in a soft flash of lightning, he saw her, and caught his breath again. Her body, smooth and pale on the furs, was spread before him in full nudity.

He ran his hands up her legs, aching to touch every inch of her, to kiss every conceivable part.

Her thighs were the softest, most beautifully rounded shapes. He trailed his fingers along the inside of one, then the triangle of soft hair above it, lingering to trace circles around her belly button, then upward again between her breasts.

"I want to feel you, too," she whispered. "I want to feel all of you, every inch." Rising on an elbow, she slid a hand into the waistband of his pants, helping him remove the rest of his clothing. Then he, too, was totally naked.

She was a warm shadow, a black luscious shape in the dark. In another flash of golden light, he watched her muscles quiver, her bare flesh rise and fall with her breathing, her watchful eyes peering back up at his.

Sliding on top of her, he melted into her curves. "Julia, I've never felt such beauty."

He clasped her hands above her head, probing her legs apart with one knee as he lowered it to rest on top of the fox skins. Being here in a cocoon of warmth, nestled in fur, surrounded by the whispering rain was an experience so potent he knew he'd have the image burned in his mind forever.

Ryan heard her breath grow urgent, felt it growing hot as she moved her body beneath him, kissing his throat and whispering in his ear. "Push it in, Ryan."

"But I'd like to kiss you everywhere first—"

"Push it in."

Who was he to argue?

He was honored and thrilled that she found it difficult to wait. She was not a virgin, and something about her knowledge, and her candor in declaring what she wanted, pleased him.

She gasped and strained against his chest as he slowly dipped inside, parting her gently with his fingers first. He loved the heat of her as he entered fully.

He would wait for her. He wanted to put her first, to

always let her know that she came first for him. And so he tried to temper his rhythm, moving in and out slowly, knowing that any quicker pace would spend him.

Moaning, she ran her palms along his ribs and wrapped her legs around his waist. He lowered his fingers between her thighs and stroked her in time to his movements.

"You're such a good lover…" She panted, then gave a soft cry. It didn't take her long to climax. Marveling at her wholesome beauty, he felt the shudder of her contractions around his shaft.

Increasing his pace, he felt her thrust up to welcome him deeper, and then he was a goner. Spasms of heat pulsated from deep within him, tightening muscle upon muscle, pounding blood through every cell and fiber, resulting in a force so powerful it shook him to his core.

"Julia…" And yet he couldn't say anything to this incredible woman who lay entwined beneath him, her heart beating against his own.

Ryan had made promises to her before that he hadn't kept, and to do so now would appear empty and weak. Words alone would never again be enough for Julia.

He would have to give her more.

Julia was lying on what felt like a sea of feathers, drifting in and out of sleep. When she opened her eyes, a smile flitted across her lips. She was with Ryan.

He was stretched out in all his naked glory beside her. As she turned toward him, soft, thick fur pressed along her bare thigh and cushioned her breast. This was heavenly.

Ryan shifted in his sleep, then his arm came around her

waist. He slid his large hand along her hip and backside, sending tingles across her flesh.

The rain had stopped. Dawn was nearly here, for the tent was no longer pitch-black, but held an underlying hue of orange. She estimated that she had about an hour more with Ryan before she had to leave.

There was enough dim light to study him. His closed lids were rimmed with a fringe of short thick lashes. Heavy black eyebrows curved above them. She liked his forehead, though she didn't quite know why. It was creased slightly even at rest, indicating he had a few years behind him. His wavy black hair was clumped on one side, mussed from sleep.

His severed earlobe didn't look too bad up close. It had been a clean cut, likely done in one slash.

Looking lower at his broad chest, she shuddered at the numerous scars that lined it. Who had done this to him? She wondered if these scars, and the amount of fighting they implied, had finally pushed Ryan to turn his life around. Whatever had changed his mind, she was pleased that he'd returned.

She tried not to think about the ramifications of their night together. It was what it was. A night of passion, a consummation of years of longing. She was a mature woman, capable of seeing life around her and understanding that they were working together here in extremely volatile circumstances.

And then there was the thought of Holt. She refused— *refused*—to think about what awaited her.

Ryan rolled slightly on the velvety furs, and Julia gazed across the expanse of his flat stomach, lingering on the handsome sight of his more private areas. She studied his long legs, heavily muscled from years of hard work, likely from galloping across the African plains with the British Army, walking and running for miles when necessary.

"What are you staring at?" His eyes remained closed, but his hand shifted on her buttocks.

"A handsome man."

He seemed to like her answer, for he smiled and stroked her.

"Who cut off your earlobe?"

"I was robbed in India and made the mistake of fighting back."

"The great Ryan Reid lost a fight?"

"Depends how you look at it," he said, eyes still closed. "I took out three of the culprits, but the fourth and fifth, the ones with my gold watch, got away."

Julia sighed. "And who gave you the big scar on your chest? The one that runs from your nipple to the other side?"

"When I first got to England, I made a living as a fighter. There was more money in it if we used knives."

"Oh, Ryan."

He opened his eyes. "Don't be too sad for me. There was a time when…I didn't want to go on, when I couldn't have cared less whether I lived or died."

"What were you so angry about?"

"That I couldn't get along with anyone. That my father thought I was useless. That I couldn't handle cattle as fast as he wanted me to."

"But you were young and growing when you first got to the ranch."

"And he was impatient. We argued about everything—

where to build the fences, what price to sell the steer, why I stayed out so late. Why I loved to fight."

"Why *did* you love to fight?"

"Because I was finally good at something."

She ran her hand along his and finally asked the question she'd been wondering for ten years. "What happened the night you left?"

He caressed her shoulders. "After I walked you home, after those two wonderful hours we spent together, I was in such a good mood I couldn't sleep. So I continued walking. When I reached the alley, someone cornered me to get into a fight. I declined, but a group of them started putting money on it. I walked away. So that drifter knifed me."

"Samual Johnstone," she said.

Ryan nodded sadly. "Self-defense, so I only meant to nick him but he moved forward on the blade. God, he died." He swallowed hard. "There wasn't much we could do for him. I went home to get help from my father. He was so outraged he called me names and swung at me. So I swung back. It woke my mother and she started crying. She screamed at me to get out. Now, looking back, I don't think she meant forever. But that's how I took it. That's why I never wrote them. I was a poor son and was nothing as a man. I'm so ashamed, Julia, at how little thought I gave to how you'd feel."

She blinked away tears.

Ryan continued with his story. She needed and wanted to hear it.

"I didn't take anything with me. Just the clothes I wore and a few dollars in my pocket. A Mountie was at the scene when I got back to it, declaring it self-defense, but I turned east and started walking."

Incredulous, she leaned against his chest. "You *walked* out of town?"

"For a few nights and days. Then I came down with scarlet fever and gave away my last two dollars to an old man I met up with, to help me through it. After a while I hitched up with some ranchers, made some money and bought my way to England. I think you know the rest."

"I didn't know you went through all that. That's awful." She listened to the birds chirping outside as she pictured Ryan on his journey.

"What you went through was more difficult. You had no idea what happened to me. You were the one left behind. I'm so sorry for that."

She was grateful for his apology, but it was still difficult to accept everything he was telling her. *She* wouldn't have left *him* like that. If the circumstances were right, would he have the heart to leave her again? Or was he a completely different man?

She wanted to believe in him.

"And now?" she whispered. "How do you feel now about living and dying?"

"Life should be taken and enjoyed an hour at a time. I'm hopeful now. Maybe I was put on this earth to help others see that. Maybe I had to go through everything before I saw it myself."

She leaned over and kissed him on the cheek. His skin was bristly and warm. Her breast dangled above the fur and touched his ribs.

"Umm," he murmured, cupping it.

"Commander?" a voice called from outside the tent.

Julia's heart slammed to a stop.

Ryan quickly covered her naked body with the loose end of the fox furs, protecting her. She didn't dare move for fear of being discovered.

"Yes, Jackson?" Ryan called.

"I think you need to come out and see this, sir." Something in the constable's tone indicated fear.

"What is it?"

"The lightning storm from last night...I think it's increased the pace of the wildfire."

Chapter Fifteen

Ryan jumped at the urgent news. He had a fire to fight, but he also wanted more precious time with Julia. "I'll be right out," he told the messenger.

"I'll wait here," said Jackson. "So I can pack up your tent as you attend to the men."

"No, I'll…" Ryan squeezed the furs above Julia's shoulder, determined to let her know how much she meant to him, how much he wanted to shield her reputation. What they'd shared this night had touched him deeply. "I'll join you at the trenches in three minutes."

"Yes, sir."

When the light footsteps diminished to nothing, Ryan swept his hand along her cool arm. The air was damp and chilled. "Sorry, we'd better run. But since he asked about packing up the tent, he's unaware you're in here." Ryan sprang to his feet and grappled with his clothes. Balancing on one foot, he slid into his breeches, then donned his blue shirt.

Julia raced to get into her own clothes, but had more to put on than he did.

"I didn't want our night to end like this," Ryan whispered, tugging one large leather boot up his leg. The spur jangled in his haste. "There's more I want to say to you."

"You've got work to do." She yanked on the ties of her corset, which made the top of her breasts swell. "You have to go. And I should check on…on…"

Holt, Ryan silently finished for her. She seemed unable to say his name aloud.

Ryan couldn't say it, either. The tent seemed like a spiritual place that belonged to him and Julia, which no other person could penetrate.

He got dressed in well under a minute, while she was still sliding her skirt over her stockings and pantaloons. She was a pleasure to the eye. All curves and grace.

Ryan tucked her loose hair behind her ear, enjoying the scent of it. He brushed his lips against hers. "We're not through here. We've only begun."

She nodded and smiled, but he was concerned about her silence.

I promise, he wanted to say, but the words would be shallow in light of the wasted promises he'd given her before. In his regrettable youth, in his stupidity, it'd been almost easy to dismiss her because she was a barmaid, but he would never do so again. "You'll see, Julia. What happened tonight was different than before. I won't cut and run. You'll see."

She nodded, buttoning her gray skirt. Although he was concerned about her, there was no time to discuss it.

Ryan left the tent. He took a quick look around in the

morning mist and saw no one. "It's all clear. Wait one minute, then leave."

"All right," she said from inside. "Don't worry about me. Be careful."

He bounded up the slope toward the steam engine, and the trenches the men had been digging. They'd stopped when the rain had started, and Mitch had been slated to take command for the few hours Ryan had dedicated to sleep. He and Julia, after making love, had caught about three hours, he figured. It didn't seem like much, but he felt invigorated after the night they'd shared.

Julia, Julia, Julia. Making love to her was a full-time occupation, he thought with a slow grin, and one he wished he had more time for at this moment.

She'd wait for him, though, wouldn't she? She'd certainly wait for him to return to her side when this was all over, so they could deal with their feelings and decide where they'd go from here.

She had Holt, but surely Julia would explain to the young man that the two of them weren't suited.

A rising tide of brilliant sunshine hit the peak of the hill as Ryan reached it. The heat instantly cleared the mist at his boots and brought deep blue color to the sky above.

At the water tank, Ryan turned the nozzle until he'd filled his cupped hand then scrubbed his face. The water was so cold on his cheeks and eyelids that the skin stung, but it was just what he needed to regain his focus on his duties. He patted his face with a towel, then tossed it aside as he rounded the front of the steam engine. He'd finish washing up in the medical car as soon as time allowed.

"Are both trenches dug?" Ryan called to Mitch, who was standing in a clearing among a dozen men. The brush on both sides had been removed, and to Ryan, the trenches looked complete.

"All done," said Mitch. With a long stride, he joined Ryan, so they could talk without being overheard.

"Good. And the ground between them looks soaked from the rain, so we don't need to pump any extra water."

"I agree." Mitch nodded toward the fire. "I had a scout just return from up yonder. Unfortunately, the fire skipped the second set of trenches, too."

Ryan cursed. "It didn't work." He ran a hand through his hair, still damp around the edges from the splash of cold water, and thought about their next step.

"We'll move out again," he decided. "Now. Eventually we'll stop on the outskirts of town. The west side of Calgary. You know the place where the tributary forks off the Bow? Old man Cooper's place, if he still lives there."

"Yeah, he still does. That fork is now called Cooper's Creek. The town almost reaches it now. The new livery stables are just a quarter mile away. What have you got in mind?"

Ryan had a plan. A bold, but risky one.

If he disclosed all the details now, he'd meet with resistance, and he wasn't ready for the drag-out fight that was sure to come. "Well, the supply train is coming in this morning, right, with dynamite?"

"Yeah, and if we leave early enough, we can head them off before they get too far out of town."

"We'll have to evacuate most of Calgary."

"Dammit," said Mitch. "It's come to this?"

"Only as a precaution. I plan to use the dynamite to blast the area at Cooper's Creek."

Mitch frowned. "You think it'll smother the fire?"

"There's a good chance." It was only part of Ryan's plan, but if he revealed the rest, he and Mitch would spend their time arguing rather than moving.

Mitch appeared to think about it, obviously worried about the dangers involved with dynamite, then nodded and turned, about to rejoin to his men. "You know I'm not crazy about using dynamite, but the trenches aren't working. The fire's headed straight toward town, so we've got to try something more drastic. I'll give the orders."

"Mitch." Ryan grabbed his brother by the upper arm. "I'd like to thank you for backing me up on everything I've asked for."

"Not everything." Mitch clenched his jaw, avoiding Ryan's searching gaze. "Only business."

Ryan sighed and released him, then he headed for the medical car to check on his patients. They were holding their own, he found.

Moments later Julia and Clarissa arrived to help with their care. With a brush of her skirts, Julia squeezed by Ryan, slipping her charming body past his as if nothing had happened between them. But she met his eyes with a shimmer in her own. He wished again he had more time to spend with her, and to deal with everything else in his charge, but the safety of his men and the town were his priorities. And obviously hers.

The next hour passed quickly.

The train rolled east toward Calgary. Ryan adjusted doses of morphine, exercised Franklin's burned arm so that the joint wouldn't freeze up, rolled Holt's ankle back and forth for the same reason, and then allowed Travis to sit up and dangle his legs over the side of the bed to get accustomed to being upright. When his brother grew short of breath, Ryan ordered him to lie down again.

"I know you're eager to get up and go, but you need more rest," Ryan told him.

Every moment he could steal, Ryan murmured an encouraging word to Julia. She was quick and disciplined in doling out water, and had developed a stamina that he hadn't expected after witnessing her initial flustered attempts. Her attention was rooted on Holt and his recovery, which Ryan wholly supported, but at the same time... Well, what did Ryan expect? A beaming, beautiful smile from Julia while she was in the presence of her beau?

Ryan tried to bite back the rush of feelings that swamped him whenever he caught sight of her with Holt. The turn of her cheek, the flash of her blue eyes, the pretty sway of her hips.

What Ryan and Julia had shared seemed so much more complicated now in the light of day, in the presence of Holt. Ryan felt guilty looking into his patient's unassuming face. The sergeant couldn't possibly know their secret, but Holt's injury and potential recovery loomed large in Ryan's mind, and the guilt started to overwhelm him.

But, on the other hand, didn't all three of them deserve honesty? If it were up to Ryan, he'd shout out his involvement with Julia for all to hear, but out of respect for her, he kept it to himself. He'd allow her to choose where and when to tell Holt.

Ryan had to believe that she *would* tell him.

Ryan's team rotated through the canteen for breakfast. He spent time with David, going over the newest entry in the journal, then with Mitch going over the specifics of where they'd plant the dynamite and how they might evacuate the town.

Just after eight o'clock, the train slowed around a bend. A man on horseback galloped past the windows—the scout, signaling the engineer that they were approaching the other train.

Within a few moments, both trains chugged to the junction in the rivers, halting as close to each other as they could. They were about thirty minutes away from Cooper's Creek. Ryan and Mitch hopped off and met in the center of the teeming crowd.

When Joseph Reid, heavy and slow, stepped off the supply train, Ryan fell silent with disbelief. He wondered why his father was aboard.

Joseph nodded. "We didn't expect you back this soon. I've come to aid my sons."

Hope sprang up in Ryan, but was quickly laid to rest when his father added, "Mitch and Travis."

Ryan said nothing.

Mitch blinked and coughed. "The fire is spreading faster than we thought. Travis has been injured, along with two other men. Another man died."

Joseph moaned, then tilted his head so that one ear was directed at his youngest son, and for the first time since Ryan had returned home, he realized his father had a hearing problem. No one had told him. He didn't seem to be a part of this family anymore.

"Injured how?"

"Travis inhaled smoke from the fire," Mitch told him. Joseph removed his hat. "Where is he?"

Ryan explained the details of all the injuries as he led his father to the medical car. He directed the troops to get started unloading shovels and dynamite, then led his father inside.

"What's all the dynamite for?" asked the older man.

"Something I need to speak to you about," said Ryan. "Right after you see Travis." It was time for him to come clean with his entire plan. The fact that all the Reid men were in one location would make the process quicker to explain, for his new plan centered on them. His stomach clenched as he thought of their reaction.

Julia was inside and Joseph quieted at the sight of her. If he wondered what she was doing here, he didn't voice any questions.

Ryan gave her a nod of understanding, silently begging for her patience with his family. There was much he had to get out in the open between Julia and his father, but it would have to wait.

Travis was surprised and buoyed to see the old man. For that, Ryan was grateful.

"What brings you here?" Travis asked his father. Travis's breathing seemed to be easier, Ryan noted, his energy somewhat restored.

"In my earlier days, I used to be good with a shovel," Joseph said, looking in Julia's direction. "The latest news is that you're digging your way to China."

Travis grinned, as if his health problems were over, and the heavy mood inside the car lifted. Ryan understood that Joseph had read Julia's newspaper with its latest update from the front. Her articles had gone back to town on the supply train and her grandpa had typeset them as promised.

"How's everyone at home?" asked Travis.

"Ma's a little tired from the trip, but it did her good to see family. Shawna's busy with the little ones. Quigley would have come with me, if it weren't for his knee. And I suppose you'd like to hear about your own wife."

Travis nodded.

"Jessica's got her apron full with those two kids. They tear around that new house like young pups. She said to tell you to rush on home so she can bake you those cinnamon rolls you like so much."

In the background, Clarissa attended to Franklin, who was dozing in and out of a medicated sleep.

Beside them, while getting Holt to sit up and drink, Julia glanced at Ryan. Her slender hands gripped the sergeant's arm, and her back was bent with the strain of supporting him.

Ryan hated that he couldn't say what he wanted. He hated that he had to sit on his hands and watch as she worked in the background, as if she meant no more to him now than she had ten years ago. Mostly, he hated that he was at a loss as to how to handle this situation. He was a commander, for God's sake, a man used to giving orders and solving problems.

For Ryan, there was more pain involved in this situation than simply watching Julia, watching Holt and standing by as Joseph Reid ignored him. Travis had recently built a log cabin for his young family on their father's property, and what Ryan was about to suggest would tear his brother apart.

"Clarissa," Ryan said. "Would you mind finding Mitch and asking him to join us? Please tell him it's urgent."

"Yes, sir."

Clarissa raced off, and within five minutes, Mitch was standing among them.

"What is it?" he asked, squeezing past the beds.

David called for Clarissa from the canteen, and she left to help him boil towels. Julia was about to leave as well, but Ryan shot her what he hoped was a pleading look. Somehow, her quiet presence gave him strength, and he instinctively wanted to include her in this very personal time with his brothers and father.

"I've got a plan to stop the wildfire," Ryan said to them.

"With the dynamite, you mean?" Mitch asked.

"That's right. We're going to plant some here at Cooper's Creek. The way I figure, we can try to divert the fire."

"Divert it how?" Mitch pressed.

"If the first line of dynamite doesn't work to smother and stop it completely, and if it jumps again, then maybe we can at least divert it away from town. We could try to do that by planting another line a hundred yards away from the first, slightly off-center to it. If we can get the fire to go in that direction, through a less populated area, there'd be a lot less damage to homes and property."

His brothers listened quietly, unaware where Ryan was going with this. But his father was getting an inkling.

Joseph swallowed hard, frowned and shuffled his feet. "*What* other direction?"

Ryan turned to look straight at him and delivered the news. "Along Cooper's Creek. I think we need to corner the fire and snuff it out between two streams. Cooper's Creek and Elk River, just north of town."

"You mean divert it to *my* property?" Joseph bellowed

an expletive so loud that Ryan's ears rattled, while his brothers stared at him, dumbfounded.

"Our ranch is out that way." Shaken, Travis inched off his cot. "Your mother and father's home, and Jessica's and mine. The house we grew up in."

Ryan remained firm. "I know that."

He looked to Julia, who stood by Holt's side as he dozed. She was watching with alarm and disbelief.

"My home is there, too," said Mitch, shaking his head.

"I'm sorry," murmured Ryan. He was doing the best he could. Of his family's homes, only Shawna's, in town, would be spared.

Joseph's face burned scarlet. "You want me to turn a blazing fire in the direction of everything I've sweated over for twenty-five years?"

Ryan nodded. "Yes."

"You want me to burn down my own goddamn house?" the old man shrieked. "The stables would go, too. The outbuildings. Everything!"

Ryan's boots felt as heavy as lead. "If it comes to that, if we need to make a choice between hundreds of buildings or six homesteads, then we'll choose the six."

"You call yourself my son?" Joseph's eyes welled with tears.

Ryan shuffled his feet, critically aware that Julia was witnessing this awful moment. Then he looked to the floor.

"You ignored your mother for ten years. You came home to disrupt our family. Now you want to destroy everything I've built?"

Ryan didn't answer. An artery pulsed in his jaw. This wasn't as bad as violin strings. There were no joints to repair with coarse gut string, no young man lying on the floor with a bullet hole in his head. There weren't twenty more fatally wounded men lined up outside, who would never get Ryan's help.

"Get out of my sight!" hollered Joseph. "You're no son of mine!"

With the weight of failure and shame spreading through him, Ryan kept his eyes averted, grabbed his hat and slipped out the door.

The wrath of Joseph Reid had frozen Julia to utter stillness. She watched the old man leave the medical car accompanied by his youngest son, and tried to shut out his horrible words. Poor Ryan. The misery he had had to endure from his father, as well as the torment that had flashed across his face when disclosing his plan, made her wonder at his courage.

Holt and Franklin, awakened by Mr. Reid's rough language, were alarmed at the severity of the fire and how the commander planned to combat it.

"There's nothing you can do, Holt, except try to remain still and get some rest." Julia touched his shoulder.

"But I'd like to be out there—"

"You will be again, one day soon."

"Do you think so? Really?" Holt studied her expression. His dark blond hair was spread against the pillow, but his firm shoulders jutted off the cot. "Do you really think I'll mend?"

He was speaking about the topic they'd both been avoiding for two days.

"Yes, Dr. Reid thinks—"

"I know what he thinks. What do *you* think?"

"I believe him. He's said that when the skin closes, you'll be up and exercising—"

"He said *if* the skin closes."

"I believe he said when."

"He said *if*."

Had she heard Ryan correctly? Who was she to argue with Holt? He was scared to the bottom of his soul, tortured by worries about whether he'd ever walk properly again, whether he'd still be capable of working as a Mountie.

"Dr. Calloway should be here soon with his wagons. Then you'll have two surgeons looking out for you. The very best of doctors."

Holt reached out and lifted her chin. "You've no idea what I've been thinking while I've been watching you take care of me these past couple of days."

"Holt, please, we're not alone." Suddenly shy, Julia glanced around the room. Clarissa, who'd just reentered, was busy helping Franklin drink a cup of water.

But Julia couldn't bring herself to discuss anything private with Holt. She didn't want to weaken him. She was no longer on a sure footing with Ryan, either. How and when could she possibly tell Holt that she'd made love to the commander?

She felt deceptive, when she wanted to be strong and hopeful for Holt's sake.

Making an excuse that she had to get some supplies, she patted his hand and sped out the door into the morning sunshine.

With her nerves trembling, she searched for Ryan. The new supplies and water were being unloaded from one car to the other, but no Ryan.

It seemed like an eternity before she found him down

by the river, watching the clear water splash and gurgle over granite boulders.

"Here you are," she said, rushing to his side.

He turned his head toward her, then looked back at the raging river.

How could they be so reserved with each other, after the night they'd shared?

"You're doing a fine job, you and Clarissa both," he said. He'd chosen a simple topic of conversation, one that didn't create tension. It was also the furthest from her mind.

"It doesn't seem like much. Our only responsibility is getting the men to drink."

"That's the most vital thing to their survival."

She wanted to tell him how awful she felt for him, how harsh his father had been, how brave and levelheaded Ryan himself had been in divulging his plan to his family. But she couldn't find the right place to start, and his square shoulders were turned away from her.

"Tell me something, Julia. Was there ever a moment when you thought you loved me?"

She looked at her hands. This was no time for half-truths. "I thought I did once, when I was much younger."

"But?"

She wove her fingers together. "But time and experience gave me clarity to...believe that it was more of a young woman's infatuation."

He groaned almost inaudibly. She didn't mean to hurt him, only to tell him her side of things.

Last night, making love with him had been the beginning of something wonderful, she hoped. But their problems were far from settled. Had he expected her to vow commitment just now? How could she, with Holt in there, needing a kind word from her as well? And how could she promise anything when nothing had seemed to change between her and Ryan's family?

She was more mixed up today about her relationship with Ryan than she'd been yesterday. She couldn't help that her guard went up slightly. She wondered whether he would retreat from her now that they'd slept together, as he had that night ten years ago, or whether he would remain by her side this time. It was up to him to prove he'd changed. It was always up to him.

He kicked a pebble into the water.

"There's so much going on now," she said. "There's the fire, and things with Holt, and there's your family. I'm not sure where one feeling stops and the other begins. Everything is up in the air. Especially your plan with the dynamite. What are you going to do?"

"I'm not sure."

"What is it that you feel, Ryan?"

"I feel like I've always felt. Alone."

Her eyes stung with hot tears, but she held them back. She knew his father's harsh words were affecting Ryan, that she shouldn't feel personally slighted. But she felt so nonetheless. "You don't have to be alone. That's your choice."

He turned then, took her hand and brought it to his lips.

"Commander!" Constable Williams called. "It's time to renew the morphine! I need help! The men are in need!"

Julia and Ryan raced back to the medical car. Once they were inside, Ryan dispensed the painkiller. He gave the order for the trains to move and for the men to eat an early lunch in preparation for the day ahead.

When things calmed down, Julia tried to catch her breath. Her brow was damp with perspiration. Walking to the counter, she poured fresh water into a clean tin bowl, rinsed a washcloth, then wrung out the excess and placed the cool cloth on Holt's forehead. It seemed to soothe him, but the morphine had loosened his tongue.

"Come closer, Julia," he said, loudly enough for everyone to hear, including Ryan, who was rinsing his metal instruments in soapy water at the counter.

When Holt called her name, Ryan stiffened. He turned his head, as if he could force himself to disengage from her and Holt's private conversation.

"I like to feel you standing here with me," the sergeant murmured. "I want to ask you something."

She hesitated for a second, caught between two men. She ached inside when Ryan twisted slightly and cast his uncertain gaze on them, while her heart broke at Holt's determination.

Julia leaned over him and asked, "What is it?"

"I've been thinking for forty-eight hours straight on this subject." Holt swallowed, as if trying to control the wavering of his voice. "I've been thinking that such a kind woman would make a lovely wife. I'm the man you seek in your ad, Julia. Marry me."

Chapter Sixteen

While the train gathered steam, Ryan could barely listen to the conversation between Holt and Julia. Ryan was losing her, and he was forced to be a silent witness to that fact. Julia would surely answer in the manner Ryan expected. With his back turned to them, he rinsed his surgical instruments briskly and placed them on the rack to dry.

"Holt, I'm very proud that you're asking me. Any woman would be. So much is going on…you're wounded…and you're not yourself."

She was being kind, thought Ryan, for she knew that he could hear every word. But she was saying similar things to Holt that she'd said to him. Next, Julia would probably tell Holt that she needed to think about her decision.

"We need more time to adjust to all of this," she said, as if on cue. "The fire's on its way and we've got to get you out of here."

It was Ryan who'd placed her in this awkward position. More than awkward. Almost unbearably cruel. He'd placed his family in the same sort of doomed situation, forcing them to choose between what was right for themselves and what was right for other folks. Everything Ryan touched and everyone he cared for suffered because of him.

He would lose Julia. He would lose his father. He would lose the town.

"But Julia," Holt said gently, "I want you in my life."

Ryan couldn't listen anymore. For the second time that morning, he bowed his head and escaped from the confines of the medical car.

It was noon and things weren't getting any easier. It seemed to Ryan that his problems with Julia and with his family were getting worse.

He wondered if she'd said yes to Holt.

And then Ryan tortured himself by thinking about it.

They arrived at Cooper's Creek. There was a crowd already waiting, which included Julia's grandfather. To Ryan's great relief, Dr. Calloway appeared with his wagon train and the wounded were transferred to John's care. Holt was drowsy from the morphine and didn't put up much resistance on being separated from his beloved Julia, although she remained quiet and sympathetic. Franklin was happy to leave.

Travis, however, refused to go. "I'll stay here where I'm needed," he insisted, rising off his cot on shaky legs.

"For God's sake, you can't breathe properly," said Ryan. "You need to rest. Go with John to the fort and start the evacuation."

"My breathing's getting better. I'm not going to lie on my back while everything around me burns down."

There wasn't much Ryan could do to stop his brother.

With a muttered breath, he held the door as Travis eased himself outside.

"The superintendent is on his way to see you," John hollered to Ryan from his covered wagon. "He'll be here any moment!"

"Good! I'll watch for him!" Before Ryan planted dynamite, he had to clear it with his superior.

Sunlight flooded the area around the aspens where he stood with his brothers and father, giving orders to the troops on what brush to clear. On a distant slope, Flanagan was talking to the men saddling horses. David and Clarissa were taking photographs. The heavy scent of smoke permeated the air. Men raced from the trains, carrying shovels and wheelbarrows.

"Start digging the trenches!" Ryan shouted.

By God, it had better work this time.

Several yards away, Julia was saying goodbye to Holt in the wagon—words Ryan couldn't make out, but the soft tenor of which made him envious. Jealousy was such a damn waste of time, but as hard as he tried to combat it, it flared within him. When Julia turned around, she was square in the middle of the Reid men, and two senior Mounties who were approaching.

She attempted to slip by them unnoticed. But when she brushed past Ryan, his breath stopped. Her clothes, bedraggled from hard work, clung to her. Her blouse, moist with perspiration, would have embarrassed some of the society women Ryan knew, but in his eyes, she looked as regal as a queen.

"I don't want to interrupt," she said, trying to step past the men.

"No place for a woman," Joseph agreed.

That made her stop.

Keep going, thought Ryan. But to his dismay, she turned to face the older man.

"I've had about enough," she said, as behind her, the wagon carrying Holt rolled away. Her voice had a frazzled edge, and Ryan noticed a swelling beneath her eyes from lack of sleep. Everyone was being affected by the emergency they were dealing with, and now was not the time to fight his father.

"Enough of what?" asked Joseph.

Ryan straightened and tried to intervene. "I think Clarissa is cleaning up in the medical car, if you're looking for her, Julia."

His father and brothers looked from Julia to Ryan, as if noticing the personal tone of his voice.

Julia didn't respond to him, but to his father. "Enough of being ignored by the Reid men."

The others looked away, some shifting in their boots, some coughing. The two Mounties said goodbye, leaving the three Reid brothers and their father behind.

Joseph scoffed at the woman, dismissed her comments and addressed Ryan. "I think I see the superintendent and his men galloping over the hill. I want to speak to him. We'll just see who gets to redirect what."

"You Reid men are all the same," said Julia, holding her ground. The sun behind her lit the auburn wisps of her hair. She had a wild beauty. "Stubborn as they come and unafraid to flaunt it. Proud, almost, that you're so bullheaded."

She stood defiant as Joseph wheeled around to confront her. "What the blazes do you know about any of this?"

"Ah, finally, a word from the almighty Joseph Reid."

Ryan sighed, suspecting there was a big blast coming, while his brothers looked on, riveted in disbelief.

Her quiet voice underscored her anger. "How dare you speak to me as if I'm your servant."

"Now listen, girl—"

"I was on that train for a lot longer than you were. I helped Travis through his breathing difficulty, and I helped Ryan deal with the other injuries."

Ryan rushed in. "I thank you very much for that, Julia, and now if you'll—"

"Push me aside, will you? The whole lot of you?" She stepped closer to Joseph so that she was nose to nose with the big man. "My shop and everything I've worked for are in the path of destruction, too, as much as your ranches. Do you think the poorest here care less about our future than you do yours?"

Her eyes blazed a brilliant blue, and when she settled them on Joseph, then on Travis and Mitch, each man flinched in turn.

Ryan's brothers seemed to register something in her that Joseph missed—determination to fight.

Joseph scowled and planted his wide, gnarled hands on his hips. "If you think I'm going to make some grand gesture to step aside and invite fire to my—"

"I've given up expecting grand gestures from you."

"Now is not the time, Julia," said Ryan. "You have a right to your feelings, but—"

"Doesn't that beat all." Flanagan came up from behind and interrupted. The old man said to Joseph, "Imagine settin' off that fire to burn in your direction. When all is said and done, I might own more than you in this world. Hee hee." He rubbed his bristly white chin. "Us, from debtors' prison, owning more than you."

Color flashed across Joseph's face. "That'll never happen."

Julia's face twitched with anger. "You might not think a lot of your oldest son, but you might learn something from Ryan if you listen. You're a damn old fool if you can't see that. And you, Grandpa, are a damn old fool if you think redirecting the fire has anything to do with debtors' prison."

She pretty much left all the men speechless.

The hot glares pivoted to Ryan.

"What are you going to do about her?" his old father demanded. "You're in charge, aren't you?"

Ryan walked to her side. "Thank you for your vote of confidence, Julia, but this really isn't the time to fight on my behalf."

Her hopeful expression faded. Disappointment registered. Maybe Ryan wasn't handling this right, but he wanted to protect her from his father's wrath. He didn't need a woman sticking up for him. He didn't need anyone sticking up for him. In fact, he felt awkward that she seemed to think he was unable to stand up to these men on his own.

"When I was a kid," Julia told the elder Reid, stepping back, "what I remember most about you was the big set of keys you used to carry on your belt loop. Remember? There were three silver ones, two gold and ours. The big brass one with the scratched ring."

The tension in Joseph's face increased.

"You used to carry them as if you didn't notice how heavy they were. Our whole lives depended on those keys, but you didn't seem to notice they were hooked on your belt loop."

Joseph swallowed as if his throat was parched. "I noticed." His mouth softened. "I tried to ignore the keys when I saw little kids staring at 'em."

Julia's eyes flickered.

Ryan took advantage of the moment to step forward. "Mitch, you've got to see that redirecting the fire is what's best for the town."

When his younger brother didn't respond, Ryan continued. "You think I don't recall the hunting trips we used to take through those woods? I remember teaching you how to scale fish and skin rabbits. Don't you think the woods I grew up in mean something to me, too? It pains me to advocate their burning. And you, Travis—" Ryan pointed to the creek "—I know that your ranch, the new one you built with your new wife, contains a dozen broodmares of the finest breeds in the territory. I know," he said, begging his brothers, "I know what this land means to you."

"I've got a wife now," said Mitch. "She has three younger sisters and a brother who live with us, and we call this land our home. What you're asking is too much."

Travis adjusted his hat while taking slow breaths, still recovering from his injury. "You've never met my wife, Jessica. I haven't told this to anyone yet, but she's expecting."

Ryan sighed. He addressed his brothers. "You'll both have time to collect your families, and herd your livestock to safety." He turned to his father. "Pa…"

The simple word seemed to affect them both.

"Pa…I'm not asking for myself. I'm asking for the town. Remember what you told me all those years ago when we crossed the ocean? Just like you did the right thing with those bribes you took in Ireland—giving them back—I'm trying to do the right thing here, for the town."

A collective gasp went up from his brothers, Flanagan and Julia. Wild-eyed, she stared at Joseph, who was trembling.

Ryan knew then that he'd gone too far. The secret shame of his father, which Joseph had confided to him after Ryan had witnessed two men beating him up on the steamship, was something Ryan had promised he would never disclose. His father had taken bribes to allow two men to escape from the Dublin jail. When it came down to it, Joseph couldn't bring himself to allow their release, since they were convicted of murder. He gave the bribe money back, but had to flee to Canada to protect his family. Two crooks followed them on board the ship and gave him a lashing for his broken promise. Ryan's mother knew the full truth, too, but no one else did. The rumors had swirled in town for twenty-five years.

The sound of galloping horses cut through the silence.

"Commander!" shouted Superintendent Ridgeway from atop his horse. "Commander, what's happening? I've been told you're cooking up a scheme to divert the fire. Is this true?" He dismounted while the others groped for words.

Mitch was the first to make his decision. "I think…I think we should do as Ryan asks. For the sake of the town."

And then Travis showed the courage he was made of by stepping forward. "I stand by you, too."

With a stone in his chest the weight of an anchor, Ryan addressed his father. "Sir, I don't need your permission to do this, but I would like to have it."

Joseph ran a shaky hand across his cheek. In the last five minutes, he seemed to have aged five years. His chin quivered as he looked from Julia, who stood stoically beside Ryan, to his eldest son. "All right. You can divert the fire across my land."

Reeling with shock and fear at what the Reids were about to try, Julia didn't wait to discuss her next move with Ryan. As soon as he told the troops that the married men had precisely two hours to arrange for their families' evacuation before reporting back to him, Julia got Grandpa to help her secure a horse, borrowed from the Mounties. She raced to her sister-in-law's home, where she found Pete. Julia fell to her knees, hugging him.

"I missed you," she said.

"I was havin' fun. Do I have to go?"

"Yes. The fire needs to be stopped. We have to help Dr. Reid."

"Isn't he a bad man?"

"No. He's a good man. I didn't understand him before, but now I do. He's trying to save everything from burning down." She whisked Pete up beside her on the horse and rode back to the site.

Most of the Mounties were single and therefore stayed to continue digging trenches. This included Ryan, since they needed his leadership especially. Many of the others, like Julia, came back with family members—wives, older children and elderly grandparents, all wanting to help dig firebreaks and plant dynamite to save the town. Grandpa took off to take care of her shop and other evacuations in town as best as he saw fit.

"Why are we bringing our shovels?" Pete asked Julia when she brought him to the trenches.

"Because the Mounties don't have enough to go around. Here, you start digging beside me and we'll work our way to the edge of the creek." She said hello to the barrister, Mr. Shapiro, as he walked by to assess the area with the mayor.

It was calming to have something physical to do. Pete did as he was told, hoisting as much dirt as he could carry. At his age he wasn't much help, but she was relieved to have him beside her. Julia felt the sun on her back as she heaved and twisted alongside her boy.

"So here you are." Ryan came to stand beside them. "Both of you."

Crouched low to the ground, Julia looked at the square toe of his cowboy boot, aged with creases and riddled with dirt, then up his long body to his face. He held a shovel, too.

"I thought I'd lost you," he said.

He seemed worried, the muscles tensing in his dark jaw. It hadn't occurred to Julia that he might look for her when she disappeared. As commander, he had everyone's problems to deal with, and she hadn't wanted to saddle him with more. She knew she was returning, but she should have made it a point to tell him.

"I went to get my son."

"You're not evacuating with the other women and children?"

Julia shook her head. "We're able-bodied, and we can dig. You need all the help you can get."

Pete strained to lift a heavy shovelful of dirt. "My ma said you need us."

"Indeed we do." Ryan gave Pete a quick smile as he swung his shovel into a mound of grass and dug. Motioning to Julia, he asked, "Where's your grandfather?"

"Helping with the evacuations on the other side of town," she said. "With my sister-in-law and her family. David and Clarissa went with him." It was odd for Julia to see Ryan digging at a time like this. She was used to watching him bark orders.

He noticed her curiosity. "The superintendent took over my command. He told me it was time to take care of my family, considering what they are about to go through. But I don't think they want my help. And I would never leave you to face this on your own."

The words and his smile gave her such hope. With a quick scan, Julia realized his brothers and father were nowhere in sight. They'd left to take care of things on their ranch.

The front of Ryan's shirt was drenched with sweat. He'd likely been at it for the time it took her to locate Pete.

"I'm sorry I blasted your father," she said.

"Don't be. It served us well. Until you blasted him, I didn't realize it was just what he needed."

He quirked his eyebrow and she sighed.

Where did they go from here, she and Ryan? For the moment, Holt was gone. Her world and everything in it might disappear into the fire. There'd be more change in her life. Change made her fearful for her future and for Pete's. It was difficult to give up the little control she had.

Ryan looked up from digging, glancing at the dozens of men and women bent over in the dirt. Children toiled beside their folks, all with a common purpose.

Ryan's pace increased. "This plan might not work, Julia."

"What do you mean?"

"The dynamite might set off the fire in two directions instead of one."

She refused to believe that. "Or it might extinguish it completely so nothing will burn. Not even the Reid ranch."

Ryan rubbed his dripping face with the back of his sleeve. "That's what I like about you."

There was something honest about the way they worked together for the next little while, Pete eagerly digging as much as he could, Julia clawing at roots and clearing shrubs. Ryan answered questions when his men asked, and pointed out what needed to be done. When it was time to wire up the explosives, he lent his expertise.

More fearful than she was letting on, Julia wiped her dirty hands across her skirt. She'd given up trying to remain tidy and constrained while fighting a fire that was unleashing hell.

Her pulse careened as she saw the clouds of smoke getting closer and closer.

The crowd had been subdued at first, but now, hours later, as the smoke and fire spewed their ugliness, the activity and shrieks got louder. Cattle being evacuated from nearby ranches passed behind them on the way to the river, lowing to each other as if sensing danger. Roosters and ducks from old man Cooper's place squawked as their cages were carried away.

Fear caused Julia to tremble. Grandpa had told her he'd go to the printing shop to pack up the essentials, then he'd head out of town on the main road. She and Pete were to catch up with him and the family there.

"Let's go," Ryan hollered, coming up beside her. He carried a burlap sack.

"Maybe I should try to meet up with Grandpa."

"You and Pete are coming with me. I'm not letting

you out of my sight. I'll make sure to reunite you with your Grandpa later, but right now it's too dangerous."

And, suddenly, it seemed so right to let Ryan lead.

"We'll go to my father's ranch. They'll need help with the livestock. If we're separated…head to the river. Fire usually skips over water."

And then she saw what he meant. Walking quickly beside Ryan, with her arm thrown over Pete, Julia looked on as a farmer herded his goats down to the river. The banks of the Bow were already teeming with sheep, cattle and people, all walking east along the river's edge, away from the fire. In case the blaze came close, they could jump into the water for protection.

Cooper's Creek, flowing into the Bow, was empty of travelers, since the fire was supposed to head north in that direction.

"Ryan," said Julia, swerving to look back at the town's buildings. "Your violin. The bank—"

"The bank will have to take care of itself."

"But Mr. Bosley would want you to get it."

"Adam would laugh at that."

"What do you mean?"

"There's no time to explain," Ryan roared above the din of the crowd. "You're worth a lot more to me than a violin—"

"I'm scared," Pete whimpered.

Julia filled with anguish as she tried to comfort him.

Ryan placed his arm around both of them and squeezed. The gesture consoled Julia.

"I'm scared, too," Ryan told Pete. "So let's stick together."

Ryan waved to two men who were directing seven

horses out of another livery. There were more animals than they could handle, judging from the restless panting of the mares.

"I'll take care of these three for you," hollered Ryan. "You can pick them up at the fort in a couple of days when this is over."

"Take 'em!" they shouted, going into the livery for more.

Ryan helped Julia and Pete to mount. Pete was a good rider, but she felt uneasy at the size of his mare. When Ryan mounted a roan and tied on his lumpy burlap sack as a counterweight to the saddlebag, she realized what it contained.

Dynamite.

Ryan looked into her trembling face and tried to calm her fears. "They might need help…my folks might need help wiring up their houses."

Good Lord. He was going to blow up each home with dynamite to try and extinguish the fire. She couldn't imagine how painful that would be for the Reids to witness.

Riding through the crowd, Julia silently praised Ryan. Though, for the first time in hours, he looked doubtful. The firm lines of his face seemed strained. The dark eyebrows were pulled together, and his powerful legs pressed tensely against his mare. The turmoil she saw him in wasn't about his plan to divert the fire. She sensed it ran a lot deeper.

He was a good commander, ably leading and managing hundreds of men. He wasn't so good with one person at a time. When Ryan saw his mother for the first time in ten years, he would once again become a man seeking forgiveness for the pain he'd caused them all.

Julia wished there was something she could do to help him with his family, or to somehow stop the fire. But she simply felt useless as doom approached.

Chapter Seventeen

In ten years' time, the place hadn't changed, Ryan thought as they galloped onto the Reid ranch. And yet everything inside him had changed so much.

"Where's my mother?" he called to two ranch hands as he, Julia and Pete dismounted from their horses. He hitched them to the post nearest the stables. "Where's Mrs. Reid?"

"Not here. Did you look in the house?" A young hired hand pulled two palominos through the stable doors. His cowboy hat blew off in the wind and rolled across the dry grass past Ryan.

"Not yet, but I will." Hanging on to his burlap sack, Ryan stomped on the hat's brim and retrieved it.

Close by, he saw Julia survey the expansive two-story home, its large veranda and the two sprawling cottonwoods at the entry. Her smart young son stood mesmerized by the animals dashing across their path—two gigantic draft horses, one dappled gray, a sorrel, and three donkeys.

It must be Julia's first time here, Ryan realized, feeling

a sense of shame. As a young woman she'd meant a lot to him, yet he'd treated their time together as if it was no more than a passing fling. She must have felt belittled when he'd left. Maybe she still felt that way.

What he'd learned in his travels was that sometimes apologies weren't enough. Sometimes suffering and humiliation went too deep for words to heal them. In this instant, as Julia stared at the veranda she'd never seen before, Ryan understood for the first time how insulted she must have felt. She'd lived in Alberta District for twenty-five years and had never been cordially invited to the Reid home.

He understood why she might prefer Holt to him.

But there was another woman in Ryan's life to whom he also had to make amends. Would his mother recognize him when she saw him? Because of her stroke, would she be too weak, too thin, too incoherent to know him?

"This way," he said to Julia, climbing onto the veranda. There was no time to dwell on how he would try to make it up to her, for they were racing against time, against the wildfire. He could see the smoke billowing from the western edge of town, beyond the fields of prairie grass and shrubs.

Ryan placed a hand on Pete's back, urging him toward the front door. Something about the contact with the boy's limber spine felt good.

Their boots clomped on newly painted floorboards, over the neat row of nails tapped into pine. Polished brass lanterns, each one as expensive as a horse—Ryan recalled when his mother had ordered them from a catalog and his father had objected—flanked the double oak doors. Lacy curtains adorned the inside of each door's windows.

No one answered when Ryan lifted the brass knocker

and banged. He kept knocking while he looked toward the distant foothills. Half a mile away stood a smaller ranch house. Crowds of people were working there, too, as well as on another ranch a mile from that one. They were likely his brothers' homes. Beyond the hills, someone was herding a hundred head of cattle and several dozen horses northward. Even the animals weren't safe yet.

Carefully hanging on to his sack of dynamite, Ryan banged on the door with his fist, then opened it and hollered, "Hello!"

The loud activity inside made Ryan realize why no one had heard his banging. Two unfamiliar men were lifting a horsehair sofa to their shoulders, while a third was removing gold-framed pictures from the papered walls.

"What are you doing?" Ryan demanded, wondering if they were thieves. But a familiar head—his father's—bobbed up in the kitchen doorway.

"Trying to save as much as I can," said Joseph in as sorrowful a voice as Ryan had ever heard.

When Ryan, Julia and Pete walked toward the kitchen, the three movers stepped outside through the back door. They loaded the items onto a wagon that was spilling over with other household goods. Ryan stepped outside to take a look. The objects symbolized decades of hard work by both his parents, but his father wouldn't be able to save more than a fraction of their possessions.

"Where are the others?" asked Ryan, stepping back into the kitchen to join his father and Julia. Ryan braced himself. "Where's Ma?"

Julia ran her fingers across a shelf of crockery, her

sleeve dangling in the air as she turned to listen. Pete, in coveralls, plopped to the floor to inspect a pail.

"Mitch and Travis took her. They're loading up as much as they can haul from their own homes. They're going to head north with most of the cattle. Did you see them outside?" Joseph pointed in the direction of the two ranches.

"Yeah." Ryan couldn't mask his disappointment at missing his mother, but she was safer and better off far from here. He couldn't bring himself to look at Julia.

"Did Ma take...do you know if she took the dress I gave her? I'd like to save it from the fire, if I can."

"What dress?"

Ryan shook his head. It was obvious that his mother never confided in Joseph. "Never mind. It's not important anymore."

"Travis and Mitch will be wiring up their ranches before they leave," said his father. "Like we agreed."

"Good."

"Did you bring more dynamite?"

Ryan held up his burlap sack. "Some." He noticed Julia's look of dismay. She grabbed her son from the floor and pressed him to her side.

"What's the dynamite for?" Pete asked.

"To starve the fire of air," said Ryan. "To smother it if it comes this way." He explained to the adults, "We'll wire each room, but we're not going to light the fuses. We'll let the fire do that if it swings this way. If it doesn't, then we'll unwire the dynamite and no harm done."

Julia sucked in a gulp of air. "Let's hope the house is saved."

Joseph looked at her, as if he realized how awkward she

felt in the midst of such luxury, in the home of her former jailer. "Look," he said, pointing to a porcelain figurine. "My wife won this at the harvest fair we started in Calgary—the very first year. It's a ballerina."

"It's pretty," Julia said softly.

"To win it, she had to toss three eggs into a bonnet without breakin' them." Joseph chuckled. "And this, this here rifle—" he walked to the fireplace mantel and removed his favorite Winchester from the wall "—is the first gun I bought when I landed in Canada. I learned to shoot geese with it."

It was the rifle Ryan had learned to shoot with, too. One winter when his father was suffering from a broken foot and couldn't walk, Ryan had taught himself how to shoot rabbits to feed the family.

Julia didn't say much, but nodded at the old man sympathetically.

"They're things, Pa," said Ryan. "They're only things."

Joseph's eyes welled. He looked down at the rifle. "They're memories."

"We've got to hurry." Ryan placed his burlap sack on a table and opened it. "Pete, maybe you can help me."

"With what?" Julia pulled her son back.

"I need someone to help me plant these sticks."

"But he's barely old enough—"

"I can do it, Ma." Pete rushed to Ryan's side and watched as he demonstrated.

Ryan handed Pete a stick. "That's it—nice and easy."

They worked as quickly as they could, Julia following them into every room, helping where she could. Ryan moved with the concentration he'd developed on the battlefield. But he found the patience to be kind and attentive to her son. Ryan answered every question Pete had and made the boy feel important, thanking him for his help even as they raced through the house.

They finished thirty minutes later in the top bedroom, with Joseph standing beside them, watching. His father's glance flickered around the room, and he shifted his weight from foot to foot.

"What is it?" Ryan asked.

"Come out in the hallway and look out the window."

Ryan, Julia and Pete crowded forward.

Joseph whispered, as if they were sitting in the front pew of a church, "The fire's reached Cooper's Creek."

Pete wiggled between Julia and Ryan to get a closer look. "But I don't hear no blast."

"Maybe we're too far away," said Julia.

"Or maybe the fire didn't divert," said Ryan.

A bang rippled through the air. The sound was as muffled as distant thunder, but there was no mistaking the huge ball of fire that shot through the air, followed by a tall puff of smoke that flared up from the trees along the river.

"What happened?" Joseph peered around Ryan's shoulder. "What happened to the fire?"

With fear pounding through his chest, Ryan swallowed. "The dynamite worked. I don't think the fire's heading toward town anymore. But it sure as hell is coming this way—stronger and wilder than anything we've seen so far. *We better run!*"

There was no time to lose, thought Julia. With her pulse pounding, she grabbed Pete by his sleeve and leaped down the stairs. Ryan and Joseph were right behind them as they reached the kitchen.

"I'm heading north with the wagon," hollered Joseph. "You three best ride out on horseback!"

"All right," Julia shouted, as Joseph tore out the back door. "Ryan!" She spun around to see where he'd gone. "Ryan!"

She dashed back to the hallway to look for him, while Pete peered into the parlor. They found Ryan turning a hardback chair upside down in the dining area.

"I don't see it," said Ryan. "I don't know where it is."

"What? What have you lost?" she asked.

"I checked every room as we planted the dynamite. I didn't see it."

"What's not here? Tell me!"

Panting, Ryan ransacked the sideboard, then rushed into the sitting room.

"What are you looking for?" Julia screamed, dashing after him. "We've got to go!"

"The violin! I'm looking for the violin!"

Julia halted in her tracks, trying to understand. "But it's at the bank. In Mr. Bosley's vault. I saw you hand it over to Jackson."

"That was a decoy. What you saw me hand over was an empty case. I threw a plank of wood inside so that it would feel like a violin, but it's not in there. I didn't want every thief from here to the Rockies knowing what I actually did with the violin, so I figured Bosley could deal with them."

"Mr. Bosley's going to kill you when he finds out you gave him an empty case." She rubbed her wrist. "So it's at the other bank, then, the Imperial? I saw you give Jackson that money. The bag was huge. You must have stowed it in there."

"No, not there, either. I wanted anyone watching closely to think that if I didn't send the violin to Bosley, then I might have sent it to the Imperial, but it's not there."

"What *did* you do with it?"

"I wrapped it up in the blue dress I gave my mother. I sent it to her."

Dismayed, Julia fell back against a table. "I remember that bag. You tucked it in there? Land's sake…" She slid her hand into her skirt pocket. "How do you know what your mother did with it?"

"I don't." Ryan towered over Pete as he reached for his hand. "I don't know if she thought enough of me to open the bag. Maybe she never pulled out the dress. Even if she did, she likely didn't realize the value of the violin. Maybe the bag didn't even get to her."

"Maybe your father took the bag without realizing it."

"I had a good look at his wagon and it's not there."

Julia raised her hands toward him in a gesture of compassion. "Oh, Ryan, I'm so sorry."

"I wanted it for you. For my family. For the town."

"That's lovely," she said, touched by his disclosure. "But I won't miss it because I never had it."

He swung Pete by the arms toward the front door. "You're right. Never mind. The violin's not important now. Let's take the horses and get out of here."

They fled the house and ran across the yard, but a commotion near the stables stopped them.

"Are all the animals out?" Ryan shouted to the ranch hand who appeared, the same one he'd talked to earlier.

"No!" cried the young man. "I thought they were, I told your father they were, but there's a number of them in the back quarter that I thought—that I thought the foreman released."

Julia froze at the awful image of trapped animals. She watched Ryan turn as pale as she felt.

"What's your name?" Ryan asked.

"William."

"Go, William. Take my horse and go!"

"Are you sure? I've got my sister and brother waiting down the road…"

"Yes, go find your family." Ryan wheeled toward Julia. "Go with William. Head to the river!"

Julia couldn't abandon Ryan any more than she could abandon Pete. William tore off, but she and her son climbed off their horses and followed Ryan into the barn.

The scents of straw and horses mingled with the heavy smell of smoke. The fire was nearly upon them. Just one spark was all this place needed to ignite into a blazing inferno. The sounds of horses snorting and stomping from behind a closed door caught her attention. Ryan barged forward. Three horses, frightened beyond sensibility, bucked at their stall boards.

"Easy," murmured Ryan. "Easy now," soothing them with a calm voice.

He released the two young stallions, then finally coaxed the aging mare, a mustang, into submission. Ryan swung onto her, bareback, and took firm control. "Easy, Charlotte, easy now."

So he knew her, thought Julia.

Sitting on top of the mustang, towering over Julia and Pete, Ryan was as tall and massive as a bronze statue. "Julia, you both need to calmly but quickly get back on your horses."

"I understand," she said, mustering a calm she didn't feel. "Come on, Pete."

Dashing outside, she helped her son jump into his saddle, then flew onto her horse and kicked it to a gallop. The three of them thundered past the house, the toolshed, the overturned wheelbarrows, the door to the underground cellar, the stables and the two big cottonwoods they would likely never see again.

Smoke and soot billowed past them. The temperature of the air had increased by ten degrees. Rabbits and small rodents crisscrossed their path as they flew over the dried grass, the fire bearing down upon them.

Five minutes later, the rush of the wind was exploding in Julia's ears. Hooves pounded the ground beneath her. She felt the mare's muscles strain beneath her thighs as she, Pete and Ryan reached the river.

"Ride into the water," Ryan shouted. "Both of you! Ride into the river!"

Gasping for breath, Julia pulled back on her reins and watched Pete do the same. His mare, much too large for his slight body, turned sharply and raced along the riverbank.

"Slow down!" Julia yelled, terror clutching at her. "The mare will trip! Slow down!" She almost sobbed with relief when she saw her son regain control and halt his mount.

The horses burst into the river with a splash that soaked Julia's blouse. Water filled her boots and saturated her clothes. She hiked her skirts higher, trying to keep the layers of fabric above the level of the water so their weight wouldn't drag down the mare.

Cattle mooed in the river beside them. There was no

sign of people, only dozens of red-brown Herefords. Smoke curled in the air around them. Pete coughed once and then again.

"Get off your horses!" shouted Ryan. "Stick to the side of the river, where it's shallow!"

Julia slid from her mount into waist-deep water. She raced to help Pete, but he'd already dismounted. The water reached his neck.

"Bend over and keep your face close to the water," she said. "Breathing will be easier in the moist air."

Heaven almighty, the fire might jump the banks and scorch them, or the smoke might suffocate them.

Greasy air bit at the back of her throat. If she inhaled too deeply, the heavy smoke clogged her windpipe.

"Use your skirt," Ryan called. Letting go of the mustang, he waded to Julia's side. Holding on to his hat, he lifted the floating fabric to her face, then demonstrated how to use it as a filter, as he was doing with his wet shirt sleeve. "Breathe through the damp cloth. You, too, Pete."

Ryan's strong arm looped around her son, and Julia felt blessed that Ryan was with them. If anyone could protect them, he could. He focused on Pete and made sure the boy was safely breathing.

"Let go of the reins, Julia," Ryan said.

She couldn't seem to budge.

"Let go of your horse, sweetheart," he repeated, stepping forward and coaxing them from her hand. "The horses are scared, too. We can't constrain them. They might injure us."

"If we let them go, they might run away."

"The animals seem to know by instinct to remain in the river."

"But," said Pete, "some of the steers are climbin' up on the other side."

"Just a few runaways. But they're doomed if the fire jumps over and ignites the far bank."

The flames were moving closer. Ryan hurried to untangle the reins of a horse that had caught on a nearby bush.

Making sure Pete was breathing okay, Julia kissed his cheek and whispered, "I love you. I'll always love you."

She watched Ryan help the frightened mare, and knew she would never feel the same about him, either. He was a courageous man who seemed to care as much about her son as she did.

Ten feet behind Ryan, she pulled her skirt edge from the water again, wrung it out and breathed through it, then looked up at the hillside, where a wall of fire spun like a top out of control.

Thick smoke blocked her view of the ranch houses, but she finally heard a loud bang, then another.

"My brothers' homes," said Ryan sadly, reaching her side again.

Julia grasped his hand. She mumbled prayers as another explosion, this one louder and closer, ripped through the air.

She felt Ryan shudder. "It's all right," she said. "You did the right thing. No matter how it turns out, you made the right—"

A blast of smoke so fierce it blew Ryan's hat off his head hammered down on them. It must have been his father's house. Ryan pushed her and Pete into the water, submerging them completely, as well as himself. Then he slowly lifted them up a few inches so they could breathe.

Surprised by the move, she and her son coughed and sputtered for a few moments.

The huge cloud of smoke around them dissipated. Breathing became easier. Inch by inch, Ryan allowed them to rise above the water. They rubbed their faces and peered through the diminishing smoke, which still clawed at Julia's throat.

The sea of cattle shifted around them. The grass at the water's edge was burning. Julia swung her gaze to the opposite bank, which was green. There was no fire visible, no fire anywhere along that edge. Her spirits soared. The fire had stopped at the water's edge.

Ryan swung his long arms around her and Pete. "It's all right," he murmured to them both. Ryan kissed the top of her head, and then Pete's. She was surprised still that Ryan's attachment to her son had come so naturally.

"It worked, didn't it?" she asked, clinging to Pete and Ryan, one small and wiry, the other huge and solid.

"I think so," said Ryan. "I think the fire got trapped and smothered between Cooper's Creek and the Elk River." He trudged through the water to grab hold of his mare, then helped Julia and Pete locate theirs. "Mount your horses."

"Commander!" A shaky voice called from the other side of the river.

Startled, Julia swung around to see a young Mountie sitting on top of a horse, with two other men coming up behind him.

"Are you all right, Commander?"

"Yes, Cole, I'm fine."

"Let me help you out, ma'am," the constable said to her. "Take my hand."

"Please help my son first."

"Ma, I can do it on my own." With youthful ease, Pete mounted his horse, gripped the reins and splashed up the side of the bank.

Julia and Ryan mounted their horses and followed, water draining from their clothing as they reached dry land.

"Was the town spared?" Ryan asked his men.

"Yes, sir. We went overboard with the amount of dynamite we planted at Cooper's Creek, and it blasted a bigger hole than we planned, but the wildfire bypassed town."

Julia murmured sweet thanks. For the first time in days, the knot inside her stomach began to unravel. She took a deep breath and turned toward the man who'd protected her and Pete. Ryan's muscles flexed beneath his wet shirt, tapering from his wide shoulders all the way down to his lean, long legs. The sight of him aroused aches and desires she couldn't control.

Water dripped off the brim of his hat and landed on his chest. "Go with the Mounties," Ryan told her.

"But you've got to come with us."

"No," he said, shaking his head. His gaze swept over her wet clothing. And a muscle pulled in his throat. Then he peered out toward the northern plains. "My family…my folks and my brothers are likely watching from there. I've got to see if anything more can be salvaged from the fire."

"But Ryan, what can you do? Everything's still burning."

"I've got to see that for myself. I'll catch up with you tomorrow," he murmured. His lips twitched at the sight of her wet skirt clinging to her legs. "Go find your grandpa and see to your boy."

Ryan turned to her son. "You've been a brave young man today, Pete. You'd make a good Mountie one day.

You've made me and your mother very proud of you. In fact, I knew your father, Brandon O'Shea, and he'd be proudest of all."

Pete smiled, nearly bursting at the kind words.

It took a moment for her to recover. Julia wanted to be with Ryan, to hold him and talk to him, but he was right. What she needed to do first was find Grandpa and take Pete away from these ruins. She needed to show her son that the town had been spared, that the right people had made the right choices.

Julia dug her heels into her mare, called to her boy and, with a fleeting glance at the man whose stark, smoke-blackened face she would never forget, galloped away. Now that the worst was over, the fire had been extinguished and Ryan was free to go, she wondered with a tremor if he would choose to pursue her. He'd made no promises to her this time. They had made love with more intensity than they had ten years ago, but she wondered how much that meant to him, how much *she* meant to him, and if he'd have any trouble walking away.

Chapter Eighteen

"What happened, Julia? Tell me what happened on the Reid ranch." Flanagan grabbed hold of her mare's reins as Julia and Pete drew up to the front of her printing shop. In the brilliant rays of the setting sun, they slid off their saddles and let the Mounties take the horses, to return them to their rightful owners.

"Gone, Grandpa. It's all gone."

The old man turned pale and struggled for solid footing.

Julia ran her hand across Pete's damp head. The two of them were wet and grimy. "Let's wash up."

Grandpa ushered them through the shop, along the back hall and into their kitchen. He had a fire going in the cast-iron stove. The wood inside sizzled and wonderful heat filled the room. Julia hadn't realized until now that she was shivering, either from the coolness of her damp clothing or the strain of all that'd happened.

Grandpa filled a pot with water and set it on top of the stove. "Chamomile tea will do you both good."

After they'd taken turns scrubbing themselves in the old

tin tub, and had changed into dry clothing, Pete begged to go see how his cousins had fared in the disaster. No sooner had he asked than his quiet cousin, Max, appeared on the back porch.

"They made out fine," said Grandpa as he poured the tea.

Before her son could reach the back door, Julia stopped him for a private word.

"Pete, sometimes people make mistakes when they judge other people."

"I didn't say nothing—"

"Not you, honey. Me." She rubbed a towel over his damp hair. "I told you once that we had to be careful about trusting Dr. Reid."

"Yeah."

"I just want you know that...I was wrong. I should have been more forgiving. People with fancy clothes and expensive haircuts can be just as kind and good as those with less. Dr. Reid protected us today and we owe him thanks."

"I like him."

"He likes you, too."

"Can I go? Max is waitin'."

She smiled. "Yeah, go on."

"Tell me again what happened," Flanagan said after the two boys left and Julia settled into a chair by the stove.

Wrapped in a blanket, she sipped hot tea. "They laced their homes with dynamite and blew them to shreds."

"Mitch's?"

"Yes."

"Travis just built his ranch and stables a couple years back. They couldn't have—"

"All gone."

"But Joseph…surely he salvaged his."

"I was there when he and Ryan wired it. It exploded into a million pieces. So did their stables and sheds."

Grandpa slumped onto a chair. He pressed his fingers against his forehead, his white head shaking. "But why would they do it?"

"You already know why. They explained. So the fire would circumvent the town."

"But I never believed… I thought when it came down to it…"

"They did it, Grandpa." Julia could barely believe it herself. "They did it so we could sit here and enjoy our tea."

Grandpa muttered. "They've got nothing."

"Mercifully, their livestock was spared."

"Joseph Reid is a proud man and this will… And poor Ryan. His family already…."

Julia closed her eyes and felt the world spin. "Do you know where Holt MacAllister is?"

"The Rossmans took him in for the night. They had to clear the fort hospital in case the fire swung that way."

She slid the blanket off her shoulders. "I've got to see him. There are things that need to be said."

"Now? But you—"

Julia sprang from her chair and headed out the door. "Right now, Grandpa."

"I knew you'd come." Holt, lying on a sofa in the Rossmans' parlor, rose on an elbow as his aunt ushered Julia in.

Julia nodded to Dr. Calloway, who was leaving after settling Holt for the night. When he and Holt's aunt withdrew, Julia could hear him giving overnight instructions to Mrs. Rossman behind the door.

"How are you feeling?" Julia asked.

"Doc says it's healing well. In another couple of weeks, if we keep up with the exercises in bed, I can try walking."

"That's wonderful."

"I heard the commander got the fire out."

"He did." She shook her head. "Yes, he did." She felt hopeful for the first time in a long while.

"I'm glad you're here." Holt motioned to a chair beside the bed, and she sat down. "We need to finalize—"

"Holt, it's not that easy."

His smile receded. He leaned back on his pillow, blond hair lifting around his ears. "What's not easy? The doc told me that my foot will never be the same, but I didn't intend on working as a Mountie forever. I always wanted to buy into a share of Rossman's Mercantile. Remember I told you I've been saving money? Well, my aunt and uncle are quite agreeable to having me start soon."

"That's lovely, Holt, that you've got such plans. I admire that in you."

His warm smile returned. "So I figure we can set—"

"I'm sorry, Holt."

"About what?"

"I feel that I've misled you. But you see, I didn't know it myself. I thought I was truly following my heart when I placed that advertisement in the paper."

"You no longer need the ad. I'm your family now. You have me."

Her lashes flickered at his omission. "And Pete."

"Yes, of course. Pete and your grandfather, too. We'll make room for them both."

Julia shifted on the hard wooden seat. Her hair, still damp, curled on her blouse.

"I can't marry you, Holt."

"What?" He sprang forward, muscles tight. "Why not?"

She twisted her fingers together. "It's not that easy to explain…"

"If it's my foot—"

"It's not your foot."

"Then don't tell me it's that silly notion Clarissa put into your head."

"What notion?"

"Our age difference. Please, I assure you that won't be a problem. I'm not the least bit intimidated and I find you…I find you simply beautiful."

Julia cleared her throat. It was difficult to go on with the pressing ache there. "And I think you're simply outstanding."

This brightened him.

"But I can't marry you, Holt."

"Why on earth not?"

"Because…I've got feelings for someone else. I always have, but didn't see it. No matter what comes of it, I figure he's got a right to know. He's done so much for this town, for all of us. If he leaves again…God, if he leaves again… I've got to let him know."

Holt pressed his back against the cushions. "You don't need to tell me who it is. I can guess."

"I'm sorry," she whispered.

"If you didn't know him, if he wasn't in the running, would I have…would you have chosen…?"

"I would have married you. Without a doubt." Rising to her feet, Julia looped her fingers into his and kissed him on the forehead.

"We would have dazzled them, Julia."

Her voice came out raspy. "Yes, we would have."

Ryan tried not to punish himself by brooding about Julia, but his thoughts dwelled on her. He wondered what she was doing and if she had reunited with Holt.

On any other day, he would have thought this a pretty summer morning. But today, Ryan was walking through the charred ruins of his parents' home. He was here alone in the orange mist of sunrise, wearing the Mountie tunic he had donned to ward off the morning chill. His wide brown hat shielded his face from the wind and flies, and a shoulder harness held his gun. He hadn't been able to salvage anything yesterday, even though he'd told Julia he might, and no one in his family had returned. He wondered where they were and if they were safe.

Ryan kicked the ashes, then stopped to pick up a shiny scrap of metal. It glinted like a silver coin, but turned out to be a useless piece of twisted tin. He turned it over in his hand.

Would his family ever understand and forgive him? Would his father know how deeply Ryan cared for this homestead? How often he'd dreamed of it in Africa?

They'd buried Ryan's grandmother on the hill just beyond the stables. She'd taught him how to read and write the alphabet on the steamship crossing from Ireland.

The mustang he'd ridden back from the fort, Charlotte,

was the mare he'd used to win his first horserace. He'd never earned a whole dollar before that day.

He'd helped build the stables, too—once the most magnificent in the entire county, now a pile of black rubbish. Most of the outlying sheds had burned to the ground, as had the wooden door to the fruit cellar just off where the kitchen used to be. Gone was the pear tree and the old wooden swing that he'd built for his brothers and sister. The only things remaining intact were two slightly charred cottonwoods that had somehow escaped the inferno.

Ryan turned the tin between his fingers. Sunlight caught its edge. This morning, he felt like this piece of curled tin. He was strong and bright on the outside, an accomplished surgeon, but once you looked closer and twisted a little bit more, the man beneath might crumble.

What should he say to Julia? They'd struggled together to bring everyone to safety, and somewhere in between, had got caught up in each other's arms. He should be feeling relief that the wildfire crisis was over, but what he felt was a sense of loss and separation.

At the faint sound of galloping hooves, Ryan scanned the horizon. He tilted his Stetson low to block the sun, but couldn't make out who was approaching. There was more than one rider coming in from town, and from the north as well.

A slow smile etched its way across his mouth as the identity of the first rider became clear. She was racing at quite a gallop, her skirts billowing, her cowboy hat tied around her throat and bouncing off her back, her loose hair flying.

Julia.

There were others behind her, but Ryan wasn't watching them. Julia reined in beside him, flew off her horse and panted, "Good morning," all in one breath.

He laughed in delight at the sight of her. Seeing her dewy-eyed and safe lifted his spirits.

"Good morning yourself. How did you sleep?"

"Fine, just fine…"

"And Pete? How's he doing?"

"Good. He spent most of the evening with his cousins. I left him there this morning. I thought he could use a day of rest. But I'll bring him by tomorrow."

"I was worried about him last night."

When she tilted her face up, her pretty hair shifted around the neckline of her lacy blouse. "Why?"

"He went through a lot yesterday. Being shoved into the water like he was, and then witnessing the fire so close, he must have wondered if we were going to make it."

"I'm keeping my eye on him, but he slept well." Julia slid the leather tie of her cowboy hat over her head. "Pete ate a big breakfast and he's playing with his usual vigor."

Ryan smiled. "Those are good signs."

She smiled back. "Thank you for asking about him."

"He's a fine boy."

Julia's expression grew serious. She fidgeted with her hat. "I saw Holt last night."

"Ah, Holt." The mere mention of his name aroused such envy in Ryan. "How is he?"

"Doing all right. He's at the Rossmans' but he's being transferred to the fort hospital today."

Ryan stared at her upturned face. "He must have been pleased to see you."

She flushed. Her lashes flickered downward, conceal-
ing her eyes. "He was."

"Ryan!" Someone hollered behind them, interrupting
the moment.

"Flanagan," said Ryan, eyeing the old man. "What
brings you here?"

"Came to see how bad it was."

Ryan pulled in a breath. If the old gent was here to bask
in some sort of misguided—

"Ryan!" called yet another voice.

He looked up in amazement as a stream of folks dismounted from their horses. Some were pulling up in
wagons loaded with shovels and saws; others carried
blankets and bedding. Women rode beside their husbands,
bringing baskets of food and sandwiches, as if they intended on staying the day. Adolescent boys disembarked
from buckboards. Some started immediately shoveling
debris out of the ruins of the stables, and kicking stumps
where the orchard used to be.

It was a sight to behold, and brought a sheen to
Ryan's eyes.

Flanagan left—to unload a wagon, he said—while
Ryan studied the welcome faces, most especially Julia's.
"Where have you all come from?"

Julia smiled as she observed the crowd. "We've come
to work. You're going to need a lot of help to clear up
this—" she glanced at what remained of the sprawling
ranch house and winced "—wonderful ranch."

Dear Julia. She'd only been here once, and that was yesterday. Yet she was back today with a sparkle in her eyes
and a bounce in her step.

"Ho there! Ryan!"

Ryan looked up as Mitch galloped onto the site. Ryan's pulse leaped as he saw that his brother was heading a procession coming in from the north. Family. Then Ryan watched the sorrow cross his brother's face at seeing the devastated ranch. Ryan wished there was something he could do to ease the hurt.

Mitch didn't allow himself to wallow in the shock. He slid off his horse, rubbed a hand along his bristly chin and looked at his older brother. "Nothing to salvage. We can build everything new, then. Right, everyone?"

Mitch turned to the wagonload of people arriving behind him—a woman who was likely his wife, and a handful of youngsters who had to be her siblings. They jumped off the wagon so quickly that Ryan had a hard time counting heads.

"My wife, Diana," said Mitch proudly, introducing a pretty, slender woman with brown hair.

Diana extended her hand, and Ryan and Julia shook it in turn, introducing themselves.

Travis and his clan rode up next. His wife was expecting a child, Ryan recalled, but the woman hadn't yet filled out, as far as he could tell. Travis helped her off the buckboard.

"My wife, Jessica," he said starting another round of handshakes. Travis still looked a bit pale from his smoke injury, but Ryan noticed he was steady on his feet and his handshake was firm. Two dark-haired children, a girl and boy who appeared to be twins, jumped off the back of the wagon and stared at the ruins.

"Whoa," said the young boy. "Nothin' left."

"Are you all right?" Travis asked the girl gently, apparently not satisfied until she nodded. Then he spoke to the boy. "This place could sure use your help. Why don't you grab a shovel?"

"Me, too!" shouted the girl, and raced off with her brother.

Ryan felt sentimental, seeing all these people. It was getting to him. He was meeting strangers who shouldn't really be strangers. Their stilted acknowledgments underscored how much time he had wasted and how little he knew about his own family.

Maybe Julia understood him and how he felt, for she stood by his side and touched his elbow.

"My God," Ryan said, looking up as the next team of horses pulled a covered wagon to his side. "That's not you, is it, Shawna? Don't tell me you're the same young girl who used to put dry beans in my bed."

Shawna still had a mass of reddish hair. She was more graceful and elegant though, as her husband came around to help her down. A baby cooed in her arms and a toddler wiggled in the front seat. "It's me, Ryan. I can't believe you've come home."

Ryan grew somber at the circumstances, especially when his sister looked around the empty land and brought a hand to her face to hide her horror.

"It seems…" he said, "…it seems I came home to destroy everything."

Shawna walked to his side, cradling her baby. "Mitch and Travis told me what happened. My house is in town, along with our pub." She looked at her tall, dark-haired husband. "So you saved our home and business by doing this. You saved everyone in town."

But she, too, was awkward with Ryan, as if assessing who he was and why he'd come back. There were no warm embraces, no kisses in greeting. Ryan glanced down at his boots, aware that Julia was still near, watching his lackluster homecoming.

When he heard the creak of another covered wagon behind Shawna's, he gazed at it intently, his nerves quivering. "Is that Ma's wagon?"

"It is. She's not the same," Shawna warned him. "Careful with her, Ryan. Her memory's not what it used to be."

Shawna peered at Julia and nodded hello. "Miss O'Shea."

Of course they knew each other, thought Ryan. They both ran businesses in town. But it was obvious their acquaintance was stiff and formal.

Julia stared at her hands. Shawna's husband, Tom—or Quigley as Ryan's brothers referred to him—was more friendly to her.

"Howdy, good to see you," he told her. "I read every word of your newspaper accounts of the fire."

"Thank you," said Julia.

"She was irreplaceable on that train." Ryan was unable to disguise his pride. "We couldn't have done it without her." He wanted to get her alone to tell her so himself.

The wind snatched her hair and flung a strand over her smiling face. She caught it and held it back, nodding to Ryan in a private way that made his desire for her surge.

Julia glanced to his mother's wagon, her blue eyes glistening. Somehow she seemed to understand that he wanted her to come with him to meet his mother.

Neither said a word as they passed the two men sitting on the wagon's front seat. They made their way to the back, Ryan tall and trim in his Mountie uniform, Julia slender and graceful in her windblown skirts.

Ryan's father was just helping his wife slide off the wagon to her feet when Ryan and Julia appeared.

Ryan stumbled when he saw how frail and weak his mother looked. A dark brown dress clung to her body. The stark color matched her bonnet, which shielded her thin face from the sun.

He felt Julia press her palm to the back of his tunic, and the warmth and steadiness gave him comfort.

Joseph, in turn, stiffened at the sight of Ryan, then quickly returned his attention to his wife, grabbing her cane from the wagon and planting it in her hand. The sheer bulk of him made his wife look more petite. Her movements were symmetrical as she walked, Ryan observed, which indicated no severe damage from the stroke. *Thank you.*

Adjusting her bonnet, she turned in Ryan's direction. His presence seemed to catch her by surprise. "Oh, good morning."

She didn't appear to recognize him.

"Good morning," she said again, looking to him, then Julia, obviously expecting them to introduce themselves.

"Good morning," said Ryan gently. He watched the color deepen in her clear brown eyes.

She stared at his missing earlobe. "Are you here, Officer, to—to help with the clearing?"

"Yes…"

"Good of you to come." She peered more closely at his face, stretching upward. "You look like someone I recall…"

Ryan's gaze careened toward his father's. No one had told her that Ryan might be here. Why the hell not? Dammit, why not?

A small sob clutched the back of his throat. Because

maybe they couldn't count on Ryan still being here after the fire. And maybe because they couldn't bear to break an old woman's heart once again.

Ryan's voice came out deep and low. "Did you like the dress, Ma?" He searched her face. "I picked it out because the color was your favorite. Blue."

"Oh…" Her voice faltered. She swallowed and tilted her chin up to stare at him. Sunlight skimmed her aged cheeks. He'd never seen more beauty in such wrinkled skin in all his life. "Oh," she whispered lovingly, "Oh, my boy."

Ryan felt the sob release from his throat.

"My Donovan Ryan…" Her arms went up around him, the first embrace from someone in his family. She felt as weightless as a snowflake, but her grip on his back was solid.

"I haven't been a worthy son," he murmured into her bonnet.

She pulled away slightly to look at his face. "From what I've been hearing, you're a man worth knowing."

The words strengthened him. The family had told her about him, after all.

"I prayed you wouldn't leave before I saw you again," she said. "You'll stay, won't you, for a little while?"

"Yes, I'll stay."

People swirled around them. His sister returned with his brothers and their wives. Shawna slid her baby into her husband's arms so that she, too, could hug Ryan. His brothers stood in the background, not about to show any physical affection. But Ryan could see by their softening stances and mellowed tones that they'd all been waiting to take their cue from Ma on how to react to the long-lost member of their family. With a burst of optimism, Ryan felt he'd finally come home.

Through it all, Julia remained in the background. She spoke when spoken to, nodded politely at the wives, smiled at the children who were shoveling up ashes. And whenever Ryan glanced at her, she returned his inquisitive look with one of her own.

She was amazing. Three times he'd gone to tell her so, but he'd been constantly interrupted with questions.

His brothers asked where he'd been and what he'd seen. His sister wanted to know how blue the English Channel was. One of the children asked if he'd seen any elephants in Africa. Thirty minutes later, laughing and talking, Ryan finally made his way to Julia's side.

But his mother followed him, so he still couldn't speak freely to Julia. Instead, he studied her striking profile as she leaned against the back of a buckboard, smiling and watching with delight the way his family tugged him in all directions. His eyes followed the line of her forehead and nose, then came to a halt where a sunbeam glistened on her lip.

"Thank you for the dress, Ryan. In return, I was hoping to bake you something nice and set you down in my kitchen next time I saw you, but..." His mother looked past his shoulder at the heap of ashes that used to be her home. The turbulence of the past few days was grooved into her face. Twice, he'd seen her wiping tears away as she'd looked at the ruins. But if he believed anything, he believed in the strength of his mother. "I don't think the beautiful dress survived the fire. I don't remember where..." She frowned and seemed to lose her train of thought.

"There'll be other dresses," he said, trying to comfort her, wishing he could snap his fingers and magically rebuild her house. "I'll buy you dresses with imported lace collars. You always did enjoy the beauty of delicate things."

His mother looked at the empty grounds and tried to absorb the devastation. "We had so many beautiful things. We couldn't save very many."

"Ma'am," said Julia, pushing herself off the buckboard and pressing forward with some urgency. She reached into her skirt pocket and pulled out a white object. "It isn't much compared to what you had, but I saved this from yesterday."

A porcelain ballerina balanced in her palm.

His mother smiled fondly. "Thank you." She accepted it from Julia and then took a good hard look at her, as if seeing her for the first time. His mother gazed at Ryan, then back at Julia, as if weighing the importance of her presence next to her son. "It's Miss O'Shea, now, isn't it?"

"Yes, ma'am."

"I'm terribly sorry about the circumstances of how you and your family met my husband so many years ago. But thank you for coming to help today."

The warm words brought a timid smile from Julia that made Ryan's hopes surge. He wrapped his arm around her shoulders and felt her shiver at his touch. Ryan no longer cared what Julia had said to Holt's proposal. MacAllister could damn well get in line, because he was here first.

Chapter Nineteen

The trouble was, Ryan couldn't seem to get Julia alone.

His family went to work almost immediately. Folks were eager to clear the ruins, scrape the ashes to ground level, pick up rusty nails and remove twisted wagon wheels. Julia jumped when she was called by her grand-father, and seemed eager to help.

In the growing heat of the summer morning, Ryan dis-carded his wool tunic. By noon he was working in his sleeveless undershirt and dark breeches, like many of the other men. It was silly to feign propriety when most of the folks were farmers and ranchers and knew what hard work was.

It was difficult to read Julia. Ryan looked for signs of affection and encouragement, but she was devoted to her tasks. With head bowed, cowboy hat anchored in place, she rummaged through the ashes and pulled out two ruined front-porch lanterns—each the price of a horse. Later she provided water and fruit to anyone in need.

When David and Clarissa arrived just before noon with

their camera and notebooks, Julia moved off to assist them in reporting.

Julia eventually approached Ryan at lunchtime, when the crowd gathered along the creek to sip on cider and enjoy slices of thick ham, as well as other food folks from town had brought along.

"Ryan?"

Oh, finally.

Surrounded by other Mounties, he smiled in the most charming way he could muster. His body reacted to her presence as it always did—with a tremor of excitement, an infusion of possibility.

"Yes?" he asked.

She blinked at him, then stared down at her notebook, pencil in hand. "For the record, what happened to the cattle and horses? Where's the livestock?"

"My brothers tell me they're fine." He looked above her head and nodded toward the north country, to the greener pastures past the river. "They're grazing on Reid property ten miles north of here, on the other side of the Elk River. There's a rotating team of ranch hands and drovers caring for them."

"Ah, I see." She scratched some words onto the paper.

He wanted to rip the notes out of her hands and demand that she look at him. Really look at him. Face up to what they were feeling, and MacAllister be damned.

Sunshine filtered through the mesh of her straw hat, casting speckles of light on her cheeks. A fountain of hair swept down her back, tossed by the wind, its colors ranging from deep auburn to mink-brown. Her lips were swollen slightly from the heat, and she pursed them unconsciously as she concentrated on writing.

"I need to see you alone," he said.

"Pardon?" She looked up.

"Don't go home tonight until we talk. *Alone*."

A smile touched her lips, curving slowly. Now that gave him hope.

Hope quickly diminished when one of Julia's friends inquired how Holt was doing, and how quickly he might get back on his feet. Julia glanced away from Ryan when she spoke, as if trying to hide her sentiments for the sergeant.

How was Ryan going to deal with Holt?

As he climbed the creek bank, he heard another woman's laughter.

Pivoting to see where it was coming from, he noticed Clarissa bending under the black cloth of the camera. David stood in front of the lens with his monkey perched on his shoulder, posing for a photo with several of the Reid grandchildren. It was strange, seeing David and Clarissa together, laughing. Ryan believed he'd never witnessed it before.

He joined the others in getting back to work. As the crowd of men and women walked from the creek, they cleared debris from their path. Even Mr. Shapiro was there in his heavy suit. The barrister didn't get his hands dirty on the ground, but he helped organize the tools on the wagons. Todd Mead, the barber, was his assistant.

By late afternoon, the pile of charred items they'd collected stood as tall as Ryan, and he figured that the crowd was turning a two-week job into a one-day affair. It was astounding.

Flanagan emerged from the group, jumped up on a flat rock and got the crowd's attention. He whipped off his

black felt hat, threw it upside down on the back of a buckboard, then reached deep into his pockets and pulled out
several coins. The white-haired gent spoke in his usual
gruff manner, addressing his comments to Joseph.

"You're still a son of a bitch, Joseph Reid!" he hollered
over the crowd. "But someone's got to start a reconstruc-
tion fund!"

He tossed the coins into his hat. "I reckon you Reids
sacrificed your homes on our behalf, so they'll need re-
buildin'. Here's ten gold pieces."

People around Ryan froze for a moment, staring from
Flanagan to Joseph, who was obviously shocked himself.

As difficult as this gesture was for Flanagan to make,
Ryan realized, the old man must have taken time to plan
it, for he would have had to carry the coins from his home
this morning.

Flanagan seemed hard-pressed to understand why everyone was staring at him. "This, of course, doesn't mean
I like ya any better!"

People chuckled and the spell was broken.

"Well, thank you kindly," shouted Joseph from behind
a wheelbarrow. He set it down and wiped his sweaty forehead with the back of his dirty leather glove. "But that also
doesn't mean I'm gonna be grateful forever!"

The respect in Joseph's eyes outweighed the harshness
of his reply.

Ryan watched his father stand in awe as, one by one,
men shuffled past Flanagan's hat, emptying pockets,
throwing in dollar bills and loose coins.

"Since we're funding it," hollered Flanagan, "I think we
should decide how to rebuild it. I vote for a simple log

cabin this time, nothing fancy. Something not quite as showy or high and mighty as before."

Joseph tilted his good ear toward Flanagan. "And I vote we don't listen to you at all!"

Ryan laughed as the two old men exchanged insults, then caught sight of Julia standing beneath one of the big cottonwoods, six feet away.

He caught his breath at the vision.

Even coated in dirt, she was lovely. The tip of her nose was smeared with soot. Perspiration dripped down her cheek. Her hat sat forward on her head as if she couldn't find the best way to shield herself from the sun. Her gaze met his above the back of someone bending over to pick up an ax, then was lost again as that person straightened up.

"Dr. Reid," said a man on his other side—the Prairie Hotel owner and manager.

Ryan grabbed a shovel from beneath a tree. "What can I help you with, Wilbur?"

"I've set aside some hotel rooms for your family, for however long you need them. Just say the word."

"How do you mean?"

"I reckon if you'd like to stay in town this evening, for the women to have access to bathtubs for the children—"

"You'd do that for us?"

"The least I can do. You saved my hotel."

Ryan shook his hand, amazed at people's generosity. "I'll allow you the pleasure of informing the rest of my family. They'll be delighted."

Wilbur smiled and went off in their direction.

To Ryan's left, Flanagan was still shouting as he lifted

his hat, overflowing with money, to pass it to Joseph. "This should be a good start toward three new ranch houses."

"Could we make it four?" asked Joseph, balancing the hat as it was passed to him.

"Whaddya mean?" asked Flanagan.

The crowd was thinning. Flanagan hopped off the rock as Joseph searched the faces and finally settled his gaze on Ryan. "Four," he said simply. It was a statement and a question all rolled into one.

With a tight clench of his gut, Ryan realized what his father was asking. Ryan found it impossible to speak. When he nodded ever so slightly in answer, sunlight beamed from his father's face.

A ruckus from the road interrupted them. Turning to see what the crowd was chattering about, Ryan spotted yet another wagon rolling in, accompanied by several riders.

Hell, he thought, here we go.

Cleveland Bosley waved frantically to him from the wagon's front seat as he wheeled onto the property. Hobbs, the antiquities dealer, sat rigidly beside him. Six serious-looking armed men on horseback rode beside them, with rifles cocked and ready.

Bosley hopped off the wagon. Hobbs wasn't far behind. Their eyes looked weary behind their spectacles. Reaching Ryan, the banker presented him with his violin case. It was still held together with the leather straps and lock.

Ryan knew the key was in his holster, strapped to his horse, but he didn't step forward to take the case.

"Safe and sound," said Bosley. His face was pale and his gray beard needed a good trim, as if he'd been neglecting it for a few days. "You don't know what I went through—"

"Listen, Bosley—"

"Here," he said, stretching out his arms, oblivious to the folks listening. "Take it. You haven't got the faintest idea what the bastards tried at the bank. I had five attempted holdups. Val Zefield and his brother are in jail right now. And then last night someone tried to saw through the bloody back of the building. I damn well had to hire four extra guards—"

"There's nothing in it."

Hobbs's pleasant expression faded, but Bosley kept on talking. "I couldn't sleep for four nights on account of this blasted thing. Why the hell did you give it to me, anyway? You're not banking with me, so I don't understand—"

"It's empty," Ryan repeated.

"I've never seen so many thieves come crawling out of the woodwork. Vicious, too. You only have to look into their—"

"Bosley. The violin's not in there."

The banker stopped talking. He looked down at the violin case, frowned, then glanced back up at Ryan.

Ryan finally took the case from him. "Thanks for holding on to this case though. No new scratches. You took good care of it." He turned to set it on the back of a buckboard as Bosley exploded.

"What the hell do you mean?"

"I never said the violin was in there."

"But you made me think—"

"I can't help what you were thinking. All I know is I asked you to lock this case in the vault while I was gone. Paid you pretty good, too. Thanks."

"W-what?" stammered Bosley. His gray suit shook. "How could you do this to me?"

"I wanted you to earn back your reputation, after you sullied it by refusing to serve me."

Bosley's mouth gaped open, and Flanagan's laughter could be heard from twenty feet away.

"And I knew it would keep the thieves away from the real violin," Ryan added.

"The other bank? Is that where you sent it?"

"Actually...no."

Hobbs stepped forward, dressed impeccably in a white linen suit and black string tie. "Please, sir, tell us where it is. I'm prepared to increase my offer."

When Ryan sighed, Julia stepped up beside him, again offering her silent support.

Ryan's mother came out from the covered wagon, where she'd been resting.

"Where's your violin, sir?" Hobbs repeated.

Ryan gazed at the burned scraps of lumber strewn over the hill. "Somewhere in this heap of ash."

"Oh, my God," declared Hobbs, stumbling to a nearby wagon for support.

"Is that what you're looking for, Ryan? The violin?" asked his mother. She gazed at the blank spot where the house used to sit, then at the charred cellar door. "I recall now. The underground cellar. I put the dress and the bag in the root cellar. I set them next to the peach preserves that used to be your favorite... I was keeping them all together, in case you came back. I was going to make peach pie."

"It's in that hole?" cried Hobbs. "Under that burned door? There can't be anything left in there!"

Ryan kissed his mother's cheek.

He and Julia strode toward the cellar. She helped him yank on the door handle, but the latch inside must have melted, for it wouldn't budge. His brother Mitch produced an ax and they chopped through the door. Ryan hopped down the cement steps and into the dark cavity. Two minutes later he came back up, carrying his mother's dress and his Italian violin—both unharmed.

Julia's laughter drifted through the air. A cheer rose from his brothers, then the rest of the group as the news rang wide.

"Thank you, Adam," Ryan whispered, running a hand along the glossy wood. "You've been a good friend." Ryan finally knew exactly what he was going to do with the violin and the money.

He delivered the dress to his smiling mother, handed the violin to Mitch, then went to his horse to get the key to the violin case, which he gave to Travis. Ryan knew his brothers would guard the valuable instrument with their lives.

"Mr. Hobbs, I'd like to negotiate a price," said Ryan. "Something good and fair, for I intend to rebuild this town better than it was. A price that'll get us a volunteer firehouse, with fancy pumping wagons and shiny hoses. Something with a team of the finest horses to pull it, and a big brass bell we can hear for miles."

Folks shouted their approval.

And that idea was just for starters. He'd disclose the rest privately to Julia.

"How much did you have in mind?" asked Hobbs.

"Not now," said Ryan, searching the crowd for her. It was past dinnertime and getting late. Folks were starting to head home. "Tomorrow."

"I can go up another five hundred, unauthorized."

"Not now." Ryan grew frantic. Where was she?

"All right, perhaps a thousand. Well, let's call it fifteen hundred. Fifteen hundred more."

"Tomorrow!" Ryan shouted, finally spotting Julia standing near her horse, unfastening a saddlebag.

The sun was setting behind the mountains and the air would chill soon. A team of horses cantered past him, and another rider quickened his pace.

Travis called out to Ryan, "We're staying at the Prairie Hotel tonight!"

"I'll see you there," Ryan replied. He waved goodbye to his family, but his sights were on Julia.

She took out what appeared to be a wrap from her saddlebag to stave off the wind, then swung up onto her mount. It wasn't a wrap, but an old leather coat.

He recognized it. It was his. *Theirs.*

With a soft hitch in the back of his throat, he realized he did mean something to her. She'd kept the coat.

Looking over her shoulder to catch sight of Ryan, as if questioning whether he would follow, she kicked her horse and then flew off at a gallop.

Filled with the thrill of a hunt, Ryan jumped onto his mare and raced off to catch her.

"Where are you going?"

The wind snatched at Ryan's hat as he galloped beside Julia, hollering. He yanked on the brim to anchor it. He was wearing his scarlet tunic, and looked again like a commander who meant business. Seeing him in his uniform, appearing so handsome and official, sent a tingle down her back.

"Home! I'm going home!" Julia admired the way he moved. He was masculine in everything he did, from the way his large hands gripped the leather reins, to the way his thighs moved in the saddle.

They weren't alone. Wagons carrying families rumbled ahead and behind them, and single riders were racing toward town.

Ryan seemed content to gallop wordlessly alongside Julia as they crossed the creek and leaped up the far bank. After being holed up for days, trapped in a train fighting back a wall of fire, it appeared that both of them relished their freedom.

The ride was exhilarating. Fresh air poured into her lungs, the waning sun streaked across the sky, and birds—which she hadn't seen in days—chirped and soared above the trees. She would tell him. She would let him know exactly what she thought.

Where could they go, and be alone to talk?

As they neared the edge of town, Ryan's pace changed. He looked troubled. He raised his arm and reached over to touch her saddle horn, indicating that she should stop.

Her cowboy hat, with its leather thong hanging around her neck, bounced along her spine. The long loose coat dipped around her knees.

"You have a right to do as you please," he said as she slowed her gallop. "You have every right to go to Holt. If you said yes to his proposal, then I suspect what I have to say won't matter much. But I need to say it, Julia. And you need to hear it this time."

Ryan thought she'd said yes to Holt? Her heart beat a little faster.

"I'll go straight to the hospital right now, Julia, and tell him what I think. I'll do it if you want me to. I'll tell him you and he aren't suited. I'll tell him you and I are."

"Oh, Ryan...I don't want you to go to Holt."

"I'll do anything it takes this time to let you know I want you. I want you, Julia. I do want you as much and more than I did ten years ago."

Tears suddenly stung her eyes and nose.

She believed he'd do it. She believed Ryan would go straight to the fort looking for Holt, and, convalescing or not, the sergeant would have to listen as Ryan explained his frame of mind.

It felt heavenly to hear him say it. She should slow him down and tell him she'd refused Holt's marriage proposal, but it felt so good to listen to Ryan trying to convince her in his own special way.

"I've changed," he said, his forearm pressed along the length of his thigh as he rode beside her. He faced into the wind with determination, and his voice rang with sincerity. "You were right. I was a bastard before. I didn't know what I wanted or needed until it was out of my grasp... until *you* were out of my grasp."

As they passed by the first buildings of town, the livery stables and the bootmaker's, she answered, "I know you suffered, Ryan. I didn't know how much until you came back."

"No one deserved to be treated the way I treated you."

With a tightening in her throat, she nodded to riders, to folks she knew. Ryan mumbled hellos, equally impatient to be rid of everyone so that he and Julia could be alone. The sun had nearly set. It was getting dark.

"I made mistakes, too," she said, shivering in the saddle. They were nearly at her printing shop and she had so much more to say. She pulled at the reins, coming to a stop in the middle of the road because she couldn't go home yet.

Beside them stood the Prairie Hotel, so she nudged her horse to the hitching post there. Sliding off her mount, she pressed her quivering hand along her skirts to keep them from riding up. The old tan coat she was wearing—his duster—brushed her thighs.

Ryan was instantly at her side, standing tall and dark. He looked toward her shop, across the street and two stores down, as if trying to buy more time with her.

"I made so many mistakes," she whispered. "One of them was blaming you for everything that went wrong in my life. You were right that I was harboring resentment and was unable to let it go."

"I'm sorry I said that, Julia, that wasn't fair—"

"You had every right to be frank."

"But I had no right to hurt you. Everything that came out of my mouth was a barb."

Catching her breath, she pressed on. "The other mistake I made, and this one was a big one—" she had to disclose it all if they were being truthful "—was not letting you know how I felt. I depended on you to speak for the both of us, when I should have let you know…how much I wanted—how much I *want* to be with you."

The streetlamps hadn't been lit yet, so he was standing in the purple dusk. His eyes glistened, capturing the glow of lantern light coming from inside the hotel. "What are you saying, Julia?"

"I can't say it out on the street. I can't just say it and

then go back to my shop as if nothing was different. Yet I can't pretend for another moment."

Ryan swung around, unbuckled his saddlebag from his mare and lifted it to his side. He peered at the hotel doors. "I'm meeting my family here later. Let's go inside and talk."

With a shiver, Julia felt Ryan place a firm hand at the back of her waist. Whether it was improper or not, she followed him into the hotel lobby.

Chapter Twenty

❧

"You're coming up to my room," Ryan told her minutes later, making Julia's pulse beat a crazy rhythm. He'd asked her to wait in the alcove at the bottom of the stairs while he went to the front desk and got a key to a room.

"I can't do that," she whispered in astonishment. "People will think—"

"Where else can we talk alone? The reception hall? If I have to nod and say howdy to one more person, when what I want to do is shut out the world for five minutes to get you alone, I'm going to shoot someone."

"But isn't there another place?"

"Five minutes." Ryan grabbed her wrist and hauled her up the stairs. "Five minutes and then you're free to go."

"Ryan…" She struggled in his hold, to no avail. She had to practically leap up the stairs to keep up with him. A hotel guest, a middle-aged man, came down as they went up, looking at the couple with a question in his eyes.

"What are you afraid of, Julia?" Ryan muttered. "That

you'll get hurt again? That Holt will discover where you've been? I don't give a damn anymore. You're coming with me."

"Hauling me around without giving me a choice is no way to treat… Didn't we just finish talking about this kind of thing?" Julia lowered her voice at the sound of footsteps coming around a corner in the hall.

A young maid with red hair and fair skin, carrying a stack of clean but worn-out towels, passed by. "Good evenin' to ye both," she said in a Scottish brogue. Glancing at Ryan in uniform, seeing the way he possessively held on to Julia's wrist while unlocking door, she turned as red as his tunic.

"Evening, miss." Ryan nodded. "How's the towel business?"

She giggled. "They're keeping me busy. Will you be needin' newpapers in the mornin', sir?"

"No, I've got my own source for the news now, thank you."

Julia bristled beside him. "This looks like the same room you had the day you came back. Did you ask for it on purpose?"

Ryan raised his eyebrows and smiled.

She was still trying to tug free as he burst through the door. He spun her around with such strength that she was tossed to the narrow bed. Her coat fell open.

Julia yelped. "I'd like to stand while I say this—"

Ryan dropped his duffel bag and landed square on top of her. "I don't care what you say to me, but you've got to say it lying down."

This wasn't fair! How did he know what she wanted to say? How could he assume she'd lie beneath him—

"Let go of me, you big oaf!"

He laughed and held on tighter. "You look good when you're mad. Your cheeks get red and your mouth puckers."

"Get…off…of…me!"

"Nope. I like it here." He shifted his weight, those firm thighs encased in dark breeches pressing against her legs. "Tell me again. Pick up right after the part where you said how much you want to be with me."

"Go…to…hell!"

"Oh, Julia, you do have a fine way of expressing yourself. I'm not the least surprised you do it for a living."

When she cursed more explicitly, he laughed and kissed her throat.

"Why don't you ever kiss like a normal man?"

That got his attention. "What do you mean?"

"When you've got me lying down, you go straight for the throat and then usually lower. Why don't you ever start at my mouth?"

"Because you're usually talking too much."

"Uhh!" She squirmed good and hard beneath him, but only managed to mold herself to his body. A body that was growing firmer.

"That's nice," he said, kissing the base of her throat. "And I like your blouse. I've never seen this one before. Peach is my favorite color."

"If I had known that, I would have burned it."

"Really? That wouldn't have been wise. You'd have to replace it, sooner or later. But no matter. I'll buy you ten more like it."

She stopped squirming. "What *are* you going to do with all your money?"

He slackened his grip. "I'm going to make some investments. There's a shop in town. I have great faith in its owner. It's just a little place, not much to it, but the workers inside are what make this place special. They never give up. No matter how hard and rough life gets, they keep the presses going."

She was shocked by the impact of his gentle words.

He loosened his grip on her then, so she knew she was free to go. Someone must have lit the streetlamps, for one glowed just beyond their window and cast a spell inside the room.

"I hear the owner can be a real handful," she said.

"I'd like to get my hands full of this owner."

Her heart hammered. Ryan lounged above her, as if they had all the time in the world. Somewhere, he'd tossed away his hat. Dark strands of hair gathered at his forehead. The light in his dark eyes had the power to turn her world inside out.

He reached up and stroked his finger along her nose, down her lips and chin, and then to the base of her throat, all the while causing spasms in her stomach.

He studied her closely, the glimmer in his eyes telling her much of what he felt. She could almost see his thoughts in the expressions drifting across his face. His sorrow for having left her, the pain of meeting her again, and now the struggle to repair everything.

"I'm a wealthy man now, Julia. Thanks to Adam Willeby. And I don't see a problem with that. I'm going to rebuild all the houses I blew up. I'm going to build a big music hall with Adam's name on it." Ryan grinned. "He'd like that. I'm going to spend money on my family, every one of them, and I want to spend it on you. You and Pete.

What does he like? Fishing poles and rowboats? What do you like? Pretty clothes and fancy meals? Name a place anywhere in the world. I'll take the two of you there. The Taj Mahal. Buckingham Palace. The southern tip of South America. The northern tip of North America. We can get away from everything. From Holt, if you want to."

"I said goodbye to Holt last night."

Ryan's finger stopped trailing along her skin. His short black lashes flew up. "Goodbye as in…"

"Goodbye as in I can't marry you."

When Ryan swallowed, his Adam's apple slid up and down. "Why can't you?"

She whispered, "Because I'm in love with someone else."

His lips opened slightly. He lay staring at her, his expression riveting her to utter stillness. Nothing mattered but the beating of her heart against his.

She watched the whirl of emotions play across his handsome face—surprise and pleasure and intoxicating joy.

"Julia O'Shea." Her name rumbled off his tongue. "I love you with all my heart."

She closed her eyes as he kissed her lids, her cheeks, laughing as he finally reached her mouth. This was what she'd always wanted, this feeling of connection with Ryan that ran so deep and true that, beside him and Pete and Grandpa, everything else in the world dimmed.

She slid her arms up and stroked his cheeks, captivated by the feel of his mouth on hers. She poured her soul into the kiss, wanting him to know how much she felt, how good it was to be with him.

He murmured loving words in her ear, sending her pulse racing and her senses soaring to the clouds. She basked in the security of his arms, knowing that he would always protect her, that he had come home to her and that, whether she was willing or not, he had yanked her back beside him, where she belonged.

Eager to show him how much she loved him, she nudged him over on his side. The bed squeaked and they stifled their laughter, still kissing and stroking and holding.

She rushed to unfasten his tunic, nearly ripping off a button, then ran her hands along the soft cotton of his undershirt. His skin smelled good, tinged with smoke and wild grass.

"You look good in breeches. I wouldn't mind if you stayed in them."

He buried his face in the crook of her neck, inhaling the scent of her hair, as if he'd just discovered it.

He slid the coat from her shoulders.

"I can parade around in my breeches all you want later, but right now, they're coming off."

She smiled at the mischief in his voice, combined with the urgency as he peeled off his pants.

"Ah, Ryan, I did miss you."

"Let's see if we can make up for lost time."

Drunk with pleasure, Julia leaned back so he could undo the buttons of her peach blouse. The lace collar flopped against her throat as he yanked the sleeves down her arms.

The muslin curtains on the windows blew aside as a breeze rolled through. "I remember this room," she said. "You looked like a beast to me that day."

"And you looked like a proper Victorian lady. I wanted to unfasten every single button you owned. Like this," he said, undoing the two on her skirt.

"You're naughty."

"Shift this way and you'll see how naughty I can be. I'm going to make love to you like you've never imagined possible. I've decided making love to you is my favorite pastime."

Her stomach rolled again. Could this really be happening to her?

He removed her corset, unlacing it so slowly it was painful to wait. She was ready for him, hot and moist, and it surprised her how quickly he could build her anticipation.

The corset flew open. Her breasts rose, soft tips pointed upward, the chilled air feeling heavenly on her nipples. If he tugged at them just once…

"Umm…" She moaned as he did. First one and then the other, with expert hands that slid over her skin like velvet.

Grasping the back of her pantaloons, he yanked them down with one firm tug.

"You have many talents," she said.

"I'd like to demonstrate them all to you."

She laughed softly. She was completely naked except for thigh-high black stockings. Reaching for one to roll it off, she was surprised to hear him say, "Leave them. You look beautiful wearing only stockings."

"Aye, aye, Commander."

He still wore his undershirt, but when he scooted off the bed, she finally got a good look at his body. He was naked from the waist down, as firm as a rock and eager to plant himself inside her.

But he couldn't be more eager than she was.

He swung her bottom over the side of the bed, wedged her legs upward around his forearms, groaned in pleasure when he looked at her, then dipped his head and suckled her breasts.

The sensation was near bliss.

Her eyes drifted shut. Her throat tightened. His tongue teased her flesh and aroused every hair on the back of her neck. She was ready for him.

But he stretched back and glanced around the room. She spotted the basin of clean water, the soap and towel on the dresser, the same time he did. She understood, and they gently bathed. When he repositioned himself between her legs and again slid her bottom to the edge of the bed, he kneeled on the carpet and dipped his mouth to the feminine part of her that seemed to be waiting just for him. Had always been waiting for him.

The tenderness of his lips on the swollen part of her aroused her quickly. She was practically drenched with moisture, but that seemed to please Ryan more. He slid his fingers inside and she ached for more of him.

"Harder," she whispered.

His dark eyes deepened with want. "Not yet. Not yet, Julia. There's more."

"Then wait," she said. "I'd like to kiss you."

He must have thought she meant on the mouth, for he bent so she could do so. She brushed his lips with her own, then pulled away and slid to her knees on the bed. He was still standing at the edge, and when she kissed the smooth warm skin of his shaft, he murmured in pleasure.

She enjoyed the sensation, the feeling of being able to give him such love, but stopped short as he reached his brink.

Julia trembled with sensation. Lying back on the bed, she positioned herself close to the edge once more.

"This is what I've wanted for so long," Ryan whispered. "I've wanted you."

Slowly, so that they could enjoy every blissful moment, Ryan slid his fingers around her moist button and gently inched himself inside. He penetrated the opening, then filled her to the brim, his hands sliding up her ribs and claiming her body as his.

He kissed a path down her breasts, and along her ribs, above her, his skin moist with a golden sheen, his face intense, as if he'd never get enough of her.

She found love in his eyes as they rocked together gently, as he pressed deeper and deeper, and she accepted everything he offered.

"I want us to come together," he said through gritted teeth. "Tell me when."

He held back, trying not to spend himself, trying to please her. With his intimate stroking and the heat of his fingers gripping her flesh, it didn't take long.

"Now," she said.

He thrust deep within her. And then it happened—the shuddering in her muscles, the explosion of power, the feeling of being wrapped in Ryan. It was an experience so powerful she tried to capture it and hold it so she could remember it always.

Thirty minutes later, wrapped in Julia's arms as she lay naked beside him, Ryan playfully slapped her rump. "An hour ago, you told me to go to hell, and now look at you."

Lying on her belly, she opened her eyes. "Cocky in the bedroom, aren't you?"

"All I know is, you're one damn fine woman."

When she laughed, her bare shoulder blades moved up and down. He loved watching the rise and fall of her ribs, the way her body, warm and soft, shifted on the blankets. When she rolled over from her belly to her side, wrapping one bare leg over his, he sucked in his breath at the sight. Her breasts spilled against each other, rosy nipples the color of raspberries. Her abdomen, softly rounded, gave way to fuller hips and a triangle of soft curls.

"Are these for me?" He cradled one breast, kneading it in his palm, marveling at the feel of Julia in his bed.

"Could be, if you play your cards right."

"I'm pretty good at cards."

"What aren't you good at?"

"Anything to do with women."

"Oh, I'd say you're pretty good with women, too."

"Okay, let me specify. Anything to do with women's expectations of me."

She took her time answering. "I love you the way you are. If you hadn't gone to Africa, you'd be a different man now. I'm not sure I'd like that person as much as I like this one."

Her words brought a rippling tide of pleasure. She seemed to know exactly what he needed to hear. He had to forgive himself for the man he used to be, but that man didn't exist anymore—thanks, in part, to Julia.

"You know what I love about you?" he asked, easing his hand along the curving side of her luscious body.

"What?"

"Everything."

"Well, it's about time."

He tilted back his head and laughed.

Julia leaned against the single pillow. Golden light from

the streetlamp outside spilled over her skin. It etched the pretty lines around her eyes and gave her auburn hair a golden sheen.

His words turned more serious. "I can't live without you, Julia."

"You don't have to. I'm here."

He leaned against her, his firm chest pressing against her soft breasts, his naked thigh brushing hers all the way down to her toes, which wiggled against his.

"My father…did you know that my father offered to build me a house on his property?"

She pulled back in amazement. "He did? What did you say?"

"I told him yes."

Ryan had finally come to terms with his family and with himself. He no longer needed to push people to *their* edge. He would still seek adventure, especially with the Mounties, but the wild part of him that hadn't seemed to realize the influence he had on people had matured into something better. He preferred to channel his energy into building things and improving life for those he loved, not wreaking havoc.

"Ryan, that's wonderful."

She sighed with such relief that he felt guilty for how long he'd made her wait.

"Your mother will love that," she said. "And it means… it means you're staying for good?"

He nodded, knowing how much Julia had to do with the change in his frame of mind. "I want you to know, Julia, how lucky I think you are in having Pete."

Julia quivered beside him. "Thank you. Thank you for treating him the way you do."

"You and I accomplished a lot of things on that train, working together."

"I've never seen a man try as hard as you. In your work, then attempting to mend things with your family. And trying to listen to what I had to say."

They lay for a moment without speaking.

"How are David and Clarissa?" Ryan asked eventually. "I saw them working together today, but it struck me as odd that David was smiling."

"Clarissa proposed to him."

"What?"

"She did. She bought a fresh onion at the market for his monkey, then went over to the boardinghouse where David lives and proposed."

Ryan laughed. "What did he say?"

"That since his monkey approved of her, so did he."

Ryan's laughter got louder and Julia chimed in. Soon it was a belly laugh, but it wasn't *that* funny. He and Julia were simply giddy from exhaustion, physical and emotional.

He traced imaginary circles on her soft shoulder. "I told you once that you're a privilege to know."

"I remember," she said. "It was the nicest thing anyone's ever said to me. It caught me so off guard I didn't know how to respond."

"Well, I don't have an onion, but please respond by saying yes." He grew serious, the tremor in his voice thickened. "I would like you, Julia, to be my wife. It would be an honor for me if you'd stand beside me as my partner for the rest of our days."

Julia squeezed her eyes closed and when she opened them again, they were moist with unspoken feeling.

There was a queasy feeling in his stomach as he waited and hoped.

She searched his face, looking thoughtfully at his eyes and nose and mouth. "That would be my privilege," she said, closing the six-inch gap between them, melting her body against his.

In sweet response, he wrapped his arms around her.

"Let's go together to tell Pete," he whispered. "I'll bring a big basket of fruit and every sweet you can imagine. And a tin of chewing tobacco for Flanagan."

Julia smiled. "Grandpa will enjoy you trying to sway him with money and things."

"You think it will work?"

"Absolutely."

She slid her warm hands around his neck. The golden light caressed her face, and when their lips met, he was grateful to Adam and his beautiful violin for precipitating this journey, for Ryan was finally and truly home.

Widow Eleanor Scarborough is out to shock Regency London!

Eleanor has always been looked on as 'the bossy American' by London society. Now, at the death of her husband, she has been appointed trustee to his estate.

Infuriated, her mother-in-law sends Lord Anthony Neale to end Eleanor's gold-digging ways and they clash immediately. He thinks she's a siren who uses beauty to entrap men; she thinks he's a haughty, cold English snob.

But someone is threatening Eleanor, and as the malicious activities begin to pile up, it's Anthony who tops the suspects list!

Available 18th January 2008

www.millsandboon.co.uk

The Regency

LORDS & LADIES
COLLECTION

More Glittering Regency Love Affairs

VOLUME EIGHTEEN

A Matter of Honour by Anne Herries

Having recently become an heiress, Cassandra Thornton
knows she needs help to bring her into style, but at least
she can now be selective about the man she'll marry.
Unbeknownst to Cassie, however, her late brother had made
five of his friends promise that one would marry Cassie –
and Lord Vincent Carlton has drawn the short straw…

The Chivalrous Rake by Elizabeth Rolls

With a broken collarbone, Jack Hamilton was in no fit
mood to have relatives arrive on his doorstep unannounced.
But the Reverend Dr Bramley and his daughter Cressida
were practically penniless, so he couldn't turn them away.
Then Jack learnt the true reason behind their plight as he
realised Cressida was in need of a husband – but was
he in need of a wife?

On sale 1st February 2008

www.millsandboon.co.uk

Celebrate 100 years of pure reading pleasure with Mills & Boon®

To mark our centenary, each month we're publishing a special 100th Birthday Edition. These celebratory editions are packed with extra features and include a FREE bonus story.

Now that's worth celebrating!

4th January 2008

The Vanishing Viscountess by Diane Gaston
With FREE story The Mysterious Miss M
This award-winning tale of the Regency Underworld launched Diane Gaston's writing career.

1st February 2008

Cattle Rancher, Secret Son by Margaret Way
With FREE story His Heiress Wife
Margaret Way excels at rugged Outback heroes...

15th February 2008

Raintree: Inferno by Linda Howard
With FREE story Loving Evangeline
A double dose of Linda Howard's heady mix of passion and adventure.

Don't miss out! From February you'll have the chance to enter our fabulous monthly prize draw. See special 100th Birthday Editions for details.

www.millsandboon.co.uk

FREE

2 BOOKS AND A SURPRISE GIFT

We would like to take this opportunity to thank you for reading th
Mills & Boon® book by offering you the chance to take TWO mor
specially selected titles from the Historical series absolutely FREE
We're also making this offer to introduce you to the benefits of th
Mills & Boon® Reader Service™—

- ★ **FREE home delivery**
- ★ **FREE gifts and competitions**
- ★ **FREE monthly Newsletter**
- ★ **Books available before they're in the shops**
- ★ **Exclusive Reader Service offers**

Accepting these FREE books and gift places you under no obligatio
to buy; you may cancel at any time, even after receiving your fre
shipment. Simply complete your details below and return the entir
page to the address below. You don't even need a stamp!

YES! Please send me 2 free Historical books and a surprise gift.
understand that unless you hear from me, I will receive
superb new titles every month for just £3.69 each, postage and packin
free. I am under no obligation to purchase any books and may canc
my subscription at any time. The free books and gift will be mine
keep in any case.

H8ZEI

Ms/Mrs/Miss/Mr...Initials ....
                                                                    BLOCK CAPITALS PLEA

Surname ....

Address ....

....

....Postcode ....

Send this whole page to:
The Reader Service, FREEPOST CN81, Croydon, CR9 3WZ